THE STORY BEHIND THE DRESS

THE STORY BEHIND THE DRESS

RAQUEL J. MOODY

To order additional copies of this book, contact:
Xlibris
844-714-8691
www.Xlibris.com
Orders@Xlibris.com
821776

CONTENTS

Introduction

"Are you almost ready?" yelled the sales associate.

"C'mon, my girl! We want to see you!" said my impatient big sister Tanya, who seemed to be more excited about me trying on a dress than I was.

I looked at myself and thought, *Hmmm . . . A little baggy here . . . Oh, but I love how it hugs my curves. God bless Mama for these hips . . . Uh-oh! A little plump in the rear . . . Oh, he's going to love how I strut in this . . . A little tailoring done here in the bust . . . Mama didn't pass down any boobs at all . . . Oh, I just love the sequins on this dress . . . The sheer brings such elegance . . . Oooooh, when I add this train to it, that there is going to be the bommmbbbb.*

"Cassie! Can you hurry up? This lady ain't got all day to be waiting for you! We still gotta get ready for revival!" Tanya exclaimed, reminding me that we had a few hours before needing to get ready for church service.

"Okay, I'm coming out right now," I responded, hiking up the hem of my dress.

I put my hand to the doorknob of the dressing room, saying to myself, *What the heck am I doing here?*

I was supposed to come to David's Bridal just to pray over dresses. Somehow, in the ambience of bridal attire, the many brides shopping around for their special day, and how blown away I was as I planted my eyes on this mermaid-like gown of my dreams, I just had to try it on. I had to!

"Cassie, if I have to come in there myself, I will! I am not playing! Come out!" Tanya shouted. I twisted the doorknob and proceeded to open the door. I looked up at both my sister and sales associate Kim. The expressions on their faces were out of this world. I knew this dress was *perfect*.

"Yesss! Turn around! Let's see!" Tanya uttered, twirling her index finger for me to perform a pirouette.

"Well, what do you think?" I asked.

"That dress is for you *all the way*, hands down," Tanya said.

"Yes, I must admit Tanya is right. You look fabulous!" Kim replied.

"Thanks, guys," I whispered as I glanced back at myself in the mirror. "I think I'm set on this one, y'all."

Kim rushed over as soon as those words escaped my mouth. She walked toward me as I was looking at myself in mirror. Then, she leaned over and said in a slow and distinctive voice, "Are *we* saying *yes* to the *dress*?" she asked.

Taken aback for a split second, I looked back at Tanya as she gestured a head nod of approval. "*Yes!* I am saying *yes* to the *dress*!"

"Woo-hoo!" they shouted as they pranced around in the lobby of the dressing rooms. They were loud enough to interrupt the other brides from trying on dresses and shopping for a gown of their own. The compliments these ladies showered me with had me feeling as if I was already put together for the big day.

"OK!" Kim said. "Now what we usually do when our soon-to-be brides find the dress of their dreams, we have them make a wish and then scream at the top of their lungs as they ring *the bell*." Kim walked over to a nearby table and picked up this perfectly fluffed gray pillow. The pillow was bedazzled with a bunch of diamond cluster cut-likes gems, with a big shiny gold bell on top. As Kim approached me with this prop, my mind began to ponder the many women who had potentially carried out this tradition. It had to be hundreds. Shoot, maybe even *thousands*.

"Are you ready?" Kim asked.

"Yes," I said.

"OK. Make a wish."

I began to talk inside myself: *I wish . . . I wish that someday, one day, I'll marry Marcus. I pray we have beautiful kids together that will carry on our ministry and that I'll be the helpmate God ordained me to be, in Jesus' name . . . Amen.*

"Scream?" I said.

"Yes."

"Aaaahhhh!" I shouted.

As the sound escaped my mouth, many in the room along with Tanya and Kim began to cheer.

Oh my gosh! This is the dress. It will be the one I walk down the aisle in. I'll be in marital bliss. I'll live the happily ever after that I have been dreaming of. I'll finally see the fruition of the revelation God presented to me years ago. I'll finally see the man that has been getting down on one knee, popping that question in equivocal attempts yet dressing it with humor, to finally, finally ask in all sincerity, "Cassie, will you marry me?" Yesss! I feel it! It's coming to pass, at last. This is it! Or is it?

1

IN THE BEGINNING
WAS THE WORD

I remember like it was yesterday. It was September 5, 2010, when I was first filled with the Holy Ghost and had the evidence of speaking in tongues. It was the most exuberating yet liberating experience in my life as a born-again Christian. I felt a high that no narcotic could ever give. As amazing as that transfiguration was for me, I had to come back down to reality.

I had a great man in my life at the time. His name was Tommy. Tommy Banks. He had a few coins. I mean, the name says it all. But he wasn't the drug-dealing type of hood dude. He worked hard for his money, the right way. He was a manager at local restaurant Delmonico's, and a teacher's assistant at North Albany Academy in upstate New York. Not only did he have two jobs, he was also attending the University of Albany and on the verge of getting his master's in criminal justice. He was any woman's dream. He knew how to cater to me physically, mentally, emotionally, and pretty much any aspect of me that I thought a man this day in age could never achieve. I mean he was *it*. He was someone I just knew I'd spend the rest of my life with. It couldn't get any better than that. I mean this man was established, he worked, he was in school, he had beautiful teeth. What more could a woman want?

Just when I got used to the idea of having a life with him, things started to change. Who would have known that one conversation on a summer afternoon would be the start of the tables turning in our relationship? I remember being on his couch watching Small Claims Court. Before the verdict was released out of Judge Judy's mouth, a thought came to me: *Start going to church.* As random as that thought was, it didn't seem quite moving to me. Shortly after, Tommy came into the living room, joining me with salmon, rice, and asparagus accompanied with a glass of moscato white wine. He knew Barefoot was my favorite. Did I fail to mention that the man could cook? Jackpot! *OK!* Anyway, as he placed the plate of food down on the living room table, he looked over at me and said, "Hey, babe, how do you feel about going to church every now and then?"

"Tommy, that's crazy you asked," I stated, as startled as I was. "Right before you came in, I had this random thought that we should start going to church."

"Oh really?" he said with relief. "OK, let's start going. We don't have to be all spiritual and stuff. We can just give God thanks and attend church services every now and then to pay our respects to him. Sound like a plan?" he asked.

I looked at him and said, "It sounds good to me, babe."

I remember looking at him in that moment, just mesmerized about how perfect this man was as he leaned over and planted a passionate kiss on my lips. I thought it would be a new chapter we would enter into together—us two, as a couple. To my surprise, what I thought would be forever would soon turn into a short-lived romance. We both agreed that we wouldn't get so heavy into being a Christian. But God had bigger plans for me. It took a while for me to wrap my mind around the scripture in the book of Proverbs, Proverbs 19:21, which states, *"Many are the plans of man's heart, but it's the Lord's will that prevails."* You see, I planned to follow this regimen with Tommy to just visit church. But it was the Lord who kept pulling me and tugging on my heart.

It was the Lord who set me apart. It was the Lord who quickened me to give my life and totally immerse myself to live a sold-out life for him. And all of that brought me to this point, the point where God endowed me with his Holy Spirit, a new form of power, and living a life of *sin* didn't feel so comfortable to me anymore.

It was in that moment where I came to grips that I was in fact changed and was no longer the Cassie that I used to be. I pondered on having to tell Tommy that I wasn't the woman he loved. I remember seeing him that night after my spiritual encounter. I told him that we needed to talk. I said to him, "Tommy, I have to tell you something. I know we told each other that we wouldn't become all deep into this spiritual stuff, but I'm changing. I don't know what's going on with me or what God is up to. All I know is that there are certain things I don't feel comfortable doing anymore."

He looked puzzled as if he already knew what I was about to divulge. "Sex?" he said. "What? You don't want to have sex anymore?"

"It's not that I don't want to. I just can't anymore. The guilt of that act overwhelms me."

I knew Tommy wasn't too happy about it, considering the look he gave me that said all within itself that I was out of my darn mind if I thought I wasn't going to be giving it up.

"Well, when do you plan on stopping?" he asked.

"I'm not sure, Tommy. I just know eventually it would have to end."

As baffled as he seemed to be, he told me he was willing to do whatever it took to keep us together. He started coming to church more and he even got baptized. I'll never forget how ecstatic I was when he finally walked down the altar one Sunday afternoon during church service. Tommy embraced Pastor Jennings with a hug as he wiped his eyes in an effort to catch the tears he couldn't seem to prevent from leaving his eyes. But as much as Tommy tried to change for me, I just knew we were coming to a close. Because you see, that was it. He was doing it for me, and a life truly lived for the Lord had to come from within. It had to come from the love he had for God and not for me. It didn't help any when the assistant pastor came over and prayed over me the following service and told me emphatically that Tommy was not the one God had chosen for me. I remember thinking to myself, *Who does this man think he is? Did he not just see my baby get baptized last week?* But in the end, the minister was *right.* Tommy held on as long as he could. It wasn't until he became so sexually frustrated that I caught him cheating on me.

On the way home one night from a night out with my close friend Saniah, I caught him kissing some girl. It didn't take a genius for me to put together that this was the same girl I caught him on the phone with the week prior, when inquiring about her choice in undergarments. As hurt as I was, I ended the relationship in peace. I saw them together many times after that. They seemed to be very happy. I looked at her and I couldn't help to think back on all the times he kept a smile on my face. After rolling my eyes and being so consumed with bitterness every time I saw them, I grew angrier. It seemed that the more bitter I became, the more run-ins I kept having with them. I finally whispered to myself one night after catching them hand in hand at the mall: *God, you know how much I loved Tommy—you know I would have never traded him in for the world, but I found myself trading him in for you. I trust you, God. I trust that because I gave up the only life I knew for a life in you, in the end, it will be all worth it. I pray that because I gave up the man I love, you would bless me with a "man of God." Grant me a man that's after your own heart. Give me a man that would love you more than he loves me. Because I know that because he loves you, loving me would just be a given. In Jesus' name, Amen.*

One year had passed since my breakup with Tommy. As happy as I was serving God, I did not understand why God hadn't blessed me with my husband yet. I grew more and more impatient the more I kept seeing pictures of happy couples all over the timeline of Facebook. We would even have many visitors at the church coming with their significant others, sharing testimony after testimony on how "Oh, the Lawd been oh-so-good to us!" God seemed to be blessing everyone around me with a mate; shoot, even my friend Saniah had a man, a good man, and she seemed to be able to keep one too and I *know* she wasn't in the Bible as nearly as much as I was. Here I was all *sold out*! Mind made up! All *sanctified* self, serving, remaining faithful and *celibate* and still, *no man*!

We had the Summer Youth Revival service at the church, *my* church, The Light on the Hill. That night, I looked my very best. I went out and bought a nice blue dress. It was fitted but still suitable for church, and I had laced my hair earlier that day with my Wet & Wavy hair I purchased from a beauty supply store. I was at the church seven o'clock sharp. I was not about to miss my "man of God" that I was in anticipation to meet that night. Sister Janet, whom I had grown pretty close with since I began attending church, didn't refrain from informing me about all the different churches that usually came to visit whenever we had revival service. She said that good-looking men from those churches would come along. My excitement was short-lived when I looked around and recognized that Janet didn't quite have the same perception I did on what it is to be *good-looking*. Either that, or these so-called good-looking men chose not to show up. Thankfully, I put my radar for men on pause due to the sermon the youth pastor had preached that night. He was the speaker for that night. His name was Bishop Howard. He preached about *waiting on God*. Oh, how fitting it was to my situation. That night I knew he was talking to me. I went from being discouraged to encouraged. The sermon moved me to trust God. God knows what he is doing, and he has an appointed time for what I have asked God for.

After Bishop Howard finished preaching, he invited anyone who needed prayer to the altar. I remembered in that moment that Sister Janet also told me how prophetic Bishop Howard was. She told me that God had blessed him with the gift of prophecy, where he can tell what God has in store for people in their future. I wasn't going to let that moment pass me by. I was determined to go to the altar. I needed to hear what God had in store for me. There were at least forty people before me in line. People were getting prophesied to the left and right. The saints were falling out on the floor, dancing, shouting, stomping, crying, yelling, running. I mean, you name it, the saints were doing it.

The lady standing in front of me was next in line. Her name was Keisha, and in the midst of Bishop Howard praying, her two-year-old son ran out in the aisle among all of us at the altar. In her frustration, she tried to grab her son to tame him. Bishop Howard stopped her in her tracks and said, "Leave him! Leave that baby alone! Parents wonder why kids don't praise God anymore, it's because you stop them every time they attempt to do so." Bishop Howard motioned Keisha back to the front of the line and said to her without relinquishing eye contact, "You better treat that baby right, he's going to get you that house." Keisha began to praise the Lord in ways she had never praised him before. She always had a mellow praise for as long as I could remember. But not that night. I began to shout for her as well because I remembered the time she told me that she was believing God for

4

a house for her, her daughter Jordan, and her baby boy Quincy. Witnessing that grew my excitement the more. At this point, I wanted Bishop Howard to prophesy to me and prophesy *fast*!

Finally, I was right in front of him. He motioned me to come close and so I walked toward him. He then put his hand up, indicating that I stop. He then looked at me. He turned back around and started pacing back and forth at the altar. He asked, "Are you *married*?

"No," I replied.

He then said to all the people in attendance, "Everyone repeat after me, *You don't need no man!*"

The crowd repeated in unison, "*You don't need no man!*"

"He needs *you*!" Bishop Howard stated as he pointed directly at me. He then said to me, "Do you go to this church?"

"Yes," I said, curious to know where he was going with this.

He then asked Pastor Jennings to meet us at the altar. When Pastor Jennings got to the altar, Howard said, "When God finally shows you who this man of God *is*, you are to bring him back to Pastor Jennings for his approval. Is that understood?"

I looked at Howard and said to him in all assurance, "Yes, I understand, Bishop."

"You don't need a man, young lady!" Bishop Howard repeated once more. "He needs you!"

I went back to my seat, a little perplexed by what the bishop said to me that night. I was fixed in my seat the same way Bishop Howard's words were fixed in my mind. I was interrupted in my thoughts about twenty minutes later when Pastor Jennings came up to me.

"Are you all right?" he asked.

I looked at him and began to look all around the room. Unbeknownst to me, service was already over. Everyone was conversing and discussing the events that took place in service and how God had used Bishop Howard, and I was just clueless. I smiled and said to my pastor, "Yes, Pastor Jennings, I'm all right."

"All right now, Cassie, you heard the Word now! When *he* comes, you bring him to me."

"You have my word," I told him.

Walking home that night, I found myself lost in those words again: "*You don't need no man. He needs you.*" Wow! It finally dawned on me. This whole time I was so needy to have a man that I didn't realize up until this point that God was letting me know that whoever *he* is needed me and I didn't need him. God was telling me that I was necessary to my husband. The man God had in store for me couldn't go any further without me. I thought to myself: *I'm needed and I am necessary. It is not so much him being an asset in my life, but about me being an asset to his. I would be the perfect mate to the perfect man, to God's man. I can't wait to meet him. I wonder who this man will be, who will be the one so blessed and lucky to have me?*

2

FLESH AND BLOOD
DID NOT REVEAL

It was in the fall of 2011 when life began to transition a bit for me. I wouldn't call it the greatest experience. By that time, rumors were going around church about me having an affair with one of the church sisters' husband. I mean, I'm telling you, just when you thought it was safe at church. Eventually I'd learn the hard way. The man's name was Johnson. Johnson was actually the person God had used to get me to start going to church in the first place. He and I worked at the same nursing home together. While God was dealing with me, God sent Johnson after me. He confirmed to me that I had a calling on my life and how I needed to get saved. He was unaware that the Lord had been dealing with me a week prior to the encounter I had with him. Johnson and I grew really close. Once I began to take being Christian seriously, friends and family vanished. Johnson became the only friend I had to depend on at the time. But Kenya, his wife, didn't seem to like that very much. Her screwed-up face and turned-up nose served me that notice every time I saw her. It wasn't too long after that when Pastor Jennings sat me down and discussed with me that being so close to Johnson was not the best idea. He let me know how uncomfortable Johnson's wife Kenya felt about it. As hurt as I was about the saints insinuating that there was infidelity between Johnson and me, I respected how Kenya felt and I kept my boundaries. After a while, I grew bitter about the loneliness that seemed to lie heavy on me, considering the vacancy of my friends and family due to my new lifestyle. I felt so alone and so out in the cold that I considered leaving the church. I felt that if church folks weren't there for me in a time of need, then what purpose is it serving in my life? I didn't want to leave church all in all, so I figured I'd just stay until the Lord led me elsewhere.

After many nights of pondering and feeling out of place, I figured I'd get my mind off things by checking my Facebook. I happened to look through my Facebook messages and noticed a previous message I had received a while back from my former mentor. I attended his after-school program a while back. It was actually prior to me being saved. His name was Marcus. He ran this nonprofit organization for troubled kids for the sole purpose of redirecting them to a brighter future.

It's funny how we met. It was in the spring of 2008. I was in my freshman year of college, Hudson Valley community college. I got a call from a friend of my little sister Ramara. Ramara had gotten into a fight. Now, I did not play when it came to my sisters. If anyone messed with them, they were picking a fight with me! I don't mean to sound tough like I can beat everybody, but let me just say this: They didn't call me Rocky for no reason. I happened to have a silk head scarf in my book bag. I always had a habit of keeping my hair neat. I caught the bus to meet my sister at their school. When I finally got in contact with Ramara, she redirected me to meet her at an after-school program, and you guessed it, Marcus was the head director of the program. When I got to the program, I ran up the stairs and bombarded the program and asked, "Where my sister at?"

No *hi*! No *nothing*! At this time, I already had my scarf on and was on "go," ready to fight. Marcus came up to me and introduced himself. But I wasn't too friendly. I was there for one purpose, and that was to find my sister and look for the chick that put hands on her. It's funny because as I remind myself on how I met Marcus, all I could hear playing in my head is the song by rap artist DMX, "How It's Going Down" and the part when he was like "Knew she was a thug; when I met her, she had a scarf on."

When my Ramara came, after I realized she was good, I asked her about the program and how she joined it. I realized it was a safe haven for her and my other little sister Paradise to attend. It wasn't long after that I decided to attend it myself. Marcus granted me employment there as payroll manager the summer of that year.

After the program would end for the day, it would always turn into Marcus preaching. Everyone in attendance listened and would go into worship. I really wasn't into all that at the time. I mean, yeah, sure, I believed in God. But I had a pretty basic relationship with him. However, I still attended Marcus's after-hours church services. Marcus had a calling on his life to preach. I can't lie; he was *amazing*. He perfected the Word of God. Even if I didn't want to stay to listen to the Word and worship, I couldn't help it. It was so captivating. But still, even after those great encounters, I would have my best friend Whitney come through and pick me up afterward and we would go out partying *every* weekend. That never stopped Marcus from being the older brother that I *never* had. To a fatherless girl, he was the perfect father figure too. Marcus kept tabs on me. He'd keep me in line. There were times he would check me when I was being a little fresh to prove it.

But between going to college, being about the party life, and having just bought my first whip, I slowly stopped coming around.

I ran into Marcus once after leaving the program. He was with his fiancée, walking through the park. I greeted them both, and he introduced me to her. It's so funny because I remember saying to him, "Wait! This is your fiancée?" thinking to myself, *What the heck is he doing with her?* His fiancée was breathtakingly gorgeous, and Marcus wasn't all that. Like not at all! He just had height and some muscle here and there, and he was dark-skinned. I only had faith in these light-skins.

I had forgotten that Marcus had messaged me through Facebook in 2010. It read: "Hey, sis! My new number 518-631-7209."

What was so funny about this message is that he sent it to me August 8, 2010, at around 4:00 a.m. That was hours before I first attended church and got saved and baptized. He was the first person I wanted to tell because I remembered how much his preaching had an impact on me, even though I wasn't truly saved at the time. But when I called his *old* number, it was disconnected.

I wrote back: "Wow! I was trying to call you too. I got baptized!"

He wrote back with so much excitement. I'm sure he remembered how paralyzed I was when we would have service back in the day. I'd be a zombie among him and his crew of worshipers. He knew that if I got saved, it was the real deal. Marcus wrote: "Wow. Congratulations. I am so happy for you! Make sure you save my new number. You are the best and God is going to use you in a major way."

I wrote back, saying, "Thanks, Pastor. I have your number saved. I really like the church I went to today. But no one can never preach and grasp me the way you can. I will be back to hear God's word through you soon. Don't stop preaching, Marc. We need the Word through you. Marc, you have a way with young people that gives us a better understanding. Muah."

Hmm! I thought to myself. *Maybe I should go visit Marcus's church.*

The next week, I went down to Miss Juanita's; she was a member who allowed Marcus to use her house for Bible study. They would have Bible study at Miss Juanita's house on Thursdays, and Sunday service at the YMCA on Sundays. Walking in, I noticed a few faces that were there that used to go to Marcus's program. A girl by the name of Jada was there also. I remember when she first started as an intern for college. Turns out, she had become Marcus's best friend. She was always so sweet to me. Even though she was about two years older than me, I always looked at her as a big sister. Then I saw my boy Jermaine. It was funny because I knew him before the program. We used to horseplay in high school together with a whole bunch of friends of ours. And how can I forget Malcolm? He was like a little brother to me. Seeing them just brought back so many memories. It felt like home being around them; even with the newcomers, it was as if I never left.

Bible study was awesome. The Holy Spirit overcame me that night. I was jumping and speaking in tongues all over Miss Juanita's living room. God used Marcus mightily. When I came down from my spiritual high, you could already tell that Marcus made previous members of the program aware of me being saved *for real,* because their faces were priceless. Marcus introduced me to everybody in the room. He didn't hesitate to make mention that he knew me when I was eighteen years old and how I was a hothead and years later I was saved, sanctified, and filled with the Holy Ghost at twenty-three. You can always count on him for embarrassment.

I continued to attend Marc's Bible study and worship services and, shortly after, became a member. Powerhouse Worship Center is what they went by. Now I always knew that I had a strong passion for the word of God. But I felt like the moment I came to the Powerhouse, it was even more apparent that I was no stranger to studying Scripture. I talk about God all the time and Powerhouse too. Next thing I knew, I was bringing everybody to church. The unsaved, backsliders; even felons I grew up with back in the day. I couldn't believe how much God was using me. I even had some girlfriends of mine back in high school tell me that they would come and visit, women that I would never expect to step foot near a church. I guess they must have thought to themselves, if God could change Cassie, he could change anybody. One woman working Burger King drive-through could tell by the attire that I had on that I was heading to church. I remember her asking me when she was handing me my change and food, "What church you go to?"

I told her, "The Powerhouse, Pastor Marcus Boyd."

"Ohhhh! *Girl*! Yeah, I know him. He is *fine!*"

Oh and by the way, remember when I said how he wasn't all that attractive? Yeah, brotha grew up nicely.

I chuckled at her response and said, "Well, you never know, girl, you can be First Lady!"

We laughed together, and I told her I hope she'd come visit soon.

About this time, fall was drifting away. I went to church as usual, bringing people as usual. Y'all, I'm not kidding. When I tell you I was bringing everybody, that means I was bringing *urrrrbody*. It was to the point where they were calling me Evangelist Cassie. Going to the Powerhouse was amazing. I never felt so loved and so comfortable. We really felt like a *family*. Everything was perfect all the way up until one particular night. This night changed my everything. Pastor Marc did his thing preaching at Bible study. It had to be mid-November of that year. I was just listening to him preach, shouting, jumping, hollering, "Preach, Preacha!" I remember sitting back in my seat, I thought, *I'm so proud of Marcus. Look how much he grew. God has molded and shaped him into this amazing, God-fearing man. God is going to use him for His glory. Marcus is going to change the world. He will need a great wife, a godly wife, one that God will use to help him do mighty works in Him. But who is she, who will she be?*

"*You,*" the voice said, so gentle, so clear. "I chose you."

3

THY WORD I HAVE
HIDDEN IN MY HEART

I couldn't believe it. Me! *His* wife. I'm thinking, *No way, Lord! This can't be. Why would he need me? I've only been saved a year. Plus he's like seven years older than me. He's smarter than me. There is no way, God! Oh my God! God, are you sure? Oh my God, I'm freaking out!*

"Hey, Cass, are you OK?" Malcolm asked.

Here I was *again*, zoned out! Totally oblivious to the fact that Bible study had already ended.

"Uh, yeah!" I replied. "I'm OK. Look, Malcolm, I got to go. I'll see you guys Sunday."

"Oh, umm, Cassie? I was actually trying to see if I can get a ride home."

Oh gosh, Malcolm, out of all nights, tonight *you would want a ride?*

"Sure, Malcolm. I'll take you."

I waited for Malcolm to gather his things so that we could get out of Miss Juanita's house as fast as we could. We started heading toward the door to make our exit, and before you know it . . .

"Sister Cassie!" Marcus said. Leaving so soon?"

I froze and then said, "Yeah, I have to go. Malcolm needs a ride home."

"Oh no, Cassie!" Malcolm said. "We can wait around if you like. I don't mind staying until whenever."

Malcolm, will you shut up? I thought to myself. At this point, my armpits were drenched. I would wear a bright red blazer that day.

"How 'bout it, Cassie, can you stay a little while longer?" Marcus asked.

"I can't, Pastor Boyd! I actually have to get home. I have school tomorrow."

Phew! I was quick on my toes. I didn't lie either. I was actually in hair school and studying theology at the time.

"Finally!" yelled Jermaine. "You finally said Pastor Boyd", reminding me of all the times they had to correct me for calling him Marcus. I had a tendency of calling him by his first name because that's how I referred to him back in the day. Jermaine always seemed to be butting in every conversation I had with Marcus. He was like Marcus's right-hand man.

"OK, Cassie. I'll see you Sunday, 2:00 p.m. sharp, *right*?" he said, giving me a look insinuating that I was always late.

"I got you, Pastor," I said, walking out the door. *Welp!* Guess I lied then. I'm *always* late.

I drove Malcolm home. He talked to me nearly the entire ride. I vaguely remembered what he was saying. At that point, my mind was all over the place. I struggled wrapping my mind around this *so-called* revelation. I tried to not think about it, but that didn't help.

It got worse as the days went by. God woke me up almost every night to pray for him. There were times I really didn't want to. If I'm being honest, majority of the time, I didn't want to. I didn't even want to entertain this so-called revelation. I felt so weird. Not only did I not see him in that way, I felt he was way out of my league. He was way too muscular. I always said to myself I don't want a man with too many muscles. Considering that I was abused as a child by my dad, I wanted someone I could take out if I had to. It was wrong, just *all wrong!*

I didn't really have many encounters with Marcus after that. I tried to stay away from him as much as possible. He would still come around me. He'd strike up meaningless conversations. I felt like God was taunting me, like seriously, God, get this man. I was so petrified to be around this man. You would think God would let up. But what was worse, Marcus had made me a part of the intercessory team with a few of the older women attending the church. We had to pray for all the church affairs, souls, and Pastor Boyd, as if God didn't employ me for that already. I was already praying for him privately; now I was publicly with my fellow sisters in Christ.

In the following year, during spring, Marcus met with all the clergy plus me and informed us on how he would like for us to attend the Pastors and Leadership Conference by the anointed Bishop T. D. Jakes in Orlando, Florida. Let me just say this: I love some T. D. Jakes. He was my everyday pastor, OK? I had him on my YouTube channel *every night*. I was ecstatic to go.

We found ourselves at the conference a month later. It was epic. There was one night where T. D. Jakes preached something serious. I went into a powerful worship. I think that night was when the church members nicknamed me Tornado. I was all over. I remember when I fell to the floor, so many people rushed over to me, people that I didn't know. They tried to lay their hands on me to pray. Jada fought her way into the crowd and practically got on top of me and began to cover me in prayer, as little as she was. I couldn't believe it. Jada always had my back. I could always depend on her if not anyone else. I remember when Jakes did an altar call. He asked us in his most infamous snarl, "How bad do you want him? *How bad do you want God?* Run! Run up to the altar!"

Before I knew it, my feet were going. I didn't care where I was or who was with me, I wanted and I need God. *Whew!* I get chills just thinking about that day. It was such a powerful service.

After the day service was over, they announced that there would be another service that night, around 7:00 p.m. We went out to the lobby and figured we'd grab some books and things before going back to our hotel to regroup and freshen up. Marcus's mom, First Lady Liz Boyd, had accompanied us at the conference. I remember I was in a line to purchase a book from Tudor Bismark's wife, Chi Chi Bismark, titled *Teach Me How to Pray*. She came up to me and asked me what book I was thinking about getting. I told her I wasn't sure yet. As soon as I had responded to her, Marcus pulled her to the side to inform her of something. I didn't think anything of it. I just purchased my books and anticipated reading them as soon as the conference was over.

When we got back to the hotel, my hotel key wouldn't let me open the door. I sat outside the door for almost an hour. I called Marcus to tell him what was going on. He didn't answer. At that point, I was a little frustrated, because I wanted to get in the shower and rest up before getting ready for service that night. Finally, I was able to reach him. By the time he came to me with an extra key for my room, I was aggravated. He apologized and said that he would never just leave me abandoned. I knew that. I was just furious how the clerk at the desk wouldn't let me get a copy of the key without him being present or getting it himself. I felt so foolish to act like this around the other church members and his mother. Not to mention, I was still trying to cope with this whole *revelation*. It was really getting to me.

At this point, I considered leaving Powerhouse. I could see how this was revelation was affecting me. I just felt as though God would want me to walk away before this thing consumed me. I made up my mind that I would make the decision whether to leave or not before the conference was over.

The service that night was more about going back home and executing the will of God and what God had called us to do for the Kingdom. Jakes had us partner up with someone to pray. And you wouldn't believe who partnered with me: Marcus. We began to pray for each other. As I was praying for him, I began to cry profusely. Praying for Marcus was so overwhelming. It was too much for me. As much as I tried to control seeing him as more than a brother in Christ, it was way beyond *me*. I had to leave Powerhouse.

When we were walking outside toward the hotel, you would not believe who walked up to me: Pastor Jamal Bryant. He came up to me and said, "Hey, beautiful, I hope you enjoyed the conference."

"I did. Thanks," I said.

"So where are you fr—"

"Bishop Bryant?" Desmond interrupted while Pastor Bryant was in midsentence. Desmond was one of the new members from the church. Marcus has recently promoted him as his armor bearer.

"Hey, Brother. How's it goin'?" Pastor Bryant replied.

"Well! Thank you, sir. I want you to meet our pastor, Marcus Boyd," Desmond said as he motioned Marcus to come and greet him.

"Hey, I'm Marcus Boyd," Marcus said trying to be as nonchalant as could be. But the sweat on his forehead set off a different kind of radar.

Marcus and Bryant shared a few words before Bryant granted us a goodnight. After Mr. Bryant walked a certain distance, everyone crowded around Marcus. They were discussing how awesome it was for him to meet Pastor Bryant. When I looked at Marcus, he looked like someone poured a gallon for water on him with all the perspiring he was doing. He was going on and on, saying, "I can't believe I met Jamal Bryant, my favorite pastor of all time. This is amazing. I will never forget this day."

"Wait a minute, you're excited about *him*?" I asked. "You are *way* better than *him*!"

Oh my gosh, I thought to myself. *Did I just say that out loud?*

When those words escaped my mouth, they looked at me in a way that was indescribable. If their looks weren't enough, the embarrassment on Marcus's face was. You can tell he felt foolish for how star-struck he was about a man that I felt he was better than. Now I must say that Jamal Bryant is prolific at what he does, but something on the inside of me just believed that Marcus was greater than him. I just didn't think those words would escape my mouth like word vomit.

The next day, we packed our bags and headed home. We flew back to NYC, where we caught the plane to get to Florida. Then we split in two vans to head back upstate. I happened to be in the same van with Jada. When we stopped to get food at a McDonald's just off the exit, I felt led to tell her about me leaving Powerhouse. She asked why. I told her that I believed God wanted me to leave and that it was best thing to do. I'm usually not afraid to share anything with Jada. I guess her being the BFF to the man I'm supposed to marry would make things a bit more complicated. Jada and I cried together. She was so choked up about my decision to leave. She said to me that they will never find anyone like me. She begged me to reconsider. I told her I loved them so much but it was something I just *had* to do. Once we got back to church, everyone split into their own cars. I guess Jada didn't bring her car and caught a ride with Marcus to get home. I kissed and hugged her, and we went our separate ways.

I decided to leave church officially that night. I didn't tell anyone but Jada. It was already difficult enough to share it with her. Besides, I knew Marcus. He would start to hound me down. Heck, he'd probably come to my house on the days of service to make sure that I was going.

It was 3:00 a.m. by the time I got home, showered, and got in bed. I thought to myself, *I'm not going back. It's way too much.* Then all of a sudden, I heard my phone vibrate. *Who could it be, texting me so late?* I thought to myself. Maybe it was Tommy. He had been hitting me up the past couple of weeks. I guessed he was trying to get me back. But we both knew it was over. I reached over to my nightstand and grabbed my cell phone.

"Ugh. Can this night get any worse?" I said aloud.

I went to the message icon and clicked on it. It was *Marcus!* What was he doing, texting me at this hour? I opened up the message and it read: "Hey, Cassie! It's me. Jada told me about your conversation with her. I'm begging you, PLEASE, DON'T LEAVE! Whatever is wrong, whatever's concerning you, we can talk about it. We can fix it. Cassie, please don't leave. I'm begging you . . . I NEED YOU!"

As soon as I read those last few words, "I NEED YOU," I immediately remembered the words Pastor Howard had prophesied to me the night I went to the youth revival.

"You don't need no man . . . *He needs you!*"

Oh my God! I can't leave. He needs me! Who would have known this prophecy would still be in my heart? God saw it fit to bring it back to my memory at this time, on this day, on this particular night.

You can't leave, Cass, I thought. *They need you, God has need of you, and Marcus needs you too.*

4

THOSE WHO MOVE IN HASTE MISS THE MARK

Even though the message I had received from Marcus moved me, I still didn't let up on the idea of leaving the church. In the same breath, it didn't stop Marcus from contacting me and hoping that I would change my mind and go back. I thought about him and the church every day. My heart was definitely all in, even if it meant that Marcus and I never got together. I loved my church and I missed it. I went visiting other places. That didn't last too long. Nothing felt like home to me outside of the Powerhouse.

I ended up going back there three weeks later. I took my good friend Trina with me. Trina and I had been friends since I was in middle school. We lost contact once I had gotten saved. She along with my other close friends used to make fun of me. They didn't quite understand my newfound love in the Lord. Trina asked me a few questions about getting saved. I gave her some pointers and even told her about Powerhouse church. I told her that it was the best church in town. Trina didn't want to go alone, so I went with her.

Everyone at church was so excited to see me. I'm not going to lie; I was excited to see them as well, even Marcus! It was surprising to me considering that I kept dodging him and stopped returned his phone calls and text messages. After accompanying Trina a few times at the Powerhouse, I was back like I had never left. Not only did my friend Trina get saved, she became a member and joined the usher board. It was so exciting for me to see souls get saved and getting *busy* for the Lord. Still, as exciting as that was, I still struggled with being around Marcus. I struggled with every task that was given to me. I couldn't pray without getting stuck. I couldn't read scripture without stuttering. As much as I tried to be perfect and not mess up around him, the more I struggled achieving that. On top of that,

God revealed to me that I was going be a preacher. Yup! Me with my Moses-like tongue. At this point, I had contemplated committing suicide. I mean, I'm not even kidding. I was losing it. It got so bad till I had to actually go to Marcus and tell him that I struggled with taking my life.

I remember the Sunday I disclosed that to him. He made mention of in his sermon. He didn't mention my name, of course, to spare me the humiliation. But he was making reference to how you never know what people are going through, and how important it is to always make yourself available to love on your neighbor. I saw how teary-eyed he got. I remember Marcus saying to the congregation that he never would have known the person who told him this *actually* struggled with suicide. He said very kind things about me—that I was beautiful and had a big heart and a promising future. I didn't really get butterflies when he said these things about me. I honestly thought he genuinely cared and looked at me no more that he would a sister. But with all those kind words, I still couldn't shake it. I couldn't shake all that I was going through off me.

I became more and more distant toward him, so much so that when I graduated the end of spring that year from theology school, I didn't invite him. I didn't tell him about it. Nothing. He found out from the pictures I posted on the Internet, on my Facebook page. I found out Marcus was furious with me. I tried telling him that I didn't want him wasting his time on me and that there would be other graduations like receiving an associate's degree in theology. This one was only for a measly certificate. It didn't matter to Marcus. He told me he did not want to miss any achievement I had or anything I ever needed him for. I gave him my word.

I started thinking to myself, *What am I doing? If I'm supposed to be with the man, then I have to stop running him away.* I had to talk to somebody about this. I ended up telling my friend Trina, and I told my boss from the salon I worked at called Layers with Attitude. My boss's name was Toni. I told her everything. I even told her the small encounters I would have with him. There was one time when the church and I went out to eat. We were at one of my favorite places to get wings. I used to always go with my ex Tommy when we were together. I was discussing with a few members of the church how I really love the wings and how I would make it my business to come at least once a week to dine there. Marcus had overheard the conversation and said to me that maybe we could go and grab some together one day. I didn't try to read into it too much because he probably wasn't looking at it any more than actually wanted to go out and grab wings.

"Girl! I don't care what you say! That man *likes* you," Toni said as she combed out the custom-made wig she just finished making for a client.

"I don't know, Toni. I don't think he's looking at me like that. I'm not really sure if I should even be looking at him like that."

"How will you know if you don't ask?" Toni asked.

"Oh no, Toni! I am not about to tell that man how I have been feeling about him for a year now. Besides, the Bible doesn't say anything about the *woman* to go after the *man*. That's the *man's* job.

"Yeah, I hear you, Cass. But what if Marcus's way of asking was telling you to invite him out for wings? I'm telling you, girl. You gonna lose out! Just ask the man."

Maybe Toni was right. Maybe he did say that as a way to clue me in on the fact that he may just be interested. Maybe I'll text him later on tonight. I'll ask him to meet me there next Saturday in the evening.

About 8:00 p.m. that evening, I mustered up the courage to ask Marcus to join me. I thought it would be appropriate to contact him at a respectable time. After all, he was *still* my pastor. It seemed like forever waiting for him to reply to my text. I had meaningless alarms going off on my phone. Geesh! Everything but him. Then finally, about an hour later I received a text. *Yes!* It was Marcus. Oh Lord, please don't let this man send me off to bed in tears. The message read:

> Hey, Cass! Thanks for the invite. Unfortunately, I won't be able to make it. I'm going to be all tied up with preparing for Sunday's service along with a number of other things. Maybe we can catch up some other time. Great night.

Really? I waited a whole hour for that? I knew I shouldn't have listened to Toni. *Another act to be embarrassed about. I'm sticking to my guns for now on. Never will I listen to her again. And never will I be the first to reach out to Marcus.*

5

THE STEPS OF A GOOD MAN
ARE ORDERED BY THE LORD

"So . . . How'd it go with Marcus?" Toni said in great expectation.

"Exactly how I knew it would go. I'm so pathetic."

"What? He said no?" she asked.

"He said he was too busy and he'll catch me some other time."

"Cassie, maybe he really was busy. You do know that he runs a *whole* church, don't you?"

"Yes, I know. But maybe it's not what I think. Maybe I'm still little sis in his eyes."

"Well, you know what they say. What's meant to be . . . *will* be."

"I guess," I said as I walked to my station to prep for my clients for the day.

I was kind of down that night. As a matter of fact, I was for the next couple days. I then realized that I couldn't continue like this. I was tired of waking up thinking about him, going to bed thinking about him. I think I struggled more with the revelation than I did with the idea of us. Pretty soon I got fed up. I figured I should put this whole Marcus crap to bed.

I had a second job working at a nursing home. I wasn't really making as much money as I intended with doing hair at the time; so I held on to my former job. I changed my position from full-time to part-time, at least until I got to where I wanted to be with doing hair. I ended up connecting with a guy there. He worked in the kitchen at the nursing facility. I knew of him when I was in high school. I had the biggest crush on him back then. I had found out that he was a family man though. He had a high school sweetheart and two kids. So I left him alone. I've never been the type to break up a happy home.

Between our run-ins at the job and basic conversations, we actually struck up a conversation about our personal lives. It turns out that he was going to barbering school and working part-time like me. I guess he was waiting for his clientele to increase also. After our many encounters, I finally got comfortable to tell him how I felt about him back in high school. I know. *Me*, right? The punk who couldn't even muster up enough courage to lay my feelings out on the table for Marcus. But see, with Quan, it was easy to be upfront. He showed interest. I could tell he liked me, and he could tell I liked him. Not only was it simple, but most importantly, we made sense.

I started spending a lot of time with Quan. Things were actually pretty smooth between us. We would hang out all the time together. He was the first relationship I had with someone that knew and respected where I stood in my beliefs. I would get into these preaching modes around him, and he would just take everything all in. He made it easy to put aside my feelings about Marcus. He was brown-skinned, good-looking, with dreads down his back, and on top of that, he was so refreshing to be around. He listened. He was supportive. He had qualities a woman would want in a man. But even with all of those qualities, it wasn't enough to put this revelation on Marcus to rest.

After a month or so of dating Quan, I invited him out to Powerhouse. Once again, God used Marcus in a mighty way. The church went crazy that night. I was shouting. I was praising. I was *all* in the spirit right next to Quan. I didn't care. I felt so free to worship God. I got to a place where I worshipped God with no limits, considering the limits I felt I had when I was with Tommy. Now that God freed me from that, no one could dictate my praise. Quan seemed to enjoy service. I was happy that he really took the time to come, knowing how much God meant to me. I didn't have to force it on him either.

When service ended, I had Quan meet all the members and then I had him meet Marcus. They hit it off really well too. Now, a person with common sense wouldn't dare have two men that they like in the same room, let alone getting them together to converse. But this whole thing with Marcus seemed to be something fleeting now that I was entertaining Quan. I thought to myself regardless of what I thought I'd heard, Marcus wasn't into me; he couldn't be. I walked over to the other side of the room to give them a moment to talk. I went and said my goodbyes to everyone and gathered my belongings to get ready to head out with Quan. I approached Quan and Marcus just as they were wrapping up their conversation.

"Ahahaha," Marcus chuckled. "That's great though. Good luck to you on that, man. Much success!"

"You ready?" I asked Quan.

"Yes. I am if you are," Quan said back to me with a smile.

"Oh, Quan! You can get more information about our services along with the prayer line we do every week on a conference call. You can go see Sister Jada. She will help you out with that."

"OK, cool. Nice to meet you, Pastor Boyd. Cassie, I'm just going to get a brochure about the church and then we can leave, OK?"

"Yeah. Sure," I said.

Quan headed over to Jada and the others as Marcus and I stood near each other. An awkward silence stood present between us until Marcus broke the ice.

"Seems like he's a good guy," he said.

"Yeah, he is," I answered. "You think maybe you guys can connect? I think he can learn a lot from you."

"Absolutely. Make sure you give me his contact info."

"That would be great," I said.

"Ready?" Quan said as he made his way back over to me so that we could leave.

"Yes. I'm ready. I see you later, Pastor," I said, giving him a hug and planting a kiss on his cheek. "Thank you for everything."

"Anytime, Cassie," he replied.

After Quan came to church with me, I thought to myself maybe we might become something. Maybe he would take on this Christian path with me. We spent a lot of time together, and we still managed to take things slow and refrain from having sex. We hung out, watched movies, went on dates. Things seemed to be going smoothly with us. I was even beginning to function a lot better at the church around Marcus. The thought of him no longer weighed heavy on me. I was even able to pray for him without getting wrapped up in a whirlwind of thoughts.

The next night I heard my phone ringing. It wasn't too late in the evening. I was laying out my clothes, prepping them for work the next day. The name Pastor Boyd came across my screen.

"Hey, Pastor, how are you? Is everything OK?" I asked.

"Hey, Cassie. Everything is fine. Just checking on you. How are things?"

"Everything's going good, Pastor," I said. I was confused that he would call to see how I'm doing, being that I just seen him at church that past Sunday.

"Oh. Okay. Cool. How are things with you and Quan?"

"Oh," I said as I chuckled realizing the reason he was really reaching out. "Things are going good so far. Still getting to know each other."

I didn't understand why he asked me that too, being that he had also asked me that question when Quan came to church that Sunday as well. Come to think of it, ever since I brought Quan to church, Marcus made a point to ask that exact question over and over again every time he saw me. I guess his big-brother side started kicking in. Lord knows I didn't want that side of him to come out. Back in the day, when I was seeing someone he didn't approve of, he'd chewed my behind right up.

"That's good, that's good," he said. "Hope things work out for you two."

"Thanks, Pastor," I said.

"Okay . . . Well . . . umm. I was just calling to see how you were, you know. Just checking on you," Marcus said, seeming like he had more on his mind to talk to me about.

"OK, Pastor. Thank you for that."

"No problem. Talk to you soon."

"OK. Goodnight."

I went into work at the shop the very next day. It was pretty slow for me and boss Toni when it hit noon. I asked her to wash and set my weave for me. She took me to the sink and started washing my hair before prepping me to go under the dryer.

"*Soooo.* How is Quan?" Toni asked.

"*Fine,*" I said. Yup! I told Toni about Quan too. She already knew who he was. Her brother and Quan were real good friends. Quan had me by three years. Not nearly as bad as the age difference for me and Marcus. Seven years? I must have been really bugging out if I ever even thought Marcus would be looking at my young butt.

"Just fine. That's it? Y'all have to be doing much better than that, being that he's still around," Toni reasoned.

"Everything is good, Toni."

"So you all done with your feelings for Marcus now, huh?" she asked.

"Yeah, I think so. That man is not worried about me and won't ever be, so *I'll be moving onnnnnnn.*" I sang.

"You can't say he's not worried about you. You never even asked the man, let alone told him how *you* feel."

"Oh my gosh, Toni, just drop it. *Please?*" I pleaded.

"Oh, now you want to stop talking about it. Before, it was *Marcus this and Marcus that.* Now it's *stop talking about it*?" she said, laughing as she mocked me.

"See, Toni, this is why I don't be wanting to tell you anything," I said, disappointed.

"I am kidding, Cassie." She laughed. You know I love my little sis. Come on. Let me put you under this dryer. Stop trippin'!"

I sluggishly walked over to the dryer. Toni always had a tendency to make me eat my words. Changing the subject, she said, "So, Cass? What are you trying to do to your hair?"

"I'm thinking probably some curls and—"

"Hey, Pastor!" Toni yelled as she gave me this sneaky grin.

"Hey, Toni! What's going on, y'all?" said Marcus.

No freaking way! What the heck was he doing here? No, this is not happening to me right now. I look a mess under this dryer. He decides, today out of all days, to pop up on me?

"What's going on, Cass?" he asked as he playfully hit my leg before sitting at the seat with the hooded dryer next to me.

"Nothing much," I replied.

"It's so funny you popped in—we were just talking about you, right, Cassieeeee?" Toni added. All I could think to myself was *if this girl don't keep her mouth shut, I am going to literally kill her.*

"Oh, really?" Marcus asked, curious to know. "What about?"

"Just church stuff," I said quickly to rebut what Toni might let fly out of her mouth. "So what brings you here?" I asked.

"Oh, I just stopped by to check on you. Just seeing how things were going."

"Oh. OK," I said, with this baffled look on my face. I couldn't help but acknowledge that Marcus had been *checking on me* for the past couple days now.

He then started asking Toni and me about business. He informed us about things he had going on pertaining to the church and speaking engagements coming up. Toni and Marcus had grown pretty close since I had brought her to the church. They formed a great brother-and-sister-like bond. Toni was a couple years older than him. Marcus asked her about her marriage with her husband and how their kids were doing. He made mention that he'd like her husband and kids to come visit soon. Toni and Marcus continued to speak on the subject of marriage, and somehow Toni decided to throw me in the conversation.

"Yeah. I try to tell Cassie that all the time. It's always important to keep the spark in your marriage. She has to start getting prepared now. The girl don't even shave her legs, talking about she will when she get a husband."

No, she did not just go there. No, she did not just say this in front of Marcus!

"Well, I'm sure Cassie will do just fine once she gets married, right?" he asked as he rested his hand on my thigh.

Now let me make this disclaimer. The way he rested his hand on my thigh was not too high up and not too far down. It was smack dead in the middle. But that's just it with Marcus. He was always in the *middle*. I couldn't ever read this man. I couldn't tell if it was just chivalry or if he really was interested in me. The back and forth of trying to figure him out drove me up the wall.

"*Yes*," I said. "I will do just fine."

The door to the shop swung open. It was Quan. I guess it was "pop up on Cassie" day for me.

"What's up, Quan?" Toni said to him as she discreetly gave me the eye. You know, like "Oh shoot, girl, what you gon' do?" type eye.

He walked to Marcus and me as we were sitting next to each other. I could tell

Quan was heading to school because he had his barbering uniform on. I thought to myself, *This can't be happening right now!*

"Hey, Pastor Boyd. How have you been?" Quan asked.

"Oh, I'm hanging in there, bro. How 'bout yourself?"

"Oh, I just came to see Cassie before heading to school," Quan said as he looked over to me. "Can I get a hug?" he asked.

"Sure," I said. I swear from the time I lifted the hood up from the dryer and stood up to hug Quan, it was *dead* silence. You could literally hear a pin drop. I put my arms around his neck and he put his arms around my waist. Though it was like a three-second hug, it seemed like forever between the hug, releasing our arms from each other, and planting myself back under the dryer.

"OK. I'll see you later, Toni. Great seeing you again, Pastor!"

"Likewise, Marcus said, responding to Quan's farewell.

A minute or two went past. Marcus broke the ice to strike up a conversation with Toni again. Marcus didn't say much to me after that. His chat lasted about five minutes with Toni before he headed out.

"All right, ladies. Good seeing you guys."

"You too," Toni and I said in unison.

"I'll see you at Bible study, Cass," Marcus said as he walked toward the door.

"OK."

Marcus left the shop. I took a moment to process what just happened before I looked up to see the look on Toni's face. When I looked up at her from the dryer, Toni had this sly *devilish* grin.

"And you saying that man don't like you? Chile, *please!*" she said.

"He don't."

"Please, Cassie! A blind man can see the chemistry you guys have between y'all."

"Toni, stop!"

"I'm serious, Cassie! I'm telling you. That man likes *you*! Trust me. I'm older than you. I know what I'm talking about, and as far as I'm concerned, you still like him too. Hell, you might even love him."

"What do you expect me to do?"

"Talk to him! Stop beating around the bush! Tell that man how you feel!"

"I'm not doing that! I did too much already."

"*What?* Ask him to meet you for some wings? So what? He didn't come. He was tied up. Big deal!"

"It is a very big deal, especially if my Bible tells me 'He that findeth a wife findeth a good thing'!"

"What the hell does that even mean?"

"It means that it's the man's job to look for his wife. Not the other way around."

"Here you go with another one of your scriptures, Cassie."

"Whatever, Toni," I said as I went to my station and plugged up my marcel iron for some curls. A few moments later, Toni walked over to me.

"Look, little sis, I just want you to be happy. I don't want you missing out on something special. There can really be something between you two. You told me God gave you this revelation. I just don't see the harm in acting on it. That's all."

"I know you're trying to look out for me. I get that. I just don't want to manipulate anything. If this is what God wants, God will do it in *his way*. You once said to me, 'What is meant to be will be.' Can we just go trust in that?"

"You're right, Cassie," Toni said. "When it does happen, can I be your maid of honor?"

We both busted out with laughter.

"You get on my nerves!" I said once I was able to speak again after laughing so hard.

"I love you, sis," she said to me.

"I love you too."

6

MANY ARE THE PLANS OF A MAN'S HEART BUT GOD'S WILL PREVAILS

My thoughts seem to find no sleep, thanks to everything that transpired that day at the shop. I seemed to be back at the same place I was once was before. I replayed all that had taken place with Marcus at the shop, over and over in my head. *Toni is crazy*, I thought to myself. *This man is not worried about me.*

I continued to hang out with Quan. Even though these buried feelings for Marcus sprouted up again, I really liked Quan. I wasn't about to throw away my relationship with him. I wasn't about to exchange a *guarantee* for a *what if.*

A couple of weeks later, Marcus started checking on me routinely, usually twice a week. He would ask me how I was doing. You know, the usual. And he still managed to squeeze in asking about Quan and me. On one particular day, I was actually glad he did. At this point, I was wrestling whether or not to share to Marcus what I seemed to be struggling with at that time. But I came to my senses that he was my pastor and I needed to trust that God led me to be under his covering for a reason. Besides, I had known him since I was a teenager.

"Pastor, I want to share with you something that I seemed to be struggling with. I hope it's appropriate," I asked. I didn't really want to ask any of the older women in the church. Some seemed to have their views on me before getting to actually know me. What is it with church anyway? Why is it that a pretty girl with a nice shape has to be up to no good? It's like whenever a girl like me enters the room, women seem to turn up their noses like a dirty-sock odor has wafted under their noses.

"No. You're OK. What's going on?" Marcus asked in the utmost concern.

"I have been having a certain feeling toward Quan. I'm almost tempted to sleep with him."

"Oh," he said. He responded as if he was taken aback by what I disclosed to him.

"I hope this isn't too much," I added.

"Oh no. It's fine," he said. He paused for a second before he continued. "The advice I would give to you is to make sure you are not putting yourself in situations that can tempt you into falling. I would advise you to go out on dates that are public. Hang out in places where it is not just you and Quan together, alone. Don't stay the night at each other's houses if you have not done so already."

I have, I thought to myself.

"If you have, try not to because that is the number one area in the day where the devil can creep in to get you to sin."

"OK. Thanks, Pastor. Do you mind praying for me before we hang up?"

"Sure. Father God, I thank you for Cassie's life. I pray that . . ."

Wow! I thought to myself. *Can't nobody tell me this man wasn't used by God. He would pray you out of something and pray the devil under something.* Marcus was favored; he was anointed.

Even if this man never becomes my husband, I would never take his love for God and his passion for being used in the kingdom from him. Marcus was amazing. He was such a blessing me and those around.

Bless this man, God, in all his dreams and all his endeavors. Look at me! Here I am in need of prayer and I still can't help but pray for this man. He won't ever know the countless nights I have been up praying for him. Never anything about him being my husband—it was always for God's protection over him and for his success. I wanted that for him genuinely.

"And in Jesus' name we pray, Amen."

"Amen. Thank you so much, Pastor."

"Anytime. Don't hesitate to call," he said.

"I won't. Goodnight, Pastor."

"I love you."

"I love you too."

The following week, Marcus reached out to me through a text asking me to give him a call. When I called, he answered and asked how I was doing. Again. The usual. But this time happened to be around mid-August. Marcus shocked me with the next statement that came out of his mouth. He asked me what I was doing the following night. I told him I didn't have any plans. He then asked, "I was wondering if you are able to go out to dinner with me tomorrow night and have a few wings and catch up."

I could hardly breathe. What would he possibly want to have dinner with me for? What was there to catch up on? Was he really asking me this? *God, seriously, what are you up to?*

"Hello, Cassie, are you still there?" he asked.

"Yes, I'm here, Pastor. Sure. About what time?"

"Let's say about six . . . six thirty?"

"Yeah, sure. That's OK with me."

"Great, I'll see you then."

"OK," I said, then I hung up.

I met up with him at a nearby sports bar. No, I was not getting lit with the pastor, OK? It is a kid-friendly bar. I was not a drinker at all, never have been. I had gotten drunk one time with my best friend Whitney before I got saved. It was not a fun feeling. *Never again!* As I walked in the bar, I met Marcus at a table where he was seated. I said hello to Jada in passing. She had dropped off Marcus's briefcase to him. She gave me a quick hello. She had on workout attire. I figured she was in a rush to go work out.

"What's up, Cass? How is it going?" he asked as he stood up and gave me a hug.

"I'm doing good," I said with an inquisitive smile, curious to see what this meet-up was all about.

"I just wanted to take the time out to see how things are going with you. I figured we can grab a few wings and chat," he explained.

"Oh, OK."

"Can I get you anything?" the waitress asked as she pulled out her notepad to take our order.

"I'll take a water," Marcus said.

"OK. And for you, ma'am?" the waitress asked as she jotted down Marcus's beverage.

"I'll take a lemonade."

"Awesome! I'll be out with those in a sec!"

Marcus struck up another conversation. He asked, "So what's new?"

"Nothing much? Working. I finished hair school, as you know, so I'm at the shop more and I'm in my second year in theology."

"Oh yeah. That's right! How is that going for you?" he asked.

"Going good. No complaints."

"OK . . . here go your drinks," the waitress said as she placed them on our table. "A water for you, sir, and a lemonade for you, dear. Are you guys ready to order?"

"I'll try some of your barbecue wings," Marcus requested.

"And for you, ma'am?" she asked.

"I'll have an order of hot wings," I told her.

"Sweet. That will be right up in a few minutes, OK?"

"Thank you," Marcus said as he took a swig of his water. My mouth was so dry from being so nervous that I did the same.

"So how is Quan?" he asked.

Dang. Again, Marcus? Why do you insist on bringing him up every time I speak to you? As if meeting you for dinner right now isn't uncomfortable enough.

"He is doing great," I said, pretending to be interested in entertaining this question for the millionth time.

"How do you feel about him? Are you guys dating?" he asked.

At this point, I felt myself breaking a sweat. "Yes," I said. "He's really good to me, he's such a nice guy," I added.

"That's great!" he said. "Where do you see yourself going with him?"

I responded by saying, "I can definitely see me marrying him." *Yup, I said that. I told Marcus those exact words.*

"Really?" he said. I could tell that he was in shock.

"Yes. I can see him being my husband," I added. *What am I supposed to say? "No, Marcus. God told me that you are. We will have a life and a future together. I know I'm much younger than you and you're probably more seasoned than I am, but we were meant to be together."* I'd sit and watch him go in marital bliss before I made a fool of myself.

"Oh. That's great. That's really great, Cassie," he said. "I'm really happy for you." For some reason, as much as he said he was happy for me, it sounded like it was far from the truth. But I wasn't sure if it was bittersweet for him to envision that about his sweet little baby sis or if he didn't like the idea of Quan and me as a whole. I didn't know. Why was this man *so* confusing?

"OK, guys!" the waitress said. "Here are your hot wings and your barbecue wings. If you guys need anything just holler 'Sarah,' and I come running, OK?"

"Yes. Thank you, Sarah," Marcus said.

The rest of the conversation seemed to run its course as we continued to dine. Besides him asking how I was enjoying my wings and vice versa, there wasn't really much we discussed. I think the whole husband thing with Quan just made way for a big elephant to make itself present right in the middle of the sports bar. After we finished eating, Marcus waved down Sarah for the check. I started to reach in my purse to get some money to pay or at least take care of my tab. He insisted on taking care of the tab. Once Marcus paid the bill, he reached for his briefcase and asked me, was I ready to go? I told him yes. Marcus walked me to my car.

"I had a good time," he said.

"So did I. Thanks for inviting me out."

"No problem. Good luck with Quan and everything," he said, reaching out for a hug.

"Thank you," I responded as I hugged him. As soon as he walked away, I immediately got into my car and drove off. I could not believe I said that to Marcus. I'm sure I lost every ounce of hope. I know the Bible says the promises of God are *yea* and *amen*, but I didn't even know if God would still stand by this promise at this point.

I drove all the way home in silence. I thought about our dinner. How handsome he was—his beautiful chocolate skin and perfectly nice haircut. He even grew in his beard. He was a beautiful man. I really fell in love with everything about him. I even loved how he stood over me. And let me tell you, that was something to appreciate when you stand at 5'7" as a woman. But I was sure I blew it. Even if he did like me as much as Toni said he did. He wouldn't pursue me now! Not after I said what I said about Quan.

I finally reached home. I went in my house and literally performed a belly flop on my bed. And then something happened. My phone rang. It was Marcus.

"Hello? Marcus?" I answered.

"Hey, Cassie," he said in a frazzled manner.

"What's wrong?" I asked. At this point I was afraid. I didn't know what to think. Was he OK? Did he get into an accident?

"I'm fine but I have to tell you something."

"What?" I asked. "What is it?"

"It's Quan. He's *not* your husband."

"What do you mean?" I asked. "What makes you say that?"

"I had a dream. I know he is not your husband."

"Well, what was the dream about?" I asked. At this point I was nervous. *Was Quan for my harm? Should I even be dealing with him?* I thought to myself.

"I don't know," Marcus said.

"Pastor, if he is of harm to me, you need to tell me. It is your job as my pastor to cover me. Tell me! What happened in the dream?" I insisted.

"OK, I'm sorry. I didn't have a dream. I just know he is *not your husband*."

Oh my God, I thought. *Why would Marcus say this? Why would he call me in such a panic like this? Did he think Quan was bad for me? But he said himself that Quan was a good guy. Was he trying to say he's not a good guy for me? Did Marcus think he was the better man for me? Was Marcus trying to tell me that he was my husband?*

7

BUT THIS KIND GOES NOT OUT EXCEPT BY PRAYER AND FASTING

I anticipated going to church that entire week. I didn't quite get the confirmation I needed from Marcus to see if he was at all interested in me or whether God told him about me being his future wife. The dinner I had with him had given me great hope that perhaps he felt the same way about me all along. It would be nice to have someone who could relate to what I had been going through. How much more pleasant would it be if he were that *someone.*

Quan made it so much easier to entertain my daydreams on Marcus. I had found out that he was doing some drug dealing on the side. I was kind of disappointed. What was worse is that he was still entertaining his kids' mother. A friend of mine caught them going out of town together. I didn't bother investigating what was going on. I thought to myself that maybe this was the will of God. I thought that maybe I had no business being with Quan anyway, considering what God had told me about Marcus. I just thank the Lord that I didn't commit any slip-ups with him and I was able to keep myself from sinning.

I was super excited to go to the next service that week. I had to skip the week prior because I had to help my boss Toni with a wedding that particular Sunday. That was the same week I went out to eat with Marcus, so it had been a while since I saw him. I made sure I looked my best just in case his eyes happened to find me in the pews. He sat in the first row of the pews. We were still utilizing the gymnasium at the YMCA. He would sit in the first row and wait for the announcements. Then songs from the praise and worship team and other program activities had to commence before he went up to deliver the sermon for the day.

When Marcus looked up and noticed me, I smiled. He did a quick smile back. His smile seemed surfaced and less friendly. I wondered if he was upset with me about our dinner the other night. Before Marcus delivered the Word, he made an announcement regarding the leaders, and yes, I was a part of that group. He said, "I need all the leaders to meet me directly after service. It is mandatory."

I hope neither one of us is in too much trouble, I thought.

He then said, "There are concerns that have been brought to my attention that we will need to discuss and go over solutions to resolve the problem, amen?"

"Amen," I said along with the rest of the congregation.

Marcus continued with preaching the message for the day. And do you really have to ask? Of course he crushed it! When service let out, we did the usual. All of us church folk greeted one another. We made small conversation with the new visitors, along with the reoccurring ones. Then the leaders, along with me, gathered the chairs up and brought them to the gymnasium's storage closet before heading up the stairs to the conference room. Marcus would take a few minutes to freshen up and prep himself before meeting us. We waited a few minutes and then the door swung open. He entered the room, accompanying Jada, who was now his assistant, and his armor bearer Desmond.

"All right," Marcus said. "How is everyone feeling today?"

"Good," we answered.

"That's good," Marcus said. "OK, we have a couple of events coming up, so I'm going to need you guys in the loop of a few things. But before I go over that, I have to discuss something that has been presented to me. It was shared to me there are a lot of women from this area that are claiming to be my wife. They are claiming that the Lord is telling them that I am the 'one.' I even had someone approach me in my office, proposing to me that they just want to be intimate with me and that we could keep it a secret. I am under attack by a *lot* of women. It also got back to me that women in this church are feeling the same and are coming here in hopes of dating me. So I need the intercessors to cover me in prayer. Pray that God keep me focused and pray that people are attending Powerhouse with the right intentions. Is there any further question?"

"No. Not at all, Pastor. We got you!" a few of the members shouted.

"I appreciate you guys," Marcus said, with a sigh of relief. "OK. Let's jump into the agenda for this meeting. So *this fall . . .*"

My throat felt like it was on fire. You know that burning sensation in your throat when you're holding back from crying? Yes! That was the state I was in. I literally prayed the rest of the meeting: *What's going on, God? Why would you have me to be so humiliated? Please, just don't let me break down in tears. Just let me keep it together, God. Please?* I kept telling myself over and over again: *Cassie, keep it together. Cassie, keep it together.* I really couldn't tell you what the rest of the meeting was about. All I was focused on was not bursting into tears.

When the meeting got out, I wasted no time and headed straight for the door. I said a general goodbye to everyone. I was able to avoid the casual conversations and even skipped out before Malcolm asked for a ride. I just needed to get to my car. I remember driving off, sobbing. Streams of tears were just coming down my face as groaning sounds released out of my mouth. I was in so much pain. I was so hurt. I started talking to God aloud: *"Why, God?* Why would you allow this to happen to me? I never asked for this. Why would you have me to be just like these other girls? I didn't come here for a husband. I came with the intentions of growing in you. Now I am just like them. I am no different from the others claiming to be Marcus's wife. I'm so hurt, God. I'm in love with this man. I don't know how, I don't know why, but I am. I feel like such a fool. Why would you give me this revelation only to make a fool of me? I need you, Lord. *Please help me!"*

I cried for another hour or so before I thought to myself that maybe I should fast. I thought that maybe if I fasted, I would get the answers I needed from God and finally move forward. It didn't matter whether what I heard was right or if it wasn't God at all telling me this revelation. I was open to any resolution at this point. I just needed answers, and I knew that if I fasted and prayed, I would get an answer straight from heaven. I decided to fast for forty days. The first three days, I didn't eat anything. I consumed nothing but water. It was the hardest fast I had ever been on. I thought that maybe I should up my game by committing to a fast that required more of a sacrifice. This wasn't an ordinary fast for me. I needed to prove to God how much it meant to me to hear from him. I needed answers. I needed his answer.

8

HE THAT FINDETH A WIFE FINDETH A GOOD THING

In the midst of my fast, my friend Soniah had a little baby girl named Breah. She was adorable. I would spend a lot of time with Breah. I felt the most pure every time I would hold her in my arms. A lot of my serenity would take place with her. I remember being led to pray for her and to prophesy over her life. I know that she will be a tremendous blessing one day. If I wasn't spending time with Soniah and her daughter Breah, I would be at home communing with God. I hadn't answered any phone calls unless it was extremely important. I didn't watch any TV unless it was a sermon. I only fed off vegetables and peanuts. But for some reason, I didn't quite get any answers regarding the revelation. The first three weeks were a struggle. At one point, I almost threw in the towel. But I stuck with it, and I was glad I did. Not only did I feel great spiritually, but also that fourth week seemed to thrust me into the answer that I had been looking for.

It was in the middle of September that year of 2012. Something took place in my fast that would switch the direction of my norm. The night before, I had Malcolm come by. He would always pop up on me at my house. I remember my sisters would be so annoyed by him showing up unannounced. I must admit I was pretty taken aback too. I knew it was out of love and concern. Malcolm was always able to tell when I was in a funk or perhaps going through. He was never too far away when I needed him.

At this point, I had kept all my feelings toward Marcus a secret. Only a few people knew. I had Malcolm out of the loop until the time was right to tell him, and there was no way I was disclosing this information to him while I was still on my fast. When it got late, I told Malcolm to catch a cab home from my house.

As he waited for the taxi, I somehow drifted off to sleep. It was about 4:00 a.m. the next day when I was interrupted out of my sleep by a phone call. It was Toni.

Toni had called, frantic, letting me know that the shop had caught on fire. The people that lived upstairs from the salon somehow caught an electrical fire through their walls, therefore damaging the salon area also. She explained to me that we had to go to the shop to grab what we could before the building was torn down. The fire didn't quite get to the shop area, but the water that was sprayed in the building by the firefighters weighed so heavily in the building that it wouldn't be able to hold up after a couple days. Eventually, the building would collapse.

Malcolm had somewhat overheard the conversation that Toni and I were having. He asked, was everything OK? I filled him in on all that had taken place, all while asking myself, *What is he still doing here?* He had found a comfortable spot at the edge of my bed and fallen asleep. He himself must have crashed and not been able to stay awake to look out for his cab. I was glad he was with me though. He was able to assist me with gathering my things from the shop.

Shortly after catching him up on the festivities of the salon, it dawned on me that Marcus had told me how upset he was about missing my graduation before and had demanded that whenever I had anything going on in my life, he wanted to be informed about it. It was so weird and random how that came to my mind. I called Marcus. I called so that he wouldn't be upset with me. I knew that if I kept this life event from him, I would have to face his fury again. So I took heed of his request. After a couple of rings, Marcus answered.

"Hey, Cassie. How are you?"

"Hey, Pastor, are you up?" I asked, thinking to myself why he was up early and enthused at four o'clock in the morning.

"Yes, and you know what, so crazy, I was thinking about you and I felt as if God wanted me to give you a call."

What he said seemed pretty ironic to me—that I would be in his thoughts so early in the morning. But I didn't think too much on his statement. I just figured maybe God was sending him a message about me in the Spirit.

"Oh, OK. Well, I just wanted to let you know that the shop burned down and I will be headed there soon to gather my things before they tear down the building."

"*Are you serious?*" he shouted. "Are you OK? Is everyone OK?"

"Yes," I answered. "Everything and everyone is fine."

"OK. Did you need me to come by and help out? I can be on my way right now."

"Oh no, Pastor! I'm fine really. I don't want you worried about me. You deal with a lot with the church and everything. I just wanted to tell you what was going on—that's all," I insisted.

"Are you sure, Cassie?" he asked.

"I'm sure."

"OK," he said. "Just keep me posted!"

"I will, Pastor. Thanks anyway."

"All right, then. I'll speak to you soon," he said before he hung up the phone.

I called Quan immediately after I got off of the phone with Marcus. We were still cool, even though I had cut him off for a bit. Quan managed to find his way back around, trying to assure me that he and his kids' mother were not together. Oh, and I failed to mention that his kids' mother had come to the shop one time asking about my dealings with Quan! Yes. That was the quickest way a man could turn me off. A man's baggage should never become your baggage. Remember that, ladies! However, I still remained cordial with him. I mean, how could I be upset with him? I was dealing with my feelings about Marcus as well.

Quan had actually lived around the corner from the shop, which made it so convenient for him to pop up on me at any time. I asked him if he could come help me gather some things from the shop. He gave an excuse about not being able to come. I was not happy with that, considering that he was willing to do whatever it took to win me over again. I just ended the call with him and got ready so that Malcolm and I could head straight to the shop to meet up with Toni and her husband Keem.

When I arrived at the salon, Toni and her husband were loading the U-Haul they had borrowed for the day. I got out of the car with Malcolm and headed over to them. By the time I came across the street, another person was grabbing items and loading them on the truck. That person was *Marcus*. I was so taken back, so surprised, and I was overwhelmed with joy. It touched me that Marcus was there for me. He really came after I told him not to, and he came by himself. I have been around where things had taken place involving people from the church and their lives, and Marcus would send people in his place to achieve a particular task to be in his stead. But he didn't send a substitute for me. He came himself, just him and only him. I felt special. I tried not to read too much into things. But one thing was for sure: he showed up. I knew that if I ever needed anything, I could count on Marcus to come through.

At that point, we had just about everything on the truck—well, everything we could save at that point anyway. News channel 10 had shown up unexpectedly and asked Toni for a quick interview about the fire. She wanted me to be in it with her, but my hair was a mess. So I asked Marcus to let me wear his hat for the taping. He let me borrow it, and I placed it on my head as I thought to myself, *Oh my goodness, this man's hat even smells amazing.*

Afterward, we retired at Toni's house right outside the city. This was my first time visiting her house. I must admit it was way more beautiful than what she described. It was *huge*! I looked over and saw the admiration even in Marcus's eyes. Maybe this was the type of house he wanted. Maybe he wanted that with me. Toni's husband Keem had asked Marcus and Malcolm to convene with him upstairs to show them around the house some more. Toni and I snuck off to get some fresh lemonade from the kitchen. We sat in front of the open bar she had veering off from the kitchen.

"Girl! What in the world is Marcus doing here?"

"Shhhh! Dang, Toni, if you say it loud enough, they will hear you!"

"My bad, girl. So what is going on?"

"Nothing really. Why? Did he say?" I asked, thinking that maybe she had the key to this whole revelation. Maybe Marcus let her in on a couple things.

"Nothing really. He just said he came to help us with the shop."

Well, there goes my answer. The guys had found themselves to us again, so Toni and I had to stop talking about Marcus. Then Toni announced to everyone, "So I want to thank you all for coming and helping out Cassie and me at the shop today. I figure I'll show my gratitude by taking you all out to eat tonight. What do you guys think?"

We all agreed and made plans to go. Once we unloaded some of Toni's things off the truck, we all planned on meeting each other at Applebee's around eight o'clock.

I had dropped Malcolm off before I went home to get some rest. I didn't anticipate going to dinner, being that I was so used to Marcus cancelling plans because of his obligations at the church. I just didn't want to get my hopes up after yet another disappointment, especially considering that I almost lost it over the last encounter we had about women claiming to be his wife. I wanted to spare my feelings, my integrity, and spare myself the embarrassment. Neither did I want to find myself being the third wheel again with Toni and Keem. At 8:20 p.m. that night, I was getting ready to get in bed. But my phone rang. It was Marcus.

"Hello, Pastor," I said.

"Hey, Cassie. Where are you?" he asked.

"I'm lying down. What's going on?"

"You're not coming out?" Marcus asked.

"You're there?" I said in my broken English, shocked that he would actually show.

"C'mon, Cassie," he said, sounding disappointed. "I said I was coming. You are always late. Get dressed and come on."

Did he really take note of all the times I was late to church and everything else? I thought. "OK. I'm on my way."

I put a few quick curls in my hair. I put together a simple outfit before leaving the house and grabbed Malcolm to come along for the dinner. After all, Toni did invite him to come. When I got to the restaurant, Toni and her husband were sitting on one side of the table while Marcus was sitting on the other. I noticed that Marcus whispered something over to Toni and Keem, and they began to laugh. It was clear that it was an inside joke he had shared with them because he was discreet in his delivery.

Dinner was great. We shared a few laughs. We all felt like the night was too young to end it at the restaurant. Toni suggested that we go to her favorite after-hours spot. It was a bar called Andy's. She thought it would be cool to grab a couple of drinks. We hoped that they would allow Malcolm in, being that he wasn't age appropriate. We arrived and grabbed seats at a table near a window toward the back of the bar. I knew that was the table where Toni usually sat at, considering the many times I went there with her for lunch.

We aimed for the same seating arrangement we had at the previous place. But Malcolm snuck his way to sit near Marcus before I got to the table. I almost feel like Malcolm probably picked up on a few vibes between me and Marcus. As Malcolm made his way to attempt to sit next to Marcus, Marcus yelled over the music, "Yo, Malcolm, let Cassie sit between us!"

Malcolm quickly switched his seat with me. We ordered a few drinks that night. I just ordered a cup of Amerada Sour. I wasn't really the drinking type. Toni and Keem helped themselves to a Henny and Coke, and to my surprise, it happened to be Marcus's favorite drink also. And poor Malcolm, he was stuck with a Shirley Temple. We shared more laughs and had more conversation. At one point, Keem made a joke. Marcus had grabbed my thigh and laughed hysterically as he rested his head on my shoulder and leaned into my neck. I thought to myself, *The pastor is being a little too friendly with me. Hmm. What is this about?*

When the drinks got the best of Toni, she got into a big argument with her husband. I think she was a bit overwhelmed with the loss of the salon and felt the need to take it out on him. Keem took a walk away from the table and went outside for some fresh air. I guess he didn't approve of his wife's behavior. It was instinctive how Marcus and I naturally went to them to counsel and console them in their heated argument. It was also funny that as we switched off from one to the other, we voiced to each other that Toni was wrong in the matter. *Look at him and me, doing our first counseling session together.* Shortly after, they made up. Toni had apologized to Keem. The night ended great in spite of their disagreement. We all wished each other a goodnight. I gave Marcus a hug and told him I'd speak to him soon. I went to my car with Malcolm and drove him home.

The next day was Bible study. I figured after work at the nursing home that day, I'd go across town to visit Soniah and baby Breah. I tried my very best that night to make it to Bible study on time because of the memo from Marcus about me always being late. But as much as I tried to be on time, it tallied on the visible chart he had under the column that reads, "Tardy."

I snuck my way into Bible study, trying to go unnoticed as Marcus was preaching another one of his exceptional sermons. To Marcus, I stuck out like a sore thumb because in the midst of him preaching, he made a statement and then said, "Cassie!" He always called out my name when he preached. He called others too, but I took note that he called out my name way more than the others. I know I'm sounding a bit thirsty. But come on! I'm trying to figure this man out here! Once Bible study concluded, I made my way to the bathroom. I held my bladder until Bible study was over. I figured I'd wait. I didn't want to be that late girl that had the audacity to go back and forth from the bathroom with the absence of punctuality.

I sprinted to the bathroom without a single hello to the other members and clergy. Once I was done, I washed my hands and looked in the mirror and put some lip gloss on before heading back out. I opened up the door, and *boom*, there was Marcus.

"Hey, Cassie, how's it going?" he asked.

"Fine, Pastor. What's going on?" *Am I in trouble for being late?* I asked myself.

"Oh, nothing. Actually, I was seeing if you are going to Toni's house next week. She's having a football party and invited a few friends. So I was wondering if you were going to be there."

"Yeah," I said. "Sure. I'll be there."

"Really? OK, then. Cool. See you then," he said, with his hand in the air in anticipation of a high five.

"OK. See ya," I said, hitting his hand to seal the high-five gesture. *What is happening?* I asked myself.

The following day, I met with Toni at this new spot she was looking at for us to do hair. She felt it would be a great idea to work at this nearby shop and rent rooms from the owner until we were able to find a place of our own. The owner requested us to pay $150 a week for our individual rooms. Toni was used to spending more than that when she had the salon. And as for me, that was my norm because I paid that same amount to Toni for booth rent. So everything worked out perfectly for us. When the owner Karen left our rooms, I went over to Toni's room to tell her about the strange encounter I had with Marcus. I explained to her that Marcus asked me if I was going to her football get-together.

"So what is this football party and when were you going to tell me?" I asked. "What are you up to, Toni? I know you."

"Cassie, what are you talking about? I'm not up to anything!" Toni said as she laughed.

"What did you do, Toni? I know you did something. I know you!" I said in a panic, thinking to myself the worst, hoping that she didn't tell Marcus anything if not *everything*.

"OK, Cassie, don't be mad at me. I told him," she confessed after she protected herself with a nearby magazine to prevent me from hitting her and succeeding.

"*Why?* Why would you say something I told you not to, Toni? Damn! Now I know I look like a fool."

"No, you don't," she said as she continued to laugh.

"What did you say, Toni? Tell me everything," I demanded.

"It actually went well," she said. Then she continued, "So remember when Marcus came by the shop the time Quan came by to see you before going to school?" she asked. I shook my head yes. She then said, "So he has been calling me almost every night, asking questions about you, like how you and Quan were. How were you at the job? It didn't matter what we spoke on, he made his way to discuss you. I even tried to change the subject a few times because I didn't want to slip up and do what you told me *not to* as far as your revelation and all. But, girl, he just kept pushing me! So *finally*, he called me yesterday and was talking to me how he had a great time the night before and said that we should all hang out again soon. So at this point, I think to myself, maybe I can get them two together again. So I said to him maybe I can have a football party and we can all chill then. Then Marcus asked me, were you going to be there? And I'm sorry, between you and him talking about each other, I couldn't take it no more, so I told him."

"Oh my *gosh*, Toni. I swear I'm not telling you anything again! You promised—"

"Wait a minute. Let me finish!" She continued. "So I asked Marcus did he like you or something. Marcus started laughing, like 'Toni, stop! Don't ask me that!' and so I said to him, 'Look, let me make it easier for you. Cassie likes you—'"

"*Toni, why?*" I shouted.

"Well, what the hell, Cassie!" she shouted. "I was tired of both of y'all beating around the bush. Do y'all like each other or not?"

"Tsst. You get on my nerves!" I said.

"Cassie, are you going to let me finish or not?" she asked.

"Go ahead!" I yelled, rolling my eyes.

"Anyway, I told Marcus that *you* like him and if he doesn't like you, he can tell me that he's not interested and I would just tell you the next time you speak on him that you should probably move on. But turns out . . . he likes you too."

"What?" I said in disbelief.

"Yeah," she confirmed. "He likes you. He asked me why you never told him how you felt and I told him how you didn't believe in going after a man and how you had a scripture reference to support that, you know the 'He that findeth a wife' thingy thing you be pumping all the time and that he has to find you? Yes! I told him that! He even went on to say that he asked his mom about you. I guess you guys went to some conference early this year and his mother took a strong liking to you and she even tried to buy you some books at the conference. But Marcus told her not to because he just knew that the other women would get jealous. He said when he asked his mom how she felt about you, his mom said, 'Son, she is beautiful. I can see you guys having beautiful kids together and, son, that girl is anointed!' He said that his mom never talked about any woman the way she had talked about you. So he said he started asking himself, could you be his wife?"

At that moment, it seemed like everything was coming back to me. I remembered his mom asking me what I was looking to get when I was in the line to buy books. I remembered how I told Marcus that he was better than the bishop we saw at the conference that he seemed to look up to. I even remembered how he called me, insisting that Quan wasn't my husband.

Wow! My prayers have been answered. I'm not going crazy. Oh my gosh! Marcus is in fact my husband*! And yes indeed! I am his* wife.

9

HIS WORD IS A LAMP UNTO MY FEET AND A LIGHT UNTO MY PATH

I couldn't believe it. I was still on a high after Toni shared all that information to me about Marcus. I felt my confidence level went up, and most importantly, I felt like I could finally have some rest about this revelation. Though I felt like I got my answer according to what was told to me, I decided to still stick to my fast until it was complete. Maybe God would have more to share with me. The following weekend, Powerhouse had a revival on both Saturday and Sunday night. I was excited. Not only that, but Toni was having her football gathering the upcoming week, and it was the last week of my fast.

Revival was off the chain. We had so many visitors from all different churches, and the speakers were incredible. Many of us were slain in the Spirit, others prophesied too, and most importantly, people gave their lives to Christ and joined the church. Every service was great. I really enjoyed all the speakers—well, except one. I can't quite remember her name, but she kind of rubbed me the wrong way. I remember before she got into her sermon for Sunday evening, she was insinuating that everyone who even thought they were Pastor Boyd's, or should I say Marcus's, wife was sadly mistaken. She was saying how she had women at her church that were suitable for him. I remember being really upset with her choice of words. As she said these things, I remember Marcus putting his head down as he chuckled to Desmond, his armor bearer. But I didn't find it funny at all. Still, I humbled myself and listened to the rest of her segment. After she was done, she spoke over Marcus's life. She said some powerful things to him and even talked about Marcus's future church building and how he would see much success. When she laid hands on him, Marcus dropped to his knees, praising God. His mom Liz went over to support and comfort him. She would visit frequently. I remember tearing up. Marcus's worship had always affected me. It made me cry. I just wanted so much for him. I believe he earned it. I believe he deserved it.

Once church let out, I said my goodbyes to everyone. As I made my way to the gymnasium exit, I saw Marcus in the lobby, standing by Desmond and Jermaine. His eyes were bloodshot red from crying. I just loved that he was so vulnerable in God. I asked him, was he OK? He shook his head yes. I just hugged him and kissed him on the cheek as I told him I loved him. Though I was moved by Marcus, I tried not to do too much or show too much at church. Besides, it's not like we had the chance to discuss our feelings toward each other, at least not yet.

The next day was a Monday. I usually went to theology school every Monday. But this Monday was different. I decided to cut school because that is when Toni was having her football party. I remember going to the nursing home earlier that day for work. About afternoon time, I received a call from Toni.

"Hey, Cassie. You're coming over tonight, right?"

"Yeah. I'll be there."

"Well, are you going to come over with Marcus, or will you be meeting him over here?"

"I guess it makes sense for us to ride together," I said.

"Well, I asked him the same question, and he's waiting for your call to make arrangements."

"OK," I said. "I'll shoot him a text."

"All right. I'm excited. I'll see you guys around 7:00 p.m."

"OK, Toni. Later."

Right after I hung up with Toni, I text Marcus: Hey, it's me. I was wondering if we were driving up to Toni's together?

He wrote back, saying: NO!

NO? What does he mean NO?

Another message followed: LOL. I'm just kidding. 7 PM, RIGHT?

I wrote back: Yes, Pastor, better yet, 6:30 PM. I'll be a half hour early.

He wrote back: Okay, Cass. I'll see you in a few hours.

I was really excited. I couldn't wait to see him that night. I could believe this was finally about to happen between us. A journey was about to start where I was no longer looking at him as a brother or a father figure. I would soon be looking at him as my soon-to-be husband. And he would find no problem in that at all.

When I got home, I hopped straight in the shower. I put something on that was casual. I wore a simple sweater with a pair of fitted jeans and some flat thigh-high boots. I put some curls in my hair. I put a little makeup on. I was so pretty that night.

I was ready at 6:15 p.m. I made sure I was more than on time. I wanted to prove that I could be on time for something. Toni shared with me that Marcus talked to her about his concern regarding me being late. That was Marcus's way saying to her that as a First Lady, I had to work on time management. He even went as far as giving an example about us having kids and whether or not I'd be on time to pick up them up from school. Like *dang!* I was that bad, huh? I made sure not to disappoint. I was ready so that when he called, he'd know that I was waiting on him and *not* him waiting on me.

In the meantime, I literally thought about how to strike up a conversation with him. I didn't know what to say. I even practiced in the mirror. I wanted to be perfect. I wanted him to see me as perfect, considering all the times I caved around him. His presence, to me, was just so overwhelming. I didn't know what to do with myself or how to act. What kind of hold did he have on me?

Marcus called me about seven-ish. He told me he'd be outside in like five minutes. I put on my jacket and got my purse together as I headed out. I thought, *Perfect! He is late! What a perfect way to start a conversation.* As I got outside, sure enough he was pulling up in front of my house. I walked to the car, and the butterflies in my stomach began to move about rapidly. For some reason, I couldn't tame them around this man.

When I got in the car, I started off by saying, "OK, is this is your way of paying me back?" I asked. *Yes! I executed.*

He laughed and said, "Oh, not at all.

"*Hmmm,*" I said. We both started laughing. The conversation went really well. He asked me how school was. We talked about the revival that took place on that weekend. He even asked me how I felt about the speaker that talked about him getting a wife from her church. I told him I didn't like her. He laughed. We just laughed and joked all the way to Toni's.

When we got there, Toni had food prepared. Toni also made her *special punch*: fruit juice with a little liquor to it. It was sweeter than I was bitter. So I was able to drink a little. A few friends of Toni were there. She also had her brother there; he is actually great friends with Quan. He also dated my sister Tanya a while back. In fact they dated for years. I knew this was going to get back to Quan. But I didn't care. Quan and I were over. It was time I lived up to the revelation God had given me about Marcus. They ended up playing a few games of Spades. I was the only one in the room who didn't know how to play. So Keem and Marcus teamed up, and Toni and her brother James teamed up. James's wife and I stood aside to watch.

As we were watching them play, Keem and Marcus were *cooking* Toni and James in Spades. It was so fun to watch. I had gotten a little comfortable and rested my arm on Marcus' shoulder as he played. He periodically asked me whether I was OK while he played. He wanted to make sure I was enjoying myself. I assured him that I was. Marcus was fun to be around. We laughed all night, and we had discussions that he would be in the center of. He was the *man* in the room. And I was eating up every second of it.

Once 10:00 p.m. came around, Marcus and I decided to head out. We both needed some rest to take on tomorrow. I had a full schedule at the shop, and he had to run the prayer line and hold meetings with members that were scheduled. We drove a few feet away from Toni's house. Then he asked, "Did you have a good time?"

"Yes, I did. I really enjoyed myself," I replied.

"That's good," Marcus said. "*So*, Toni shared with me that you like me."

I looked over at him and saw a slight smile on his face. "Yeah, I do. It's just crazy that I feel this way about you though."

"Why didn't you say anything?" he asked.

"I just believe a man should go after a woman. It should never be the other way around."

"*Oh.*" Marcus laughed. "He that findeth a wife, right?"

"Exactly. Besides, I was extremely intimidated by you."

"Really? Why?" Marcus asked.

"I guess it's because at one point, I looked at you as my brother. You're a lot older than me. Well, by seven years, which means you have to be a lot more mature than me and probably more ready for marriage and all that comes with it," I explained.

"I felt the same way about you, Cass. You know I said to myself, she is *beautiful*. You don't even know how much the guys at the church talk about you. Why would you want me? Why would you even like me?"

"You can ask God that question."

"So God told you I was the *one*, huh?" he asked. "What else did he say?"

"Well, he did make known that we cannot have sex until we are married!"

"Oh, that's funny, because that is exactly what I want. I want to wait," he said.

"So you asked your mom about me?"

He laughed and said, "You know what's so crazy? When I had asked my mom about you, I did disguise it at first by asking my mom about a couple of the other women before getting to you. I really just wanted to ask her about you, but I didn't want her to notice that I had feelings for you. But the way she talked about you, I was like *My God!* My mom has never talked about anyone the way she talks about you."

"Really?" I asked.

"Yes, really, so I started asking myself and started asking God, could you be my wife?"

We took a moment of silence once he told me that. I had thought to myself that Toni was telling the truth. Everything she had told me added up to all he had said. I couldn't believe it. God really shared something to me, and I was starting to see the fruits of it now.

"I guess we're here," he said.

"I guess we are."

"I had a great time with you tonight, Cassie."

"I did too. I really enjoyed myself."

"So did I," he said.

"I guess I'll see you at Bible study on Thursday," I said.

"On *time*?" he asked.

"Yes." I chuckled. "On *time*!"

10

SHE SHALL BE CALLED WOMAN FOR SHE WAS TAKEN OUT OF MAN

I felt as if I was floating on air after hanging out with Marcus. I didn't really have any intentions of jumping into a relationship with him just yet. Of course we'd need time to get to know each other. I couldn't believe I was literally at a place where I now knew how Marcus felt about me and that marriage would possibly be in our future.

I only had a few days left until my fast was officially over. Marcus and I snuck in phone conversations every chance we could get. We both were pretty tied up between work and school for me and church for him. Marcus practically lived in the house of Gods. He made plans to pop up that Friday at the new shop Toni and I were working at. I was not mad about that at all.

I was pretty slow for the day as far as clients went. Some of our clients were adjusting to our move. When Marcus arrived, I was just finishing up with my last client for the day. I could tell he was so happy to see me. The smile he had literally brightened up the room. We made our way into Toni's room to chill with her as she was working on her client. Toni's room was way better than mine. She had a TV and snacks for her clients. It was more of a social atmosphere than my room. Toni was servicing one of her regulars. Her name was Brittany. She was light-skinned, beautiful, and the way she held a conversation let me know that she was really smart. Marcus didn't hesitate to converse with Brittany, considering that he was wise himself. It didn't bother me at all. I knew that Marcus was very social. I mean, the man is a *pastor*. It was something I found no fault in. Besides, I am far from the jealous type.

Everything was going well. I was happy just to be around him. Everything about him excited me. Toni finished Brittany's hair. Brittany looked in the mirror and was ecstatic at the results. After she cashed out with Toni, Marcus told Brittany that it was a pleasure meeting her and hopefully he'd see her around. Once she gathered her things, Marcus said to Toni, "Toni, what's her name again?"

"Oh, that's Brit. She has been coming to me for a while now."

"Really? She's beautiful and really smart," Marcus said.

"Yeah, that's my girl," Toni said.

"Is she seeing anybody?" Marcus asked.

"I believe she's single," Toni answered with a puzzled face as if she was confused as to why he was asking her this, especially in front of me.

"Yeah. See, that's the type of girl I'd go for," Marcus said. He was into the light-skinned type, which was another reason why I thought I didn't have a chance, because my melanin was poppin'. Then he said, "That's the type of girl I'd marry.

Marcus continued to discuss Brittany right in front of me as if he was interested in getting to know her. What man in their right mind would inquire about another woman right in front of the girl he just confessed his feelings for a few nights ago? I was appalled. I felt completely disrespected. He embarrassed me in front of Toni. You'd think he'd catch the awkwardness in the room, but he didn't. He just kept going on and on about Brittany and girls he dated that were like her physically and mentally. I decided to walk out of the room in the middle of his conversation. Why would I be a part of it?

I walked across the hall to my room and noticed that a walk-in client was heading up the stairs to get some of my infamous curls in her hair. I was so glad she came so that I could tackle her hair as I coped with my heart feeling like it got ripped out of my chest. I was pissed. I was upset. I remember thinking, *There is no way this man can be my husband.*

After a few minutes, Marcus entered my room. One thing about me is when I am upset or experiencing any kind of emotion, I wear it like a highlighter. It is very hard to disguise, and quite frankly, I wasn't trying to hide it either.

"Are you good, Cassie? What's wrong?" *Did he really just ask me that?*

"Nothing," I said.

"Yes, there is. I can tell something is wrong."

"I'm *good*, Marcus," I said nonchalantly.

"No, you're not! Tell me what's wrong!" he insisted.

"I said I'm *good*!" I exclaimed. I'm sorry I did not entertain foolish questions. If he didn't know what ticked me off, then I'd act just as dumbfounded.

"No, you're *not good*! How do you expect us to resolve an issue if you don't communicate?" he explained.

"OKAY! YOU'RE DISRESPECTFUL!" I yelled.

"What? How?" he asked. I couldn't believe this man was actually confused.

"Because!" I said. "You don't come to my job to see me and then humiliate me in front of my boss and discuss an interest in another woman *right in front of me*! That's how you are disrespectful!"

"How is that disrespectful? It's not like we're together."

"It is disrespectful to not consider my feelings about you that you are aware of by discussing and inquiring about another woman. I don't care if we ain't together. So what, because we are not together, that means you get to disrespect me?" I asked.

"Asking about another woman is not disrespectful," he said.

"Yes, it is!" I said.

"OK, let's ask Toni," Marcus said as he went across the hall to get Toni. I guess he thought bringing her to the room would defuse the matter.

"Toni, is it disrespectful to ask about another girl if I am not with Cassie?"

I couldn't believe it. *Is this man delusional?* I thought to myself. *I know Toni is about to shut this down!*

"No," Toni said.

"No? Toni, it is OK for a man to come ask about another woman in front of me, in attempts of getting to know her to potentially date her, all while visiting me at my job when he knows I'm feeling him and vice versa?"

"That is dead wrong, *hmmm*," said my walk-in client as she got up from the chair and I released her cape off her.

"Thank you, girl. Thirty bucks," I stated as I attempted to ring my client out.

"How is that wrong though?"

"It is wrong, Marcus! See you later, sweetheart. Let me know if you have any issue with your hair, OK?" I said as I mellowed my tone, giving the client a farewell as she made her exit.

"Well, Toni and I don't feel like it's wrong," Marcus stated.

"So you think that just because Toni sided with you, it's supposed to change how I feel? I don't even know why you came," I said.

"I can leave," Marcus said. "That's not a problem."

"Well, bye!" I exclaimed.

Marcus grabbed his jacket and started for the door and then stopped. He turned back and sat in a chair across the room from me. I then turned my back to him and sat in a chair on the opposite side and faced the wall. We were quiet for *ten minutes* straight and didn't care to break the silence. I thought to myself, *I'll be damned to let a man feel comfortable disrespecting me. I nearly left a man I was going to marry to serve the Lord. I know the man God has for me will know better than this! God, this is who you have for me? There's no way he's the one.*

"Hey, y'all!" Keem said as he came into the room. He must have stopped by to hang out at the shop with us. I assumed Toni told Keem that Marcus was there.

"Hey," both Marcus and I said in a monotone voice.

"What's wrong with y'all?" Keem asked.

"They over there arguing." Toni shouted from across the hall.

"Oh naw. We can't be having that. This is the pastor, Cassie," Keem said. I guess he thought reminding me of Marcus's title was enough to let him off the hook. That was an epic fail.

"C'mon, Pastor. Let's go grab a drink."

Marcus got up from the chair as he gave Keem the pound. Keem and Marcus left my room and left the salon. I decided to straighten up my room to blow off some steam, wondering whether or not this short-lived romance with Marcus was over.

Then Toni came over toward my room and stood in front of the doorway. "That was crazy, right? Marcus was real disrespectful for asking about Brit!"

"Oh, *now* he's disrespectful, right? Just a few moments ago, you weren't talking that."

"I know I just didn't want to be involved with you guys arguing."

"Well, you shouldn't have involved yourself, Toni, because now Marcus thinks there was nothing wrong with his behavior," I said. I took to heart that Toni justified Marcus's behavior. I've seen so many people around him at our church that would see no wrong in what he did or at least didn't want to acknowledge it. I didn't expect perfection out of him. I just saw better in him. I didn't like when he did things that were questionable. So I always spoke on it. I believe the people around Marcus, including me, should always push him to be greater. I saw greatness in him, and I'm sure that was just a small depiction of what God sees.

"You're right, Cassie. I'm sorry," Toni said.

"I mean, c'mon, Toni, how would you feel if that were you and Keem?"

"I know. You're right, sis. I apologize. But, *girl*, you *told* him!"

I laughed. "You're so stupid, Toni."

We hung around for Marcus and Keem to get back. I had a guy walk in for a hair service. He wanted get his dreads retwisted. I figured that would kill time until Marcus and Keem got back. If he did come back anyway. Once I got halfway through my client's hair, Marcus had called my phone. He told me to open the door for him and Keem. I ran downstairs to open the door for them. Keem and Marcus were carrying on, laughing. He was not as poised as he usually was. It was kind of nice for him to enjoy himself. I'd never seen him in this light. Keem went darting up the stairs to check on Toni. I was walking up the stairs as Keem led the way, and then suddenly, Marcus pulled me from my belt buckle to him as he was a few steps below me. Then I turned around to him.

"I'm sorry," he said.

"I'm sorry too," I said as I put my arms around his neck. Marcus put his arms around me as we hugged each other for a couple of minutes. I could just feel all the bitter feelings I had about our argument releasing from my spirit. At that moment, I just felt safe in his arms, and the fact that he apologized made me realize that he did care about how I felt.

Marcus and I headed back up the stairs. Toni suggested for us to go to the movies after I was finished with my client's hair. I finished the client's hair. The client told me to follow him outside to his friend's car because he left his money in it. When we got to his car, he had to scrabble up the money to pay me for the hair service. Once I received his payment, I headed back toward the salon. I noticed Marcus standing there, making sure everything was OK. Toni let me know later on how Marcus went downstairs to protect me in case he needed to. I love that in a man. I am big on protection.

We headed out to see the movie *Taken 2*. We decided to catch a ride with Toni and Keem. They had a nice van we could all comfortably sit in and enjoy for the ride. Toni had the music playing. Toni and Keem had their side conversation, and Marcus and I had ours.

"Don't play yourself again," I said, playfully coming at him about our argument earlier.

"Don't you play yourself," he said, grinning.

"What are you going to do if I do?" I asked, provoking Marcus.

"You'll see."

"Why wait? Do something about it now," I said as I got really close to his face.

"Don't be trying to kiss me," he said jokingly.

"What, are you scared?" I asked him.

Marcus just looked at me. He then kissed me—just a peck. I wasn't trying to do all that tongue action in the beginning. When we got out of the car, we all laughed and made jokes while we made our way into the mall, to the theater. I remember before we got upstairs to the concession stand, Marcus was telling Keem and Toni, "Cassie kissed me. She kissed me." I thought to myself, *Let me find out Marcus kisses and tells.* He went on and on, saying, "How Cassie gonna kiss me when she fasting?" Toni's eyes lit up after she had recognized what Marcus was chanting. She pulled me to the side and told me to go with her to the ladies' room.

"*Oh my goodness, girl, you kissed Marcus?*" she asked as she pranced all over the bathroom.

"It was not that serious," I said as I laughed, thinking to myself why she and Marcus were making a big deal. You would have thought I just lost my virginity.

"Give me the details all the details, Cassie."

"I just gave him a small peck—that's all. He is making it bigger than what it was."

"*Girl*, I knew you guys would hit it off. Now aren't you glad that I said something when you told me not to?"

"Yes, Toni. I'm glad," I assured her.

"Girl, I'ma be your maid of honor!" she said.

I'm sure in her head, she was already planning our wedding. "C'mon. Let's go watch this movie."

When the movie was over, we made our way to Andy's for the second time since Marcus and I had been around Toni and Keem. I waited until 12:00 a.m. to order my wings. I was now ready to get back to my normal diet. My fast was officially over! *Yay!* We ate and socialized for a bit before we all decided to end the night. I think at that point we all had our fair share of fun-filled events for the day. Toni had to bring Marcus and me back to the salon to get our cars before heading home.

"Cassie," Marcus said, "I'm going to follow you home, OK? I just want to make sure you get home OK."

"OK, that's fine," I told him.

We both walked over to our cars and drove to my house. He followed me all the way home. I thought that was so sweet of him. I couldn't believe it. Marcus was actually following me to my house. Not as a brother, not as a friend, but as someone that was interested in possibly dating me. We arrived in front of my house like ten minutes later. I didn't live too far from the salon. I parked my car and then I headed over to Marcus.

"Thank you for making sure I got home safe."

"Anytime, Cassie," he said.

"Have a good night."

"Wait," Marcus said, leaning over to the passenger side of his car. "Why don't you come sit for a bit?"

"OK," I said. I was glad that he was not in a rush to go home so soon. He didn't want the night to end, and quite frankly, neither did I.

I opened the door and sat in the passenger seat. I was so nervous. I just knew this night would change the direction of our relationship, whether it be us being friends, or a little more. I was frozen in my seat. But with all those mixed feelings, I knew I wanted to kiss him that night. Like *really* kiss him.

"I really enjoyed myself," Marcus said.

"So did I."

"I can't believe we are really here in this place. *Little* Cassie. Someone I used to look at as my little sister."

"I know," I said.

"Why me, Cassie? You can be with anyone else. You're beautiful. You have everything going for yourself. Why me?" he asked.

"You have to ask God that question."

Marcus looked at me and leaned forward, and we *kissed*. People would say when it's *true love*, it's like fireworks. I have never believed such a thing until I kissed Marcus. It was the most perfect kiss I ever had, even the way he held me. I literally felt myself sinking in his arms. Our kiss was passionate. It was heartfelt. It was in fact fireworks.

"Umm, hold on," Marcus said as he stopped kissing me. "Oh my God, Cassie! I don't know what it is . . . but it's like . . . It's like I know your body. I have never felt that before."

I was silent. I was caught off guard myself. I had never felt this in a kiss before.

He then said to me, "This is crazy. Cassie, you're not a little girl anymore. You are a *woman*!"

I was in awe of the moment. I couldn't believe it. I was having a moment with Marcus. Everything seemed like it was coming to pass. Everything was happening like God told me it would. I was really going to marry Marcus. As I was drifting into thought, I noticed he was playing Jagged Edge. The song was "Promise."

"You listen to Jagged Edge?" I asked him.

"Yes. They are my favorite R&B group."

"You're lying!" I said in excitement. "That's my favorite group. I love them. My dad used to play their songs in his car all the time." Listening to Jagged Edge always reminded me of my father. It made me feel close to him at times whenever I got sad about his death. It just brought back sweet memories of him and his big beautiful smile. I can just see him now, trying to sing like it's nobody's business. I couldn't believe Marcus was a fan also.

"Wow. That's crazy. I like them too," Marcus said.

I smiled at Marcus as he looked at me. We kissed *again*. We kissed the whole night away. I couldn't believe this was happening. The way we touched each other made it seem as if we had been longing for this moment together. He held me so close. He took charge. I felt safe. I felt protected. I could feel it in his grip of me. He was a lover. I felt it in his kiss. I knew in that moment, I was safe with him. Though we had so much passion toward each other, he didn't touch me inappropriately. You could tell he respected my wishes to wait for sex until I was married. It was refreshing to know that he wanted the same. We kissed some more; we held each other and then kissed all over again. We both knew it was getting late, but for some reason, we didn't care.

After about two hours, Marcus said to me, "I think I should go home now."

"Yes," I agreed. "It's getting late."

"Play Jagged Edge tonight and think of me. I will do the same," he said.

"OK."

"Go on Pandora. Type them up and they will play all night," Marcus explained.

"OK, I will."

"I'll call you when I get home. Go ahead so that I can make sure you make it in the house."

"OK. Good night, Marcus." I kissed him one last time before I headed out of his car.

As I walked toward the house, it felt like my legs were made out of Jell-O. I swear I could walk. "Oh my God," I whispered to myself. "I can't walk right. Just get in the house, Cassie. Don't fall. Please don't fall."

"You OK, Cass?" Marcus asked.

"Yes, I'm fine," I said. I whispered to myself, "Cassie, just make it in the house. Please don't fall." I finally got to the door and waved goodbye.

"Thank you, Jesus!" I said to myself as I ran to my apartment door. I started to get undressed so that I could shower and head to bed. Then my phone rang. It was Marcus.

"Hello," I said.

"Hey. It's me. Are you inside?" he asked.

"Yes." I chuckled. "I'm good. How about you?"

"I'm good," Marcus answered. "Still driving home. Did you put Jagged Edge on Pandora?"

"I didn't get a chance to. I literally just settled in.," I said as I smiled to myself thinking, *This man really likes me. He really wants me to think about him all night even though I planned on it anyway.*

"OK. I'm almost home OK. I'll call you when I get home."

"Sounds good," I said.

After I got off the phone, I took a quick shower. Then I put on my night clothes. I plugged my phone up on the charger near my bed and rested my phone on the bed. I put Jagged Edge on my Pandora radio as I waited for Marcus's call. About twenty minutes later, he returned my call.

"Hey, Cassie. I'm home."

"OK."

"You're playing the songs, right?"

"Yes, they just stopped when you called."

"OK, good. I'm going to let you go, all right?" Marcus said.

"All right."

"Have a good night, Marcus."

"Sweet dreams, mamas."

When we hung up, I just lay down in my bed. I just thought of everything that happened between us, from the first argument we had up until we kissed. It was such a great day. I remember thanking Jesus. I was thanking him for showing up and revealing this man to me and possibly revealing me to Marcus. As I reminisced, the song "Promise" came on again. I smiled to myself, thinking, *yeah, that's our song.*

You're the only one I want in my life
I promise everything is all right, babe
You're the only one I want in my life
I promise, promise, promise, promise you, babe.

11

BY THEIR FRUITS YOU
SHALL KNOW THEM

I fell asleep to Jagged Edge that night. I even drove to the shop the next day with it playing in my car. I didn't have any appointments in the morning, so I played it in my room at the shop on my stereo. I didn't even greet Toni. She was with a client anyway. I was riding on clouds. Marcus had me in la-la land. I was so happy that day. As I was listening to music, someone walked in my room. When I looked up, it was Marcus.

"Oh hey, Marcus," I said as rushed to turn down the radio as if he didn't catch me reminiscing.

"Hey, Cassie," he said with a smile. You could tell he was pleased by my choice of music. "I just wanted to stop by and see you and have you to meet my nephew."

He introduced us. He was a cute little fella. I believe it was his sister's second oldest son. Marcus told me that he was with him for the weekend. You could tell he would be a great dad. His nephew adored him. After a few minutes, Marcus told me that he'd see me at church on Sunday, the next day, and that he would be playing uncle for the day. He assured me that he was going to call me sometime later. I was so excited to see him. It really made my day. It only made me anticipate going to church on Sunday even more. I love praising Jesus. Now that Marcus was added to the equation, that had me a little excited too.

It started picking up at the salon once early afternoon hit. I had about five clients. My last client came around 6:00 p.m. that evening. I had about an hour of down time to kill before my client arrived. I figured I'd check my cell phone for messages. I had a message from my friend Trina, one from my mother, three from my sister Paradise, and one from Marcus. I decided to check everyone else's messages before I got to Marcus. When I opened his message, it said, "Should I be worried?"

What? Should you be worried? I asked myself as I replied back. I wrote: Worried about what?

He then wrote: About us? That you would tell people?

I was taken aback by his response. Why was he asking me that? Why would he think I'd tell everyone about us? And if I did, why was he so concerned? What could he be trying to hide? I felt a dagger in my heart for a split second. I decided not to respond. *Who did he speak to? Who did I tell? I didn't tell anyone what happened between us last night.* I racked my brain, trying to figure out what was on his mind and whom he had spoken to. Just when I began to sink in those thoughts, my last client showed up.

"Hey, Cass?"

"Hey, Melissa."

"What's the matter? You are never this dry with me," she added.

"Oh, I'm fine, girl," I said. Melissa was one of my very close clients that I spoke briefly to about Marcus. She could tell just from getting her hair done that Marcus and I had a sweet tooth for each other. People would see right through us. Well, my clients anyway, *especially* Melissa. I told her that I liked him and I thought I would marry him one day. I also told her he was a pastor at my church. I didn't tell her anything else. As far as me getting to know Marcus, the only person who knew mostly everything was Toni. But I didn't tell her about our make-out session yet.

"Well, I know what will pick you up," she added. "Guess who I just saw in Walmart?"

"Who?" I asked.

"*Marcussssss, darling,*" Melissa joked as she mimicked Eartha Kitt's voice in the movie *Boomerang.*

"Oh yeah? What happened?" I asked, wondering what she could have said. She knew what he looked like because I had invited her to church before.

"I was just like, 'Hey, Pastor.' He asked me how I was doing. I told him I was fine and was on the way to see Ms. *Cassieeeeeee.*"

I knew right there that if she said my name to him like she did just now to me, then that explained why I had received that message from Marcus.

"Was he with anyone?" I asked.

"Yes, actually. He introduced me to his mom, his nephew, and the assistant girl Jada was there also," Melissa explained.

Oh no! That is why. The family and his best friend Jada may be feeling like something is going on after running into Melissa.

"Oh, that's nice. How would you like your hair today, babe?" I asked. Lord knew I needed to change the topic and *quick*! To be quite honest, I thought that

Marcus would reconsider seeing me because of his encounter with Melissa, but he didn't. I believe he trusted me. I did make sure, however, that I was very discreet about how I spoke about him and who I spoke to from that point on.

The next day, Toni came to visit our church. Most of the church members were around us, and Marcus was talking to Toni and was telling her how much fun he had at the house and he was inquiring about her having another football gathering. There was this girl named Destiny that chimed in the conversation and said, "When is it? I would love to come too." Toni was quick on her feet, and she said, "Oh, the football parties are only for the men." I remember Marcus and I thanked Toni for covering him that day.

The alone time I had with Marcus was at Toni's house for the most part. I remember a time we stayed so late that she had to put out an extra mattress for us to stay the night. We would leave about 6:00 a.m., just in time to host prayer line. Marcus and I would hang out every Monday. That was his day off. I would work at the nursing home until about 3:00 p.m. and then meet with him to grab wings at the sports bar we ate at the first time we hung out. That became our spot to dine and catch up. We would hang for hours until it was time for me to go to theology school at 7:00 p.m. There were times when I'd skip school just to enjoy him. Outside of Mondays, he would stop at the shop on the weekends to see me. I really loved the thrill of it all. It was sneaky, and it allowed me to get to know who he was outside what I once knew: big bro, pastor. I was getting to know Marcus.

His visits at the shop weren't limited to weekends. He stopped by periodically throughout the week. He was around so much that he started getting acquainted with a few of my regulars. One client in particular, named Diamond, he became very close with. She would chime in on our little relationship debates. Diamond was one person that he didn't mind knowing about us. Everything was going all too well for Marcus and me. But then some things began to change.

I noticed that Marcus would get very paranoid being around me. He'd be scanning the room when we would go out to eat. He'd be lurking around Toni's house, wondering if people saw us pulling up together when we'd go there and he would even speak in code as we would text each other.

One night in particular, I remember it was a Friday night. We were at the shop, hanging out in Toni's room. We were watching a movie called *I Spit on Your Grave*. We were supposed to go out to dinner after watching the movie. I was excited because it would have been our first night out together publicly on a Friday night. It was a huge step from our Mondays and secret locations. I thought maybe he was ready to go public with me. As we were watching the movie, someone had texted his phone. Normally, I am not one to pry, but I couldn't help but look over when the notification came through his phone. It was Jada.

I remember a while back when Marcus and I were together riding in his car, he shared with me that Jada felt I didn't like her. It was so bizarre to me for her to feel that way about me when I was more close to her than anyone else, even more than Marcus at a point. Once he told me that, I started noticing the distance between her and me. It was so unexpected. One time, she lashed out on me for making a decision without consulting Marcus on a church assignment. I didn't know our dynamic felt different.

I didn't get to see the message at all. I just remember Marcus jumped up.

"I have to go," Marcus said.

"Why? Is everything OK?" I asked.

"Yes. I forgot that I had to prepare for my sermon for church on Sunday."

"I thought you did them on Saturdays," I said, remembering that he had told me that, in one of our many conversations.

"Oh no! I told myself I'd start it tonight," Marcus explained.

"Oh! You can't forget to do that," I said, laughing it off, trying to cover up my disappointment.

"Can you walk me out?" he asked.

"Sure."

Marcus began to gather the rest of this things. He said his goodbyes to Toni, and then, Marcus and I headed down the stairs. We went out the back door to the garage where he parked his car. He kissed me and said, "Sorry about tonight. I'll make it up to you."

"I know you will. But you know God comes first," I said. I always wanted him to know that his relationship and purpose for God was always more important, and I never made him feel bad about it either.

"I'll call you before I go to bed, OK?" he asked.

"OK."

We gave each other a long kiss. Then Marcus abruptly stopped. I opened my eyes and looked at him to see what he was startled about. He noticed that there was a car out back that looked like Jada's car.

"Oh my gosh! Is that Jada?" he asked.

"Where?" I inquired.

"In that silver Honda?"

"No, Marcus," I said to him in an annoyed manner, at the same time wondering why he was yet again so paranoid.

"I'm sorry, mamas," he said. "If I don't stop by tomorrow, then I'll see you at church Sunday."

"OK," I said.

Marcus had leaned over to kiss me again. We shared an even longer passionate kiss. This time, the owner Karen interrupted our kiss. She was heading out to her car to head home. Marcus and I had awkwardly parted, embarrassed that we had been caught kissing in front of this poor white woman. I felt awful. I hoped she didn't mention it the next time we were before each other to pay my booth rent.

Marcus didn't call me that night like he had promised. I was a little disappointed, but I figured he had been working on his sermon and possibly grew too tired to call. I knew that if I didn't hear from him that night, he would definitely call me in the morning.

The next day, on Saturday morning, I went over to Miss Kenya's house. Yes! Johnson's wife Kenya, the one that wasn't too fond of me because she thought her husband and I were having an affair. She and I grew really close after I left the Light on the Hill. She ended up reaching out to me. We both were in theology school together and became each other's accountability partners, as well as prayer partners. We became great friends, and yes, she was someone I had confided in, about Marcus. I went over her house to do a load of laundry because my machine was down at home. Kenya just so happened to live a few blocks away from my house. How convenient. *right*?

As I was doing my laundry, my phone began to ring.

"Hey! What's going on, Cass?"

"Good morning, Marcus. How was training?" I asked. Trina had told me that Marcus was starting fitness training for some of the leaders that week. Glad that I didn't have to be a part of it.

"Oh, it went well! I feel refreshed and ready to enjoy the rest of the day," he added.

"Well, that's good," I said.

"Listen. I called to let you know that I saw Diamond out to eat last night."

"Really? What were you doing out to eat? I thought you were going home to work on your sermon."

"I was, but I started feeling down so I just went to grab a bite to eat," he said.

"Why didn't you tell me? I would have gone with you," I said.

"Oh, it's cool. I just needed a moment to myself," Marcus said.

"I understand," I said, really *not* understanding. "So you went by yourself?" I asked.

"Yeah. I just needed to clear my head. But listen, good talking to you. I'll see you at church tomorrow."

Why so short with me? I thought to myself. "Okay. Cool. See you tomorrow!"

The moment Marcus and I hung up, I started feeling a *feeling*. You know, a woman's intuition kind of *feeling*. It was at this very moment that I felt Marcus wasn't being truthful to me. I started battling whether or not to call Diamond about her encounter with him. It didn't take too long for me to eventually dial her number.

"*Girl!* You must have heaven on speed dial!" Diamond said, in anticipation to tell me some of what she'd like to call *tea*.

"What do you have to tell me, Dime?" I asked her.

"So you know Justin and I are trying to work our *thang* out, right?"

"Yes," I confirmed.

"So he and I went to eat last night, and I ran into Marcus. At first he was looking all scary to see me, but then he walked up to me and said hi to me and Just. So I said hello and gave him a hug. Then he introduced me to someone he was with."

"*Really?*" I asked. "What did she look like?"

"Cassie, she was short, light-skinned, and she had a long weave in her hair," Diamond explained.

Immediately I knew it was Jada. It was so funny because come to think of it, I remember when Marcus told me that she felt I didn't like her. I remember a couple of days later, she asked me for Toni's number to book an appointment for Marcus's mother Liz to get her hair done. Jada told me that she would have booked Liz with me, but she knew I didn't specialize in short hair. And the very next day, she went to Toni to get extensions put in her hair. And for as long as I had known Jada, she had never worn extensions. So between Jada feeling like I didn't like her, posing to book an appointment for Marcus's mom just to get her hair done, Marcus paranoid that her car was possibly in the parking lot the night before, and him going out to eat by himself when he was really with Jada, yes, something was *definitely* going on!

"Thank you, Diamond," I said.

"Anytime, Cassie. You know I gotchu. I'll see you in a few weeks for my weave maintenance," she said.

"OK. Later."

After we hung up, I immediately texted Marcus. I texted:

> Listen . . . I know what God told me regarding you. If you decide to be anything but what he has told me, then PLEASE, let me keep my dream and you continue to do what you are doing. Please don't taint the image of the man God showed me you are. Let me keep my dream and you can go about your business.

It hadn't been more than five minutes that had gone by before Marcus was calling my phone. He called me back to back at least eighty times. I ignored every single call. I refused to go through all I had gone through in my past relationships to turn around and be played by a pastor and a man of God, at that. I got calls from Toni that day as well. She left me a voice message informing me that Marcus stopped by the shop and at her house, looking for me. I didn't call her back, nor did I let her know my whereabouts because I was afraid she'd tell him where I was. I didn't want him to know. I wanted him to know that wherever he was, what he did was not OK. I deserve someone who is honest with me. The Bible says, "By a person's fruits you shall know them," and his fruits showed dishonesty. He wasn't honest at all. *How, God? How can you tell me this man is my husband?*

12

TRUST IN THE LORD WITH ALL YOUR HEART AND LEAN NOT UNTO YOUR OWN UNDERSTANDING

I was not looking forward to seeing Marcus at church that Sunday. But I knew I wasn't about to miss church over his behavior. I love God too much to prevent myself from learning more about him. Even though Marcus disappointed me, I didn't let my feelings get the best of me. After all, I'd be First Lady. A First Lady should never let her feelings get the best of her in public. Service was amazing that day. I was crying and caught up in worship. I knew I had to give all my cares to the Lord. I got lost in giving thanks, and I felt in that moment that as I was serene in him, my trust in him built the more. I knew that if God in fact started something, he would surely finish it. As I was worshiping, Marcus was on the mic, walking through the aisles of chairs that were considered the pews where the saints sat. I heard him getting closer and closer to me as I had my head down and hands lifted up, giving God praise.

"Hallelujah. Thank you, Jesus," Marcus whispered as he grasped my shoulder. I didn't know why he would be so bold in touching me after the lie he had told.

When church let out, I immediately left with my sister Paradise. I didn't want to socialize and I didn't want to be in the presence of Marcus longer than I should, so I took my exit. I drove off in my car with my sister and headed out to a restaurant called Friday's. That was where we went to eat most Sundays after church. As we were driving, my sister's phone began to ring.

"Whose number is this?" Paradise asked aloud.

"What's the number?" I asked, a little concerned.

"It's five one eight . . . six three one . . . seven two zero . . . ni—"

"Don't answer! Don't answer!" I shouted as I abruptly interrupted her.

"Well, who is it?" she asked.

"Pastor."

"Oh. Well, why are you ignoring him?"

"Because he lied and told me he was going home to work on a sermon when he actually went out to eat with Jada," I explained.

"Oh. How did you find that out?"

"Diamond," I said.

"Your *client*?"

"Yes, Paradise," I said as I chuckled.

"Do you think they are seeing each other?" she asked.

"I don't know. He said she is just his best friend and like a little sister. I never questioned that, until now. It makes me wonder if this is the reason she told him I didn't like her—she probably didn't even tell him that at all."

"Wait! Jada told that to Pastor? Why would she think that?"

"I have no idea, Paradise. I know I never gave her a reason. All I know is that this is what Pastor told me and he even told me not to address it."

"Hmm. That's strange," said Paradise.

After Paradise and I went out to eat, we went home to shower, relax, and watch a couple of movies together. I needed to get my mind off Marcus by doing things that would occupy my time. That was short-lived until my phone went off. *Toot, toot* was the sound that came from my phone indicating that I had received a text message. I reached over to grab it off the edge of my bed to see who sent me a text. "*Of course!*" I said to myself. "Marcus!" The message said,

> Hey, Cassie. I have been trying to contact you for the past few days and didn't receive a response. Look, whatever I did, I apologize. Just tell me what I did that upset you, and I swear I'll never bother you again. I hope you enjoy the rest of your night . . .

Reading Marcus's text didn't make me less mad with him, not to mention he really tried to relay to me that he had no idea why I was upset with him. I vowed to myself not to answer him until the morning. I just needed him to sweat. I needed him to know that I wouldn't tolerate being lied to or played with.

The next day, I returned Marcus's phone calls. After about a ring and a half, he sent me straight to voicemail. I called a second time. The same thing:

voicemail. *Oh no!* I thought to myself. *I refuse to let him flip this around on me like I'm the problem.* I conjured up a text and sent it to his phone. It stated,

> Marcus, I'm not about to keep calling you like I did something wrong. I'm just going to let you know why I was upset with you this past weekend. We had plans to go out to eat Friday night, and all of a sudden, you receive a text that shifted the plans you made with me. You told me you needed to rush home to finish your sermon for Sunday's service. Then I spoke to Diamond and she told me that she saw you out to eat with Jada. If you made plans with Jada already, you should have just told me, and I would have understood, considering that you guys are best friends. Then you called me the next day and acted like you went to grab food on your own when you were with her, which only makes me feel that you guys are more than you say you are. So now my questions to you are, is she your girlfriend and also who does she stay with when she is in town for the weekend? [Marcus made mention of her staying in Albany every weekend, honoring her dedication for the ministry. It didn't take much to assume her choice of stay.] Have a good day.

I sent the text message. Once a few moments passed, my phone began to ring.

"Hello, Marcus!" I said.

"Cassie, I think we should end this," he said.

"That's fine, Marcus, but could you answer my questions? I think you owe me that," I asked, disregarding his request to end things.

"Jada and I are nothing but friends. She is like a sister to me. I love her as a sister. *Nothing more, nothing less!*" he exclaimed in an attempt to convince me of this notion.

"Then why lie about going out to eat with her? Can you acknowledge why I would think something otherwise by you lying?" I asked.

"Yes!" he agreed. "I just didn't want you to be upset. That's all! How would it look to tell you I cannot take you out anymore and then my best friend has something troubling her and I take her out instead and then tell you just that?"

"It looks like the truth. Lying makes me think there was something more."

"I am sorry, Cassie. I'll be upfront about it next time."

A few moments of silence passed before I asked the next question. I asked, "Who does she stay with when she's out here?"

"Jada stays either at a hotel, with Veronica, or myself occasionally," he explained.

Now, Veronica is someone that Marcus considers his little sister also. Veronica has an older sister that was really close friends with Marcus's ex-fiancée. So he kind of embraced them as family, being that they all became so close. However, what Marcus did not know was Veronica and I happen to spend a lot of time together outside church. We just happened to click after one intense conversation about dreams and goals we set for ourselves that led us to become each other's accountability partners. In that moment, I began to do what is called the process of elimination. I thought to myself: *You see, common sense tells me that if I was Jada and I had a best friend who has a place where I can stay at for free, I wouldn't waste money to stay in a hotel. This thought only leaves me with the choice to believe that she is staying with Veronica and Marcus. I am going to figure out a way to ask Veronica if Jada stays with her at times. If she says no, then Marcus and I are going to have a problem!*

"You have to trust me, Cassie. I will never try to hurt you," Marcus stated as he interrupted my thoughts.

"OK!" I agreed. "Can you promise to be open with me and not lie to me from here on out?"

"I promise," he said. "Promise me this—that if you ever have any doubts or feel any way toward me, you won't ignore me and you'll communicate instead."

"Agreed," I said as I held the phone to my ear, smitten all over again.

"Cool. I have to go now, OK? I have some work to do at the church. I'll call you later so that we can grab some wings."

I chuckled knowing that he knows the way to make me happy is to bring me to our favorite sports bar for some hot wings.

"Later," I said as I prepared to hang up and rush to work.

"Talk to you soon, Cass."

I was on cloud nine all over again. Maybe he was afraid to tell me. Maybe he was afraid to hurt my feelings, so he lied to protect them. *He's so sweet. I'm so glad he wanted to make it right. I'm going to take him at his word for now on. I mean, I doubt if he would lie to me again, right?*

13

ASK AND IT SHALL BE GIVEN

I met up with Veronica later that week. Normally our meet-ups would take place in the Albany Public Library in one of the conference rooms. Veronica and I talked about our goals and what we were doing to achieve them. I must admit, our conversations were always amazing and intriguing, but all I seemed to be interested in that encounter was finding out the truth behind Marcus and Jada and the nature of their relationship. I wanted to know if Veronica was someone that she was staying with when she'd visit for the weekends. I tried to take Marcus at his word. But something in me told me that I couldn't. I mean, it didn't help that whenever she came to town, it was as if I didn't exist until Mondays, and this particular week wasn't any different.

Even though I had so much on my mind about Marcus, I tried to stay engaged in conversing with Veronica. But I knew before I ended my time spent with her that I'd find a way to ask about Jada. We spoke for just about another hour and made plans for our next meet-up. It was about 8:00 p.m. on a Friday night. The library was getting ready to close. We started heading out of the library and making our way toward my two-door Acura. Veronica wasn't driving at the time, so I'd usually give her a ride. She seemed to be super pumped about our weekly meeting and had no problem making it known on the ride to her home.

"Cassie, I am so excited that we are doing this. It feels refreshing to know that I can trust someone and be able to have them hold me accountable and for me to do the same."

"I know, right?" I said, pretending to be just as enthused. I mean, don't get me wrong, normally I am. I just needed to get to the bottom of this whole Marcus-and-Jada thing.

"OK, Cassie, what's up with you?" Veronica asked. "You haven't been yourself all night."

"I'm fine, V. Just had a long day at work—that's all," I said as I was searching for a way to inquire about Jada staying at her house. I mean, I couldn't just blatantly come out and ask. I need to find out in a way that was not so noticeable. *How can I go about asking her?*

"OK, just checking," Veronica added. "So I was thinking, how's next Saturday for you?" Veronica asked, as far as setting up our next meet-up.

"Saturday is fine with me," I agreed. Then it dawned on me: *This is my opportunity—I can bring up the fact that Jada spends the night*, I thought. I then said, "Hey, V, I was thinking maybe we can invite the other girls from the church too. Have like a ladies' night. What do you think?"

"That's a great idea, Cass! We can play games, and I can rent a few movies from the library. Yes, that sounds good. Let's plan!" Veronica shouted in excitement.

"Great! Let's do it!" I said. "It will be me, you, Kim [Kim was another young lady at the church who had an amazing shape, might I add], and *Jada*. You can let her know when she stays over," I said, sliding that comment right on in.

"When who stays over?" Veronica asked.

"Jada," I answered. "She stays with you when she comes into town, right?" I asked.

"No!" she replied. "Jada doesn't stay with me."

"Oh," I said, with such disappointment. "Well, Saturday at what time?" I asked, being quick on my feet.

"I'm thinking around 6:00 p.m. Is that cool for you?"

"Yes, that's perfect," I responded, as I was pulling up in front of her house.

"Great!" she said. "I'll see you next week Saturday."

"OK, V! Later."

"Bye," she said as she got out of the car.

I waited for her to get in the apartment building as she waved, indicating that she made it in safely. Marcus lied to me, *again*! How could he lie to me? I trusted him. I believed him. God, how can you send me a man that would lie to me, that would deceive me? There is no way he's *the one*. My heart was breaking. I thought to myself: *He's with Jada! I know he is! I am such a fool. Why would I think he'd be true to me? He lied. This was all a lie! A big fat lie!*

I drove away from Veronica's house with so many mixed emotions. I was sick to my stomach just off the thought alone that Marcus was seeing Jada. I wanted to just block the thoughts out of my mind, but the more I tried to suppress them, the more they magnified. *Was this the reason she told Marcus I didn't like her? Or did she ever tell him that? Was that his way of driving a wedge between me and the girl I once looked at as my sister? Was that her way of making me out as a bad person once she took notice that Marcus was interested?*

These thoughts began to run rampant in my mind. It was as if they were seeds desperate to find root in the soil of my mind, and they succeeded. The thoughts were planted. I was convinced that the man that God had me praying and fasting for, the man that I wanted God's best for, the one that I believed God for and wanted nothing shy of great for, was nothing close to what God told me and was not the man God intended for me.

While I was in a state of being despondent, my phone began to ring. When I looked over to see who it was, to my surprise, it was Quan.

"Hello?" I answered.

"Hey, Cassie. What's up?" Quan asked.

"Nothing much. On my way home," I said, with such hopelessness in my voice.

"Why do you sound like that, are you OK?" Quan asked out of concern.

"I'll be fine," I responded.

"OK. Are you sure? I know we haven't been on it like that, but if you need me, I'm here."

"Thanks, Quan," I said as the peace from his voice overwhelmed me. Quan was always so sweet. What we had wasn't perfect, but he was always very kind. If Quan wasn't anything else, he was always honest to me.

"No problem," he said, interrupting my thoughts of approval toward him.

"Have a good night, Quan," I said, preparing myself to end the call.

"Cassie, are you sure you are OK? If you want, you can stop by the house if you need someone to talk to," Quan suggested.

Maybe I should stop by. I'd rather do that than have Marcus on my mind. At least I know Quan's motives are pure.

"Sure. I'm just a few blocks away."

A couple of minutes later, I arrived at Quan's house. I gave him a call informing him that I was outside. As I was approaching the doorway to his house, you heard the rummaging in his attempt to unlock the door. I approached the door just in the nick of time it took for him to pry the door open. He greeted me with a long hug, and his embrace made me feel assured that everything would be OK. We walked into the house and took a seat on his comfy brown sofa. I secretly smiled to myself, reminiscing about the times we would watch *Family Feud* late nights on that very couch.

"What's new, Cass?" Quan asked. "You didn't sound like yourself over the phone."

"I had a long day. Don't really feel like talking about it."

"OK," he said. "Hopefully, hanging out with me will make you feel better."

"Thanks," I said with a sigh of relief.

Quan took a seat next to me and began to peruse the channels on TV, looking for something for us to watch. I noticed one of my favorite movies was on BET as he was skipping through the channels.

"Oh, that was *Madea's Family Reunion*!" I exclaimed with excitement. "Turn it back!"

"OK," he said as he laughed. It always tickled him whenever I got overly excited about a movie or show I loved to watch.

As we began to watch the movie, Quan asked me to get up from the couch. When I stood up, he lay down on the couch and then motioned for me to lie in front of him so that we could cuddle like we did back when we were together. I smiled and joined him on the couch. As he wrapped his arms around me and rested his head on mine, he kissed me on the cheek and said, "Everything will be OK."

As we lay there a while longer, Quan began to kiss me again. He kissed me on my cheek, my neck, and managed to plant one on my lips. Before you know it, we were making out. And you guessed it. We got intimate. A slight pause to place as he reached in his pocket for a condom. He had already removed my pants and undergarment along with his. The act happened so fast that it took my mind moments to catch up to the fact that I was having sex after I vowed to God that I wouldn't before marriage and that I would save myself for Marcus, the man God told me would be my husband.

I began to cry out loud. Maybe Quan mistook my crying for how he believed we felt about each other—that we were finally having this moment. A moment we thought we would never have, knowing the love I had to please God in all that I do. I felt like I was dying inside. I was crushed. I thought to myself: *I disappointed God! I disappointed myself!* And even though Marcus and I weren't together, I felt like *I cheated on my husband.*

14

FAITH IS THE SUBSTANCE OF THINGS HOPED FOR, THE EVIDENCE OF THINGS UNSEEN

I woke up the next morning, hoping that this was all a dream. It was as real as the guilt that overcame me that day. I was so disappointed in myself. I didn't want to be one of those Christians that say one thing and do another. Not only was I devastated about letting God down, I quivered at the thought of telling Marcus what I had done. Sure, he lied, but I didn't really know what went down between him and Jada. I mean, even if it did go far, I'm not the type of girl that would go out of my way and do something like this. I was so mad at Marcus. I blamed him! His lying to me caused me to do something I would have never done. I was angry with him. I wanted to call him and tell him what he drove me to do and how ashamed I was and that it was all his fault.

I was in such a battle in my mind. Before you knew it, my fingers began to dial the numbers to Marcus's phone.

"Hey, champ! What's going on?" Marcus said over the phone. I used to hate him calling me champ. It seems that he would use this term to water down who we were and what we had with each other.

Ignoring his greeting, I said, "You lied to me!"

"Hold on one second," he said as he moved to a quiet space. "What did you say, Cass?"

"You lied to me!" I repeated as my voice began to crack. I arrested my tears from escaping my eyes.

"What do you mean, Cass? What did I lie to you about?"

"You told me that Jada stayed with Veronica when she's out here, and she doesn't. She stays with you!" I explained, backing him in a corner.

"Cassie," he said, "listen to me. Jada is very discreet with her whereabouts. If Veronica told you that she doesn't stay with her, it's because Jada told her not to tell anyone. I told you I would never lie to you again and I meant that. I need you to *trust me*!"

I began to cry. *I don't get it!* I thought to myself. *Was this the enemy that made me believe all this stuff? Was Marcus really telling me the truth?* I was so confused I didn't know what to think.

"Are you crying, Cassie?" he asked. I didn't answer him. The sniffling sound escaping my nose gave him that confirmation.

"Cassie? Listen to me. Are you listening?"

"Yes," I answered as I wiped away my tears.

"Cassie, I told you I would never lie to you again. I really care about you and would never hurt you. You just have to trust me, OK?"

"OK," I said, crying the more.

"Cassie, stop crying. Please stop crying," Marcus said, genuinely concerned. What he didn't know was that the sinful act I committed last night held me captive to my discontentment. Marcus stayed on the phone with me a little longer until I was able to get myself together.

"Cassie, I know I wasn't honest with you in the past. Please believe that there is nothing going on with Jada and me. She's like a sister to me. Nothing more, nothing less. In order for us to move forward, we need to be able to trust each other. I'm not perfect, but I will never do anything to hurt you. Do you understand?" Marcus asked.

"Yes," I answered.

"OK. Let's move forward. Let's not revisit this again, OK?"

"OK," I said.

"All right. Look, I have to get back to the leaders. We are out to eat right now. I'll call you later on when I'm free. Love you."

"Love you too," I said.

I took a couple of days to myself before I reconnected with Marcus. Bigger than rationalizing whether or not to believe or entertain Marcus and cutting off things completely with Quan was getting myself back in good graces with my Father in heaven whom I love so much! I made plans to meet with Marcus to grab wings. Instead of our normal Monday meet-ups, Marcus switched our Monday for a Thursday that week. Now that he stepped out of the norm by going out publicly with me on another day, it made me feel twice as bad about my actions with Quan. In the midst of us eating, conversing, and sharing laughter, something came across my news feed on Facebook that I thought was hilarious. I handed my phone over to Marcus to share with him what I found amusing. After he took in the joke, out of nowhere, he screamed, "*Quan?*"

I quickly snatched my phone from his hand in an effort to prevent him from seeing anything that Quan could have texted that would give him displeasure. When I viewed my phone, I realized it was only the news I saw on my news feed staring right back at me.

"Wow!" Marcus exclaimed.

"Wow what?" I asked.

"You're keeping something from me."

"No, I'm not."

"Yes, you are! I can tell by your reaction!"

I grew silent. I didn't know what to say. I was afraid to tell him about what happened with Quan. Would he walk away and never talk to me again?

"It's nothing!" I said.

"It's something. It's in your reaction."

Just tell him, Cassie! I thought to myself. But I kept silent.

"Excuse me, miss?" Marcus said to the waiter. "Can we get the check?"

Marcus was done with me. We shared no words. We stayed at the table silently as Marcus waited for the check. The waiter came with the check, and Marcus rummaged through his wallet to get the cash for the food along with a tip.

"Ready?" he asked me.

"Yeah," I said.

He grabbed his blazer from the chair he sat in and headed for the door. He waited for me to reach the door. Marcus held the door open until I was arm's length, and he let go in time for me to hold it myself. He pressed the unlock button on his car key, which released a sound indicating that his car was ready for access. We both sat down in the car, buckled our seatbelts, and Marcus sped out of the parking lot from our favorite wing spot. As he sped on the highway, I couldn't take the silence anymore.

"What's your problem?" I asked.

"Your reaction!" he yelled.

"Did I do this to you when you lied about Jada and the fact that you are seeing her and that she's staying over?"

"What?" he said in shock. "*Seeing her? Staying over?*"

"Yeah. You think I wasn't going to find out. Derrick told me when I met up with him and Mother Green for prayer!"

This was another thing I kept hidden from Marcus—that I found out from Brother Derrick when he was asked one day to grab something from Marcus's house prior to going to church. As he was grabbing things, he couldn't help but notice there were Victoria's Secret bags and personal belongings of a woman that seemed as if she were staying there. It was a no-brainer that I put Jada's face to it. It also made me curious to know whether or not this was the reason Marcus refused to let me come over as he got ready to take me on a date. Instead, he left me at the 7-Eleven. So many men coming in and out of the store tried to shoot their shot and spit game to me. I remember my phone even died, so I had to borrow the store clerk's phone to tell Toni about it and let her know I was catching a cab home. Before my cab arrived, Marcus pulled up to get me. I was upset the entire night. Toni was furious and made Marcus apologize and even said to him if his mom knew about how he handled me, how would she feel? The bouquet of flowers he bought and brought me the next day showed me just how his mother would have felt about his actions. Anyway, back to the matter at hand with Brother Derrick spilling the beans on Marcus and Jada . . .

"*Derrick said what?*" Marcus screamed.

Marcus went from driving the speed limit to eighty miles per hour.

Scared that we could possibly get into a car accident, I told him, "Slow down!"

Marcus continued to speed. "We're going right to his house! He's going to tell me to my face what you just told me!"

"No! No! We *cannot*!" I exclaimed.

"Why not? He can say all this stuff to you, so I want him to say it to my face!"

"Because number one, how does that look, for you to go to his house and confront him about this? And two, you are a pastor."

"Look, Cassie, I already told you that she is my best friend. Yes, she stays with me at times, but that is all there is to it. For him to make assumptions about Jada and me and share that to you without actually knowing what's the nature of my relationship with Jada is wrong of him to do."

"Well, it's not like he didn't have reason to think the situation was what anyone else would have thought it would be had they seen what he saw," I explained.

Marcus began to slow up the car, bringing it back to the speed limit after realizing that my point was well taken. Then he said, "Well, there is nothing going on between Jada and me. But this is not about her. It's about you and why you reacted the way you did when you thought I'd seen a message between you and Quan. Is there something that I need to know?"

"I did meet with him," I replied.

"And . . ." he said.

"Well, I was down because of what I thought you were doing behind my back. So I just talked to him about how I was thinking about leaving the church, but I made it seem as if it was something pertaining to you and me, in regards to the ministry."

"Well, what was his advice?" Marcus asked.

"He said that he thinks you're a cool dude and that I should have a meeting with you to work out any differences."

Marcus shook his head in disapproval as he signaled to get off the exit to drop me home. I could tell that Marcus was upset that I even hung out with Quan, knowing that he was aware of my dealings with him in the past. I wanted to tell him what happened with me and Quan. I was afraid. I mean, if he was mad about me having a conversation with him, I could only imagine his response if I told him I slept with Quan. Marcus pulled up in front of my house and parked his car. He turned the car off and took the key out of the ignition. We sat there for a few moments in silence until he decided within himself to speak.

"Look, Cassie, I forgive you for meeting up with Quan. I just need us to communicate better. You don't have to worry about Jada and me. We are *not* together. Nor will we ever be. I only see her as a friend, nothing more, nothing less. I need you to trust me, and if you are feeling some sort of way about something, just ask me."

I so badly wanted to believe him, but I didn't. Derrick was one of the very few people that I trusted at church, and he had always been honest and had integrity. I didn't press Marcus further about the issue. I left it alone. Besides, there was so much heat on my back about Quan. Turning his attention on accusations with Jada gave me the relief I was after.

"OK, fine," I said. "I'll see you later. I have to get ready for work tomorrow, and I have to meet with Veronica afterward."

"OK. Can I have a hug?" he asked. I gave him a hug and kiss on the cheek. "Later. I'll call you tomorrow," Marcus said.

"See you soon."

The next day was a drag. I went to work with so much on my mind that it took a toll on how I performed at my job. When I was done at work, I went to check with Veronica as planned. We always had such great conversation, but to be honest, I felt like I needed to tell her about how I purposely asked her about Jada staying with her to see if Marcus was lying. She and I grew so close that I felt like I needed to be honest with her about that because it didn't sit well with me that I kinda put her in something that she was unaware of. I was just tired of Marcus lying. I just knew he was not being truthful about Jada.

Once I told Veronica about it, she was upset. She said she didn't want to be in the middle of it. She still stuck to her story about Jada never staying at her house, but she felt by her telling me, I had driven a wedge between her and Marcus. I came clean to her about Marcus and how we were seeing each other and how I was just desperate to get the answers that he refused to give. I also told her that all she did was be honest and that I didn't put her in anything. She understood my point, and she was disappointed in Marcus. She never came out and said it, but her body language and facial expressions exposed her true feelings. I also asked her that if she had any info on Marcus and Jada seeing each other, she would tell me. I expressed to her that she didn't have to tell me details. I just needed to know so I could walk away from Marcus for good if it were true. She told me to seek God about it, and if I didn't have peace about it with him, then I should probably let him go.

I didn't understand why Veronica wouldn't give me a straight answer. Considering how I made her the blind mouse to the trap of Marcus, I really couldn't hold it against her. When we prayed together, it definitely gave me peace that night and released me from the burden of figuring things out on my own. I would need God's help for this one.

I was reminded of a scripture that night, Hebrews 11:1: "Now faith is the substance of things hoped for, the evidence of things unseen."

"This is where it counts, Cassie!" I whispered to myself. "Will you believe in spite of what you do not see?"

15

LEAVE THOSE THINGS THAT ARE BEHIND ME

Marcus and I still continued seeing each other. He seemed to get over the incident with Quan pretty quick. Can't say the same for me regarding Marcus and Jada. I seemed to wrestle back and forth with the thought of them having something more than just friendship. It didn't help that at church, the congregation became so isolated toward me. Looking back, I'm assuming at that time, rumors must have been going around about me.

I remember I was an intercessor at that time, and we had an assignment to pray for a few of the church members. Each intercessor was assigned one person. The lady I had was a woman who was a drug addict, and she had a heart and love for the lord. She in confidence shared with Pastor Boyd (Marcus) that every time she attempted to pray and get in God's presence, she couldn't. When the head of the intercessors department, Evangelist Ashley Sparks, Kim's mother, had me pray for the member I was assigned to, I couldn't pray. I remember crying and shaking my head, motioning to them that I couldn't. Come to find out, I was actually having an out-of-body experience. I was feeling and acting out the lady's struggle in getting in God's presence. Instead of Evangelist Ashley looking deeper in the Spirit to see why I was acting the way that I was, she accused me of being lustful. The other intercessors jumped on the bandwagon, with the exception of my friend Trina and another woman named Dria. I remember she came at me before in a church meeting. An attractive young man had joined our church. I was excited about seeing men join our church, being aware of the vacancy of this particular species not being present normally in the house of God. Evangelist Ashley said to me, "All right, Cassie, settle down now," as she gave a look to put me in check as if I was checking out the new guy. I assumed she was still salty about Marcus sitting her down for the attack on my character.

A few services later, her daughter Kim gave me this huge skirt to wear for church. I wore it, thinking it was a nice gesture for her to think to buy me church attire and she probably just didn't know my size. I did however scratch my head and wonder why she came to church a service or two with her dress unbearably tight and above her knees. I thought then that there must have been something Kim and her mother Ashley had against me. Dodging all the jabs from those two and the side-eyes from Jada and a few other girls, I still pressed my way and got what I needed from church. After all, the main attraction was and is God anyway.

If the petty beef in church wasn't enough, Marcus's inconsistencies threw me for a loop. He would have no problem communicating with me and seeing me throughout the whole week, but as soon as the weekend came around, he played the role of Wesley Snipes better than him on *Disappearing Acts*.

One weekend, Marcus's mom fell ill. He had to go to the city, to the Brooklyn Hospital Center in his hometown, where his mom was admitted. I planned on addressing Marcus's topsy-turvy ways, but considering all that was going on, his mom's health was far more important. I was upset that I found out through a church group text and not from him. Instead of getting caught up in my feelings behind that, I tried calling him. I prayed and hoped that all was well with his mom. I know First Lady Liz Boyd is his world.

I waited patiently for him to get a chance to return my calls. Malcolm stopped by the salon that day. We needed to catch up anyway. We talked about a lot of stuff he was planning to get started career-wise in his life, and I was giving him some pointers on a few of his ideas. I always enjoyed talking to Malcolm; the boy was brilliant. Our discussion was interrupted when Malcolm received a call from Marcus. Marcus was just updating Malcolm on his mother's health status. All went well, *thank you, Jesus!*

I didn't understand how Malcolm received a call from Marcus, considering all the times he expressed that he wasn't too fond of Malcolm. He didn't like the brotherly bond that I had with him. Marcus *always* insinuated that it was more feelings outside of the bubble *brotherly* that he claimed Malcolm had for me. He didn't like Malcolm in the least but he felt the need to call him outside church duties and confide in him about matters so personal, about his mother?

When Malcolm ended the call with Marcus, I sent Marcus a text. It went like this:

> Hey, Marcus. I've been calling you nonstop to see if things were okay with your mom. I was with Malcolm when you called. I am worried about you. Please call me. Just checking on you and your family." LOVE YOU! (SENT)

I waited a couple minutes for a response. After about fifteen minutes, he texted back, saying,

> Cassie, everything is not about you! This is my mother we are talking about! I am with my family! I don't have time to entertain you and argue with you about why I didn't get back to you! GOOD DAY!

I texted back, saying,

> Marcus, are you serious? I was only checking on you! I was worried about you—that's all! Sorry I even cared! Later!

I was so confused on how short he was toward me. Why was he so defensive? He then texted back and said,

> Sorry, Cassie. I was just upset and thought you were making it about us and not about my mom. Everything is fine. The doctor said she will recover. How are you?

I read the message and didn't respond. I wasn't really sure what his switch-up was about, but I was not about to keep letting him be cool with me one minute and then have a problem the next.

It didn't take us long to kiss and make up. Every time we came back to each other after an argument or disagreement, we couldn't keep our hands off each other. Whether we were in my house or in his car, our foreplay with each other was insane. Still, I managed to keep my vow with God to not go all the way with him. Besides, his bipolar behavior made it easy for me.

Malcolm called me one afternoon. It was actually February 12, 2013, just a few days before Valentine's Day. He asked if we could meet up because he had something very important to tell me. I went to go pick him up before I headed to the local beauty supply store. I was low on a couple of products at the shop. I figured I could kill two birds with one stone bringing Malcolm along.

"So what's up, bro? Whatchu gotta talk to me about?" I asked in my broken English.

"Cass, you need to be mindful about who you call 'friends'!" he said as he made quotation gestures with his hands.

"Elaborate," I said.

Malcolm picked up right where he left off. "So . . . Toni is not your real friend!"

"Why you say that?" I asked.

He continued, "So Pastor, Jermaine, and I were playing basketball this past Monday night like we always do. As we were in the middle of a basketball game, you were brought up. Jermaine out of nowhere said, 'So you know who I think is beautiful?' Marcus asked Jermaine, 'Who?' Jermaine then said, 'Cassie!' Marcus chimed in and agreed and said, 'Yeah, she's beautiful but she likes me. Toni told me!'"

Malcolm continued by saying, "You need to be careful. Toni's spreading lies about you and she's not your friend!"

I was furious! Malcolm didn't know anything about Marcus and me. Nobody did, except the few people I told. I wasn't mad at Toni because she was the *few* in the number of confidants. Marcus and I made a pact to keep things quiet between us for the sake of his *title*. He and I were well aware of what Toni knew. He told Jermaine and Malcolm information that was only supposed to be between Marcus, me, and Toni. What made me so upset is that if Marcus was to let anyone else in on this information, he should have told the truth.

Don't go telling Jermaine and Malcolm that I like you and not tell them that not only is it mutual, but also we are seeing each other. Because Malcolm was oblivious to the full truth about me liking Marcus. I said, "I'll talk to Toni about it."

When I got home after shopping and dropping Malcolm off and telling him thanks for looking out, I called Marcus without hesitation. Marcus picked up, saying, "Hey, champ!"

Great! Not only was he calling me the name I *absolutely hate*, he also broke my trust by exposing my feeling toward him to others.

"Did you tell Malcolm and Jermaine that Toni told you I like you?"

"Huh?" he said in a pitch that had guilt written all over it.

"Goodbye, Marcus. I'm done!" I exclaimed, and I hung up the phone.

I was so upset that I went back outside and drove to my mother's house. I figured I should take the opportunity to leave my home, knowing that Marcus would play his pop-up game with me and stop by, as I ignored his incoming phone calls. Eluding him was an epic fail, considering the fact that pulling in my mother's driveway would land him and me on the same street. Jermaine's mother lived down the block from my mom's house. He must have dropped him off after their weekly workouts. Pulling up behind my car, Marcus asked, rolling his window down, "Cassie, can you talk to me for a second, please?"

"Marcus, I'm over it. You want to put my feelings for you out there for people like we're not seeing each other? Cool!" I said.

"Cassie, what are you talking about? None of that happened."

"So the person that told me is just going to sit here and lie to me, right?" I asked.

"Cassie, please don't make a scene. Please, get in the car and talk to me. I'm a pastor. I can't be out here arguing like this."

Considering his title, I got in his car and planted myself in the passenger seat.

"Now what are you talking about?" Marcus asked.

"Malcolm told me that you, Jermaine, and he were playing basketball, and you guys were talking about how pretty I am and you came out and said to them that Toni told you that I like you. Considering that we established that about six months ago, why was it necessary to inform Malcolm and Jermaine about that and fail to tell them that we were seeing each other?"

"Cassie, that is a lie! We can ask Jermaine right now. Matter of fact, Jermaine is coming down the street right now," Marcus said as he noticed Jermaine. "We can ask him!"

Jermaine noticed Marcus's car, and Marcus called him over and asked, "Jermaine, did I tell you and Malcolm that Toni told me that Cassie likes me?"

Jermaine was quiet for a second too long. Then he answered, "No. Marcus didn't say that to us."

"Thank you!" Marcus said with a sigh of relief, as if Jermaine lying for him got me off his back.

"I'ma talk to Cass for a bit. I'll catch up with you though, 'Maine!"

"All right, cool," said Jermaine. He gave Marcus the pound and waved bye to me as he walked away.

Waving back, I continued with a smile to Jermaine's farewell as I addressed Marcus: "It's pretty low using the kids, Marcus." I chuckled. "You expect me to believe Jermaine? Please! You could commit a whole crime in front of him, and he will explain five ways on how you didn't do it!"

"So you believe Malcolm over me?" Marcus asked.

"Why wouldn't I? Unlike you, he has never lied to me, and on top of that, the whole purpose of him telling me was to tell me to watch out for Toni. The only thing he got wrong is the person he told me I should watch out for."

"You know what . . ." Marcus started as he shifted his car from park to reverse. "I want him to tell me this to my face."

Pulling out of my mother's drive way at full speed, he started heading to Malcolm's house.

"What are you doing?" I asked in a panic.

"We're going to Malcolm's. I'm sick of him. He gonna say this to my face!"

"What are you mad at Malcolm for?"

"I'm sick of him being disloyal!" screamed Marcus.

"How is he being disloyal when he wasn't even trying to come at you? He told me this for me to look out for Toni. He doesn't know anything about you! Why are you trying to come at him? You are in the wrong! Not him!"

"I'm not wrong about him liking you though."

"Marcus, you can say what you want! At the end of the day, you were wrong, and you are probably the reason people are feeling a way about me at church. If you are that free to tell people you don't talk to like that, about my feelings for you, God only knows who else you told," I said to Marcus as I reasoned what else he could have said or did.

Driving back toward my mother's house, after Marcus busted a U-turn as he came to his senses, we were quiet the rest of the way there. He finally broke the silence when we returned in front of my mother's home.

"Cassie, please believe me. I didn't say any of that."

"Marcus, it's hard to believe you when you still don't want to tell me the truth. More than anything outside what we have, you are my pastor first. For you to exploit my feelings for you considering all the attacks and accusations that were placed on me, you didn't make the situation any better. I reconsider you as my friend, the man I want to marry, and my pastor. I need some time to clear my head," I said, holding back my tears as I got out of his car and headed toward mine. Marcus didn't even respond. He just drove off. I was in his rear-view mirror. Maybe it was time for him to be in mine too.

When I got home that day, my feelings were all over the place. I even prayed to God and asked him, *God, did I hear you right? Is this really the man you want for me?* I was so tired of the back and forth between us. We had too many episodes of these up and down spells and still Marcus had yet to make up his mind about making things with us official. Seeing that he had now betrayed me, I had to part ways with him at this time. I texted Marcus that night to put in my resignation to leave Powerhouse. Maybe this is why I felt so strongly in the Spirit to leave before. Maybe God seen all of this manifesting. The message read:

> Hey, Pastor Boyd! This is Cassie. I'm deciding to leave Powerhouse. I just think it's best for me to remove myself. I cannot follow a pastor I do not trust. Considering that you were aware of the many attacks I have faced under your covering, you put me in a position to be preyed upon. Wish you guys all the best. Take care. (SENT)

A few minutes later, my phone was ringing, with Marcus hoping to get through. I ignored him a few times. I just felt like it was pointless to have a conversation when my mind was already made up. However, I couldn't bear the nuisance of the back-to-back calls Marcus was making. I finally returned his call after he sent a text saying,

> Cassie, I received your resignation. I don't mind releasing you as a member from the Powerhouse Ministries. I would need to ask you a few questions before I can release you from the ministry. Please give me a call back at your earliest convenience.
>
> Best regards, Pastor Boyd

When I dialed Marcus's number, the phone barely made it to a ring. I guess Marcus was attempting further countless phone calls to me. He picked up and said, "Cassie?"

"Yes," I replied.

"I understand you are desiring to leave the ministry. Is it OK if I ask you a few questions before granting your release?"

"Sure," I said, entertaining this questionnaire he made up as an attempt for me to break the silent treatment I had subjected him to.

"OK. Great! First question, Why have you decided to leave the Powerhouse?" he asked.

"My pastor broke my trust and shared information about me to other members."

"OK. Question two: What are the things you liked most and least about the ministry?"

"I love the praise and worship and the depth of the Word preached at the ministry. As far as what I like the least, it's the drama, which makes it extremely hard to focus on the reason we are all there in the first place, to worship God," I replied.

"OK. Lastly, what advice can you give to the church that can help us to be more effective to the people we serve going forward?" Marcus asked.

"When a person goes to their leader in confidence about what they may be dealing with and what they have shared, it is important that the leader not breach confidentiality," I said, shooting my comment like a dart to a bull's-eye.

"OK. Thank you for that. Cassie, before you go I would like to say I'm sorry. I didn't mean to hurt you. I just wish I could take it all back. I love y—"

Blah blah blah blah blah. After a while, I tuned out everything he said. I was done, ready to bury this revelation. I didn't want a liar. I didn't want to be with someone I didn't trust. I wasn't able to recognize myself. I was doing things I would have never done had I not been toyed with. I was over it, ready to move on. I was ready to forget about Marcus. He was now behind me. Well, was he?

16

PRESS TOWARD THE MARK OF THE HIGH CALLING

A few months passed since I left the church. I'm not even going to lie: I missed it like crazy. It didn't stop me from praising the Lord and staying in constant communion with him. I did visit other churches frequently. It helped my healing process with all that I have endured. Even though I cut off all communication with Marcus, that didn't stop him from reaching out to me. Marcus sent me a text nearly every day, saying, I pray all is well with you! I miss you! We miss you! I love you! I loved that he was trying to get back in my good graces. But I just couldn't go back. I knew my worth. As far as I was concerned, Marcus was playing with me when I was real with him. I believed all that God said I was. I am a virtuous woman, fearfully and wonderfully made. I wasn't going to put a stamp of approval on anyone who treated me any less.

It wasn't long after that I started spending time with Quan again. He made it easier to get my mind off of Marcus. Quan knew my worth. Quan respected my walk with God. He even started going to church himself, keeping church services as his weekly routine. But that didn't stop us from being intimate after a while. I battled a lot with keeping celibate until marriage. But every now and then, I kept slipping up with him. I would be so broken up about having sex with Quan. Every time, it ate me up! It was a door that I opened up in vulnerability that I had a hard time to close. I found myself even more susceptible to fornicating whenever I tried to flee the very thought of Marcus. Finally, I had enough! I could take it. The thought of potentially being seen as a hypocrite nearly robbed me of my peace. This wasn't getting me anywhere. I started feeling empty and void of God. It was time to end things with Quan, time to get on the straight and narrow. It was time to return back to my first love, my Lord, Jesus Christ. So I made the decision to go on a fast. I needed a spiritual cleanse. I needed God's help to pull me out of this trap of fornication. I had to walk away from Quan. I had to get it right. I needed to make it right with God.

I went on a thirty-day fast. I only ate within the hours of 6:00 a.m. through 6:00 p.m. I limited my time spent on social media. I made sure that I only listened to gospel music and watched sermons and God-centered shows. I found myself consumed in the teachings on the best whoever did it in the kingdom of God, Bishop T. D. Jakes, having his sermons both old and new I had on rotation. Between listening to him, praying, and being in the Word, I was *finally* out of the grip of fornication.

I was back on track! I loved it! I felt free. It was nothing I could not do or set out to conquer. I started to put up written sermons for people online to be encouraged and give their lives to God. The sermons that God put on my heart to give to people were so good that people would always ask me, "Where can I download this app?" Like seriously, people thought what I was putting out there was an actual app. My work ethic as a hairstylist had catapulted to a whole other level. I had a bit of a setback because I was supposed to become a business partner with Toni. She left the Powerhouse Ministry after I was treated poorly. It still didn't stop us from working together. We started looking for a building after she told me she'd make me her business partner. That was short-lived when she was the first of us to find a building for the salon. Toni backpedaled on her proposal to us working in partnership. She said she'd be more comfortable with me booth renting from her like I was prior to the fire. I didn't accept her offer. I just so happened to get prophesied to at a local church convention I attended the weekend before with Malcolm. The guest pastor told me that the Lord said he was going to *bless me* with my own business.

I took that prophesy and left the salon that Toni and I worked at temporarily. I brought my belongings home with Malcolm's help. I could always count on him! Anyway, I created my *own salon* set up in my bedroom slash living room my younger sisters Paradise and Ramara gave to me in our shared two-bedroom apartment. I started servicing my clients from home. My older sister Tanya saw the many clients I had, when she would come by and visit. She suggested that I come up with a name for my salon. Tanya said that she would get me started with business cards that would have the shop name and my phone number. I thought it was a great idea. I figured we could revise the business cards by adding the location of the salon once God saw fit to bless me with one. I named my salon Slay on the Way Hair Salon. My mom came up with the salon name, being that I didn't have a locked-in stationary spot for the shop. Slay on the Way meant that I could travel to people and *slay* their hairdos. I was doing my thang! I was tapping into ministry and building my business and brand. I had everything just right in my life, but as much as I tried to move on with my life, I still couldn't get Marcus off my mind.

Apparently it was the same for Marcus. He never stopped texting me. He never stopped calling me even after his failed attempts to get in contact with me. It was around mid-July 2013 when I finally broke the silence with Marcus. I only allowed communication through text. I gave short responses to his consistent "hoping all is well and miss and love you" texts with very seldom "I'm good" and "Gee, thanks!" I refused to get caught up. No! Not this time! I had great distractions all around me. There wasn't any room for potential bad ones. And to my delight, I came across the best distraction of them all, T. D. Jakes' "Woman, Thou Art Loosed" conference. I saw the flyer for it as I scrolled through and perused my Facebook timeline. They had the breakdown of the itinerary for that entire weekend. They had so many celebrities that were attending, preaching, and performing. I had to go!

I called my cousin Mimi. She was my travel buddy. It's never a dull moment with her. And she was saved now too. We were going to have a ball. I wasted no time calling her. "Pick up! Pick up! Pick up!" I whispered to myself as I anticipated hearing Mimi's voice.

"Hey, Cassie!" Mimi said in her squeaky voice.

"Hey, Mimi! What's going on?" I said, relieved and excited that she picked up.

"Nothing much. Just doing laundry and watching TV. What's up?" Mimi asked.

"So I'm over here looking at this flyer on the mega-fest "Woman, Thou Art Loosed" conference. How would you feel about going?"

"Heck yeah! Let's go!" Mimi replied. "I hope I run into Marvin Sapp. That's my boo!"

"Ahahaha. You're so stupid! It's from August 29th through the 31st, so block out your schedule and I'll work out all the details for the trip."

"Yay! I'm so excited, Cass!" Mimi exclaimed.

"Me too! OK, later, boo," I said, and I hung up the phone. *OK now!* I thought to myself. *Dallas, Texas, here we come!*

July came and went, and before you knew it, Mimi and I were on our way to Texas to the mega fest, and guess who was the first celebrity we ran into once we got our layover flight in North Carolina? The "Never Would Have Made It" artist himself, Marvin Sapp! And yes, Mimi lost her mind when she saw her boo. Prayerfully, she was able to get through a photo. We even ran into Tye Tribbett. That was my guy. I had him on repeat when I first got saved. We were stoked. But all that came to a halt the moment Mimi and I were forced to sit with strangers and not each other. Our airline tickets were purchased last minute. I had the pleasure of sitting next to a really nice middle-aged woman.

"Hi. How are you? My name is Cassie," I said, initiating a conversation.

"Hi, sweetie, I'm Latrice. Doing well so far, enjoying the flight. It's nice to get away."

"I know," I agreed. Tell me about it. "What brings you to travel to Texas?"

"I'm actually going to the mega fest."

"Oh my gosh! Me too. That's so funny. I'm so excited!"

"Me too. I can't wait to soak up everything from this experience and bring some things back to my home church to grow it and make it better. I can also use some spiritual food myself," Latrice explained.

"Girl! Nothing like a good Word going forth. Home church? That's awesome!" I continued. "What's the name of it?"

"Zion Baptist Church in New Jersey!"

"OK, are you a part of the clergy or just a member and want to help better your church?"

"Oh, honey, I'm a little more than that," Latrice said as she chuckled. "I'm the First Lady."

"Oh. I'm sorry about that."

"You're fine, sweetie. How were you supposed to know?" Latrice said, assuring me that no offense had been taken.

"How long have you and your husband been together?" I asked, now that curiosity enticed me. I always loved a good love story.

"It will be twenty-five years in September. September 28th."

"That's awesome! How did you guys meet? I hope I'm not bugging you with all my questions. I just love *love*," I said, hoping I wasn't being a pest.

"It's OK, we've only got two hours to kill on this flight, nothing but time on our hands. Besides, I jump at every chance to tell my testimony."

Latrice continued. "I met my husband at his up-and-coming church that we are at right now. I went there, got saved, and he was honestly the furthest thing from my mind. One day, I was in prayer, and the Lord told me that he was my husband. It wasn't long after that I started looking at him, imagining what life would be like with him and me being a First Lady. I still remained focused at church. Outside of the trusted confidants I had shared this profound news to, I kept this secret to myself. A few months later, my husband introduced himself to me. It wasn't long after that he asked me out on a date. We dated for about two weeks. We went out to dinner a couple of times before he blindsided me by telling me he met a young lady that he was dating as well and he wanted to pursue her and it was better that we just be friends."

"OMG! Really? That is upsetting. How did you take that?" I asked.

"I was a little disappointed," she said. "I knew what God told me and didn't quite understand why my husband pulled the rug from under me. However, in his defense, he had no idea about the revelation God had given me, and he was a very single man at the time. He had the right to date and get to know people until he found who best suited him. At least that's what we do when God isn't involved in our choices."

"OK, so what happened after that?" I asked as I leaned in closer to her to get more into this intriguing love story of hers.

Latrice continued. "I watched my husband date this girl for about a year. He and I remained good friends. *Just friends!*" she exclaimed. "I actually decided to date someone myself. I still believed what God had told me, but I did understand that God grants us *free will*. My husband had to put himself in a position where his will became *God's will*. It wasn't something I could force him to do. So I started dating a guy, and shortly after, my husband called me up and asked if he could meet with me because he needed to talk to me about something important. I met him that night at a nearby diner. He shared to me that God had told him that I was his wife and he had to break things off with the girl he was seeing at the time. That is when I felt it was the right time to tell him what God had told me about him a year ago."

"Oh my goodness! That is such a crazy love story," I said to her. I couldn't help feeling that her story sounded so similar to mine. In that moment, I sent a quick prayer to heaven, asking God, *God, I know you—this is not by accident. You are a God who makes no mistakes. I'm not sure if this is your way of telling me that Marcus and I are supposed to be together. If this is you, let her say something to me as a sign to let me know that Marcus is who you want me to marry. In Jesus' name, Amen.*

"So what happened after you told him that God told you the same thing?" I asked inquisitively.

"Oh, he was ecstatic," said Latrice. "We decided to pray and fast together to seek God about whether or not this was the right time to get married. Shortly after, we got God's approval to go forth. We met each other's parents, put the wedding plans together. And Marcus and I've been together ever since."

Wait! Did I hear what I think I just heard? I thought to myself. "I'm sorry. What did you say his name was again?" I asked.

"Marcus," she said. "Marcus Shepard. You know him?"

"No, I don't know. It's just mind-boggling because listening to your story is reminding me of my own. We have very similar stories. I too was told by God who my husband was, and his name is Marcus," I explained.

"Really? His last name ain't Shepard, is it?" She sneered.

"Oh, no no no," I said, laughing. Dang, the First Lady role jumped off her real quick. "His name is Marcus Boyd."

"Oh, child. Look now. We was about to have a Holy Ghost showdown on this plane," Latrice said jokingly.

We laughed together.

"I just think it's ironic that God would have us come together as total strangers. You share this story that is very similar to mine, and you are a First Lady married to a pastor whose name is Marcus just like the man God told me I'd marry who's also a pastor and his name is also Marcus? That's crazy to me!"

"That's not crazy, sweetheart. That is a *sign* from *God*!" said Latrice.

This is my sign, I thought to myself. *This is my sign from God. Marcus is who God still has in mind for me to marry. Was I supposed to leave the church? Was I supposed to walk away? Was I supposed to stay?*

"What in the world is going on? This is crazy," I said aloud to myself, with Latrice being able to hear my thoughts.

"Well, what is going on with Marcus now?" Latrice asked.

"I don't know," I said in defeat. "I walked away."

I felt comfortable to share my story to Latrice. I told her everything I could with the limited amount of time we had left on the plane ride to Dallas Fort Worth International Airport. I couldn't help the stream of tears escaping my eyes, reliving all that I had been through with Marcus.

"Honey," Latrice said, "there is a reason why God had me to share my story with you. Maybe you need to go back and figure out why." Latrice gave me the sweetest embrace. She gave me one of those mother-to-daughter type of hugs. Latrice encouraged me some more. Once our plane landed, Latrice and I exchanged our contact information. We also shared our Instagram accounts to one another. She told me to keep in touch, and we went our separate ways. My cousin Mimi met me at the doorway of the plane.

"Cassie, you good? Why are your eyes so red? Were you crying? What's the matter?" Mimi asked, concerned.

"Long story, Mimi. Long story."

"Uh-uh," she said. "Come on! Whatever it is, we're not doing that! We are out here in Texas. We're going to enjoy this trip, this weather, and this conference. Not today, devil, not today!"

It wasn't the devil, I thought to myself. It was God, all God. It was the Most High God. He was calling me. Maybe I wasn't supposed to leave Marcus or the ministry. Maybe I was supposed to press. Press toward the mark, whatever mark that is.

"You're right, Mimi. Come on. Let's go have some fun."

17

STAND STILL AND SEE THE SALVATION OF THE LORD

The mega fest was explosive. Everyone who was someone was there. I met stars like Erica Campbell, Pastor Sheryl Brady, Michelle Williams, Christian Keyes, and more. In the house were Megan Good, Brandy, Joe, Steve Harvey, Jazz Sculark, and Tyler Perry. I mean, the list goes on and on. The teaching from T. D. Jakes was so profound that I gave a thousand dollars as a seed offering, believing God to open up doors for my business. I had such a ball. I met so many people. So many divine connections and encounters. I left empowered and ready to take on the world and whatever was waiting for me back home. I had purchased a lot of books and DVDs and sermons to keep me on track.

I had an influx of clientele waiting for me when I got back. I knew that getaway would have me pay for it once I returned home to my clients, who had been eager to see me. I spent my first week back working a lot. I also had an overwhelming feeling that I was about to come into a building for my salon. I went to banks and start-up business seminars to get a loan out to help me jumpstart my business. I was turned down by every single one. Still my faith was never shaken. It was more firm especially when God spoke to me after all my attempts to get a loan. He said to me, "Don't worry! When it's time, you'll know it's me the moment you walk into it!" I wasn't worried. Instead, I studied scriptures and material from the mega fest. I needed to get my faith and boldness in God back up. I need it more now that I had to face what I thought I wouldn't have to face anytime soon, going back to the Powerhouse. I knew God was leading me back there again—to face the church, to face Marcus.

I went to visit the Powerhouse the following Sunday after the mega fest. I was so afraid, thinking to myself, *What are they going to do? What are they going to say? How will they react? How will Marcus react?* I was ready for whatever was going to be thrown my way. Well, if I wasn't, I'd be forced to get ready anyway.

When I arrived at the church, I said a quick prayer:

> God, I thank you for this day. Thank you, God, for giving me the very air I breathe today. I ask, God, that you cover me and that your will be done as I go in this church. I know it's been a long six months since I've been here. Cover me as I go and hear your word. Let your will be done in Jesus' name, Amen.

They were already in the middle of praise and worship when I walked in the church. I saw a couple of new faces, but for the most part, it was the same people who were among the congregation before. Desmond, Kim, her mom Evangelist Ashley, Jada, and a few others were all the way up in the front, in the row directly behind Marcus. Jermaine was sitting next to Marcus. He was front and center, still serving as his armor bearer. He would armor-bear in rotation with Desmond. Anyway, that's beside the point. I took a seat in the back.

When praise and worship was over and the atmosphere was set for Marcus to take the stage to preach the Word, he walked up to the pulpit and addressed the crowd to give God praise.

"Come on, put your hands together! Come on, y'all can do better than that! Come on, come on! If it had not been for the Lord who has been on my side, I don't know where I'd be. Come on! Look at your neighbor and tell your neighbor, 'You better *give God some praise*!'" Marcus shouted as the church went in an uproar of worship.

When the congregation settled down, Marcus told us the Scripture reading and the topic of the sermon and started to deliver to the people the word of God. As he preached and perused the room toward the crowd, he noticed me. We locked eyes for the first time in six months. He stopped for a second too long but not to where the congregation would notice. But I noticed and I'm sure he did too. Marcus had a habit of saying people's names individually as he preached. I happened to be the first name he called out once he got in the groove of preaching.

Once my name was heard, I noticed Jada turn around, and I looked over back at her and she turned back toward Marcus as he continued to preach. After church ended, Jermaine, Kim, and a few others welcomed me and made small talk. As I conversed with them outside, I noticed Marcus easing his way through the crowd, heading my way. I could tell he was trying to get to me faster, but the greetings from both visitors and members slowed him up a bit.

Marcus finally made his way to me. I held a conversation with a new member I just met. I had a habit of being occupied whenever Marcus tried to have the slightest encounter with me. He made conversation with a bystander until I was available to talk. I wrapped up the conversation with the new member, once our chitchat calmed down, with an "It was nice to meet you" farewell. And then, the moment I could no longer avoid finally showed up.

"Hey, Cassie."

"Hi, Pastor," I said.

"How are you?" Marcus asked.

"I'm doing well," I said.

"How was the mega fest?"

"It was amazing," I said, but in my head, I was thinking: Had he been keeping tabs on me?

"That's great. It looks like it was amazing." *Yup! He was keeping tabs on me.*

He asked me a couple of questions about the speakers and the things that had taken place at the mega fest and then he told me it was good to see me. I said the same. Then he went back inside the church. I lingered around for a little while, before I got ready to leave. When I started heading toward my car, I was stopped by Desmond.

"Hey, Cassie?" Desmond said as he jogged toward me.

"What's up, Des?" I asked.

"Pastor wants to see you upstairs in his office."

"OK. No problem," I said to Desmond as I awkwardly followed behind him. I was nervous about what Marcus would possibly have to speak to me about, considering that we just spoke to each other. When Desmond and I got to the office, Marcus was facing the window.

"Pastor, she's here," Desmond said as he ushered me in. I entered Marcus's office and stood on the far side of a long table he had in the room, parallel to him. Desmond stood by the door attentively as Marcus turned around to face me. Noticing that Desmond was still by the doorway of the office room, he excused Desmond.

"We're good. Thanks, Desmond."

"No problem, sir," Desmond said, shutting the door behind him.

There was a moment of complete silence before Marcus spoke.

"I knew you were coming back. I fasted and God told me you were coming back."

I just looked at him. I didn't know how to respond. I didn't know what to say. I didn't trust that I could come back and tell him what happened to me at the mega fest and how First Lady Latrice told me all that she did. I didn't trust him. I wasn't ready to speak to him about us yet. I needed to process where I was at, mentally, and focus just on coming to church, and possibly work on being friends again. And whatever will be, will be.

Marcus and I played catch-up for a bit. I told him how I started doing hair on my own at my house and how I took quite a spiritual journey. I shared that I started putting out encouraging words on social media and things of that nature. He shared with me that he was focused on growing the ministry and the measures he was taking to get there. After the small talk between us, I told him I had to get going. He gave me a hug and told me it was good seeing me, before I left.

I started going to the Powerhouse every week like I used to do. Things seemed to be looking up. With the exception of Jada, everyone embraced me. I'm not going to lie: it still hurt that she still didn't want anything to do with me. But I couldn't force her to like me. It was clear her mind was made up about me. Marcus stayed consistent with his texts checking up on me. Considering that he just closed on a deal and purchased an official home church for the ministry, it was nice to know he was still thinking of me. I kept my distance though. Besides church and basic text messages, that was as far as our interactions went. But playing distant didn't last too long between us.

It was exactly three consistent Sundays I had been going to Powerhouse. I decided to bring my mom along. This was her first time visiting my church. Marcus was preaching a sermon. Even though the sermon title slipped my mind, I remember God was using Marcus in a mighty way. The things God was using him to say were all up in my *neighborhood*. In the climax of Marcus's sermon, he said,

> God never told you to leave. He never told you to deviate from his plan. No matter how tough things got, you were supposed to stand still and see the salvation of the Lord! If God has to send a whale like he did in the day of Jonah, to swallow you up and spit you back to the place he called you to be, he will do just that. Look at your neighbor and tell your neighbor, "Get back on track!"

Every word that was coming out of Marcus's mouth hit me like a ton of bricks. On the surface, you would have thought the sermon preached had no effect on me, but inside, it was eating me up. I knew what God was telling me to do. I knew he wanted me back at the Powerhouse officially. But I was fighting it. I didn't want to go back. I refused to go back. I ignored the altar call to discipleship and all. I darted straight to the door the moment the benediction was announced. I waited in the car for my mom until she made it into the passenger seat. Then I drove off immediately.

"Church was really great, Cassie. Thanks for inviting me," she said, enthused that she was able to make it after all the times I had invited her before.

"Yeah, it was pretty good," I said, covering up my true feelings on the service that day.

"Are you OK?" she asked.

"Yeah, I'm fine."

"What's wrong, Cassie?"

"Nothing, Mom," I said as tears began to roll down my cheeks. It was as if my tear count increased the farther I drove from the church.

"Talk to me, Cassie. What's wrong?" my mom asked in concern.

"God wants me to go back. *I am afraid*. I don't want to go back!" I explained.

"Aww, baby. It's OK," she said as she held my hand.

"I don't want to, Mom. I went through too much. But I know I have to follow *him*."

"I know, baby. I'll go back with you."

"Thank you, Mommy," I said, relieved that if I couldn't depend on anyone other than God, I surely could depend on my mom.

I made a U-turn and headed back to the church. I double-parked in front, put my hazard lights on, and ran back inside the church. It was as if my feet were doing what my mind didn't want to. When I got inside, I went up to Marcus as he was finishing up speaking to Desmond about armor-bearing duties.

"Hey, can I speak to you for a second?" I asked.

"Sure. We can go inside the office," Marcus said as he motioned me to follow him. We went inside Marcus's unfinished office. You could tell that he was in the middle of getting things unpacked to decorate.

"What's going on, Cass?" Marcus asked.

"I have to come back. God is telling me to come back, and I'm scared! I can feel the attack!" I said, overwhelmed with wailing. I just kept saying over and over again, "I can feel the attack! I can feel the attack!" I remember like it was yesterday.

"OK," he said. "Hold on. Let me get the leaders in here." Marcus stepped out of the room and gathered a few of his leaders and had them come in. He then said, "OK, leaders. I brought you guys in here to share with you guys that Cassie has decided to come back to Powerhouse. I brought you all in here so that I can let you guys know that there is nothing going on and make you aware of her decision to come back as a member."

I didn't really understand why he made it such a big deal to announce that I was coming back and moreover that there was nothing going on between us to the leaders. Afterward, the leaders all lined up to give me hugs and welcome me back, some more genuine than others. However, I didn't put any more attention on the matter. I was more mitigated to have the weight of going against the idea of coming back, off my shoulders. I entertained the false love bombing from leaders who weren't too fond of me. I came back to be focused on ministry and ministry only, and if God saw fit to bring Marcus and me back together, it would have to be God, *all God*!

18

I WILL MAKE YOUR ENEMIES YOUR FOOTSTOOL

Before you knew it, I was back in the groove of things at the Powerhouse. I joined the intercessory team again, along with the cleaning committee, and even found myself on the praise and worship team. Being on the praise and worship team came by surprise to me and others. One day in my prayer time, God led me to call Marcus and encourage him by singing an old church hymn, "I Love You, Lord (And I Lift My Voice)." Maybe he was probably going through something at the time. I left it on his voicemail, and before you knew it, I was the new member on the praise and worship team. I made a decision to give my all this time around, and if I was going to be there, I was going to be all in.

I was focused, and I was back focusing on my first love, the one I was all in for: *Jesus!* I went to every church meeting, every rehearsal, and every prayer meet-up, all while building my business and clientele, believing God for a building. I kept my distance from Marcus. If it had nothing to do with church, I stayed away. In fact, I isolated myself from a lot of the members. I just couldn't afford any distractions or disappointments from anyone if I was going to remain focused. Besides, it was very hard to trust anyone, especially Marcus. A lot of what he did and said to make things right between us was more in the dark than in the light. I didn't believe you could ever fully trust someone who could humiliate you in public and simultaneously give you heartfelt apologies in private. But that all soon changed at one particular Sunday service at the Powerhouse.

After Marcus shared the Word that afternoon, he randomly called me up to the altar. He then said to me, "Cassie, I called you up here to tell you, I am sorry. I take full responsibility for all you have endured here at the church through myself and the other leaders."

I put my head down and began to cry. That was my heart's desire. I needed that apology. I really gave my heart to the church. I gave my heart to Marcus. All I wanted was for him and everyone else to acknowledge the hurt they brought to me.

"Put your head up, Cassie," he said. "Look at me."

I lifted my head and looked him in his eyes.

"I'm sorry," he said as he gazed into my eyes. It was like this undeniable nonverbal assurance he was communicating to me that he meant every word. And I believed him. Marcus then asked the leaders to come up to the altar. He had all the leaders gather around me, and he had each of them hug me and apologize to me. Then he had them all surround me and pray for me and he had Jada to kneel in front of me and lay hands on my feet. In that moment, I knew God had avenged me. He in that moment made my enemies my footstool.

Just when I thought he was done, God used Marcus to get my salon. Marcus had been going to this barbershop called Adore Cutz, and the owner of the barbershop owned the salon next door. He happened to be speaking about renting to someone who was looking for their own salon. Marcus happened to be in the midst of the conversation. He was aware that I had been looking for a salon for quite some time now and that I had been doing hair in my shared apartment with my sisters.

Marcus called me as I was in the middle of doing a sew-in on one of my loyal clients.

"Hey, Cass! Are you busy right now?"

"Hey, Pastor," I said as formally as I knew how. "Yes. I'm in the middle of a head right now. What's going on?"

"So I am at the barbershop and the owner is looking for someone to rent out and take over the salon next door. I told him I had someone looking for a place. I thought of you," he said.

"Oh wow. OK, I'll come check it out when I'm done," I said. "I'll call you right back."

"OK, cool," said Marcus.

A good five minutes went by before Marcus was calling my phone again.

"Yes," I answered, tickled at the thought of Marcus being excited for me.

"Hey, Cass. Sorry to bother you again. The owner's name is Kevin. He said he can meet with you around 5:00 p.m. if you are available."

"It's cool," I said as I laughed. "I won't be available until about 8:00 p.m. tonight. I still have more clients to take."

"OK," Marcus said. "Well, keep me posted. I can even clear my schedule and come with you if you want."

"Cool. That will be great," I said. "I'll call you as soon as I get done."

"OK. No problem. Get back to work," said Marcus.

"All right, later," I said, and I hung up.

Another five minutes went by. My phone rang off the hook again. Yup! You guessed it. Marcus!

"Pastor?" I asked.

"Yo, Cassie! This place is mad litty!" he shouted.

"Pastor, really?" I said as I chuckled.

"I'm serious, Cass! You have to come check it out!"

"I will, as soon as I'm done."

"OK. You gotta get this spot, Cass. It's to the point where if you want, I'll go into business with you."

I hesitated when those words came out of Marcus's mouth. I thought to myself: *Is this what he was calling me so much for? Does he want to go into business together? Why didn't he have the same tenacity when I sent him a picture of my salon setup in my bedroom shortly after I joined back at the church? I remember he ignored it. No prayer, no encouragement, no conversation about it. Is he genuinely trying to look out or looking out for himself, as a business opportunity? Am I questioning his motives because of how I feel about him? What is his motive?*

"Cass?" Marcus asked.

"Yes, I'm here," I responded.

"Did you hear me? I said I'll even go into business with you. I'll put up a percentage and everything."

"Yes. I hear you, Pastor. I have to go, OK? I'll call you as soon as I'm done."

"OK," he said. "Don't forget!"

I hung up. I couldn't go into business with him. Was that what he wanted? If I did that, how foolish would that be? I didn't know what to do. I mean, was this what he wanted me to do? My mind was all over the place. I started feeling God's peace leaving me as I feared disappointing Marcus. I sent a prayer up to heaven:

> God! I love you, Lord, and I know what you promised me. If it is in your will for Marcus and me to come together in business, then let your will be done. But if not, let something take place that would prevent us from coming together in business before I head to the salon to meet him. In Jesus' name. Amen.

I got done a little earlier than expected that night. I'd say that my last client was done about 7:00 p.m. that evening. I called Marcus to see if he wanted to head over to the salon as promised. Marcus didn't pick up. I saw that Toni had called. We hadn't seen each other since we decided to part ways in business. We didn't have any ill feelings toward each other. We both had been super busy. I returned her phone call. Toni told me she was at the mall and wanted to know if I could meet with her. I figured I had a good hour of idle time, and considering that the mall was about a five-minute drive from my house, I didn't see the harm in meeting up with her briefly before heading to the shop with Marcus, if he ever called me back or answered. Toni met me by the movie theater entrance.

"Hey, sis. Long time no see," Toni said as she greeted me.

"Hey, what's new?" I asked as I embraced her.

"Nothing much, just getting a little shopping done. Figured I'd invite you out to shop with me."

"I can't stay too long, girl. I have somewhere I have to be," I said on God speed with my response being discreet about my whereabouts.

"Aww, sis, come on! Shop with me . . . Uh-oh! What they want?"

"Who?" I asked.

"Powerhouse," she said. "They just sent me a text."

"Oh, maybe they are trying to invite you to Sunday service. It's Marcus's birthday weekend, and you haven't been there in a while," I explained.

"I don't plan on it either, not after how he tried to play you," Toni said, still disappointed in how Marcus handled me while we were seeing each other.

"Oh boy, Toni," I laughed.

"Well, if he acted right, maybe I'd still like him," Toni stated as she opened the text message from the church. "Oh really?"

"What? What does it say?" I asked.

"Pastor is having his thirty-first birthday bash out in Brooklyn tonight. The church is throwing a surprise birthday party for him."

"I had no idea about it. I didn't get a text," I said in disbelief.

"Girl! I don't know why you are so shocked by that. You know Jada don't like you. You know little Miss COO of Powerhouse is not going to invite you anywhere around her *man*."

"Well, I guess that explains why he didn't return my calls yet."

"You're expecting a phone call?"

"Yeah. I was supposed to meet up with him about a couple of things. But look, I gotta go," I said as I hugged and kissed her.

"Don't let that sh** get to you, Cassie!"

"Language, Toni. And please, I got better things to worry about!" I said as I walked away, heading back outside to my car.

I was bothered. I'm not going to lie. Like why was I not invited to his birthday party? I thought all was well when I got back. I'm a part of the church. More a part than ever and they don't include me? Why? Then a voice came into my head: *The one they have made an uninvited guest will soon be the life of the party. Trust me!*

"God, what are you up to?" I asked aloud.

I got home that night. I was getting ready to end my day with a nice shower and some shut-eye when all of a sudden, I heard my cellular ring. I thought it was *Marcus* returning my phone call. Maybe he was just reaching out to reschedule our meeting with Kevin for another day. Maybe he just found out about the surprise birthday party and could no longer make it. I reached out to the nightstand to grab my phone. It was an unfamiliar number that came across. I ignored it. I figured it was a client trying to get their hair done. I was closed, and the next day was Sunday, the Lord's Day. I didn't do hair on Sundays. The number kept calling back to back, over and over again. I finally decided to pick up.

"Hello."

"Hi. Is this Cassie?"

"Hey. Yes, it's me. Who is this? I asked.

"How are you? My name is Kevin."

Oh shoot, the owner of the salon. "Hi, Kevin? How are you?" I asked as I turned on the switch to my *professional* voice.

"I'm great, couldn't be better. Listen, your pastor Marcus—Marcus Boyd told me that you were interested in renting the space and taking over the salon next door," he said.

"Yes, I am very interested," I said.

"OK, great. Marcus said that he wanted to hold off the meeting until he got back from out of town. But if you are up to it, I'd love to meet you tonight."

Wow! Marcus found time to schedule my appointment without even telling me but never called to let me know that he couldn't make it? Is this God's way of answering my prayers? Am I supposed to meet Kevin alone? Is this the monkey wrench God threw in? Was it God's original plan for me to go into business by myself?

"Cassie? Are you still there?"

"Yeah. Uh, sure! I am excited to meet you and to see the place. Is 8:00 p.m. tonight still good?"

"That's perfect. I look forward to meeting you, Miss Cassie."

"Great. See you soon."

I wasted no time. Being that I had a good fifteen minutes to get there by eight, I was heading back out of the house. I got there just in time. When I got inside the hallway part of the place, it was two different buildings parallel to each other. There was a barbershop on the left-hand side. It was very busy and loud. And on the right was the entrance to the salon. It was dark and quiet on the inside, but because the door was shut, I didn't get too great of a view.

"Hi," I said, greeting everyone from the barbershop.

"*Heyyyyyy*," some of the random fellows said with their failed attempt to flirt.

"I'm looking for Kevin. Is he here?"

"Yeah. He's in the back. Yo, Kev!" Paris said. Paris was the head barber at the shop. He helped Kevin a lot with running the shop.

"Yes! That's me, that's me!" Kevin yelled from the back. "I'll be with you in just a sec. Just let me grab my keys."

"No problem," I said.

A tall, stocky dark-skinned man that looked like he was in his mid-forties came out the back, with a bunch of keys in his hand. He was walking at great speed toward me. He was looking through the handful of keys in his hand in an effort to find the key needed to enter the salon portion of the building.

"Cassie?"

"Yes! Kevin?" I asked.

"Yes. That's me. How are you?"

"Good," I said with a huge smile showing off my eagerness to see what could potentially be my very own salon.

"You can follow me," Kevin said.

"Great," I said as I followed Kevin to the salon side. As I was walking toward the door, I noticed a very handsome man sitting in a waiting chair. I thought he was a client. I soon found out that he was one of the barbers and he was also Kevin's nephew. His name was Mahdi, and he was *fine*. Anyway, I wasn't focused on that. My focus was on seeing this salon that Marcus was raving about. We got in front of the door. Kevin put the key in the doorknob to unlock it. When he opened it up, I felt like I had entered heaven. It was stations, salon chairs, swinging hairdryers to put clients in for wraps and wet-hair styling, and more. It had a waiting section with chairs for the clients. It also had a couch with a fifty-inch screen TV mounted on the wall for clients to watch while waiting to be serviced. My spirit leaped. I knew this place was mine. I knew this was what God had promised me.

"Oh my gosh, Kevin. I love it!" I said as I began to tear up.

"Really? I'm glad to hear," he said, enthused. "When would you like to start?"

Oh shoot! I thought. *I don't have any money for a down payment, first month's rent, security, nothing!* I said, "Mr. Kevin? I love the space—it's just that I don't have any money to start. Bills wiped me out. I have a good amount of clientele, I can have the money for you my first week. If that's OK with you, I'd love to take over here." I hoped he'd approve of my proposal.

"Cassie, I tell you what. The rent for your salon is $1,200 per month. I'll have you pay $600 every two weeks. Heat, water bill, cable, and Wi-Fi included. And you don't have to worry about first month's rent or security. You can start as soon as possible. It's all yours."

"Are you serious?" I asked in astonishment. "Oh, thank you. Thank you, *Jesus*!" I shouted as I went into a brief praise break.

"Like you, young lady, I am a person of faith. I am humbled to be of help to a young woman like you who has the guts to step out and do something with the talent God has given you. If you need help with anything, I got you," Kevin assured me.

"Thank you so much," I said as I hugged him. And just then, I heard a still voice say, "Like I told you, when you get it, you'll know it's me!"

I cried as I drove all the way to my mother's house. The whole family happened to be there: my sisters Tanya, Ramara, and Paradise. We also had two other younger siblings, our baby sister Snow and our youngest and only brother Hermano. My mom Dakota was there also. I told them the good news. They all jumped into the two-door Honda I had at the time. They were excited about seeing the new place. We celebrated. It was a milestone to remember. *Me*, Cassie, having my *own* salon. Who would have ever thought God would bless me like this? Who would have thought that he would use Marcus to do it?

19

IF YOU HAVE AN AUGHT AGAINST YOUR BROTHER

I decided to text Marcus that night. I felt it was my due diligence to give him a heartfelt thank you. In spite of him blowing me off, he was kind enough to consider me for this business opportunity he came across. I sent a text saying,

> Hey, Pastor, I just want to thank you for recommending the shop. All went well with Kevin. I am all set to move in. I want to thank you for being the bait to this big catch. You are the best. God bless.

> SENT.

I waited all night to see if Marcus would send me a text back. Time came. Time left. Nothing. For someone who was enlivened about this business move, Marcus sure dragged his feet to text back so much as a "You're welcome." Maybe he was enjoying himself at his surprise birthday party. "Well," I said, "there's always tomorrow."

I didn't get to go to church the next day. My family and I cleaned the shop and decorated, preparing it for the upcoming week. Afterward, we decided to hang out at the shop for the rest of the night. We normally had Sunday dinner. We had it at the salon instead. We ordered some good ole pizza and wings from the local I Love New York Pizza. As we were watching movies while eating our *cuisine*, a text from Marcus came through.

Hey, Cass! Good to hear. Anytime! Glad I can be of help.

—Best regards, your pastor

Yeah! He was highly upset. I could tell by the plastic surgery on that text he sent. It didn't help that as soon as he texted me, I had like ten other messages follow through, all from the leaders at the church. Nice to know they all knew my number to dial. Just curious to know why it was such a challenge to use it to invite me to Marcus's surprise party. Go figure! The congrats and the "Oh, I'm so happy for you" kept wheeling in. It amused me that whenever Pastor felt a way, good or bad, about anything, there was like a "fall in line" rulebook they must have abided by. I don't know if I was a rebel or just had a mind of my own. Though each message came off extremely falsified, I responded with a pleasant "thank you" to them all.

Kevin had called to meet me to drop off a duplication of keys to the shop. I posted them on my IG page and captioned it, "Ownership! BUT GOD!" Before you know it, all my clients, friends, and loved ones were sending a bunch of comments and emojis under the picture, congratulating me and showing me so much love. As I looked through the comments, I saw one from Jada come in. The message said,

> Congratulations, Cassie, on your salon Slop on the Way. I tell
> you, man, when my pastor speaks a word, it just happens. Man!
> Jermaine, our pastor is a beast!

"Ugh! I swear I can't take this girl," I said, extremely agitated.

"Who? What happened?" my older sister Tanya said as she took my phone out of my hand. She then started texting really fast on my phone. It was clear that she saw Jada's comment.

"Tanya, don't even sweat it. It's cool!" I encouraged her.

"No! I'm sick of them! They're not 'bout to keep coming out their mouth!" she shouted as she continued to text. "There!" Tanya said as she handed me back the phone. Apparently, Tanya signed me out of my account and signed herself in and put a comment as well. It stated,

> ALL glory to God, not man. SMH. I've had enough of the fakes
> and foolery. Eyes, ears, and mind on God. That's it!

"Cassie, I swear to God! If anyone of them say something else smart under that post, I am blowing up Pastor spot! I'm dead serious. Everyone gon' know what was up with you and him, and I'm dead serious! You better not delete my comment either! Let them play if they want to!"

"What happened, Tanya?" Ramara asked.

"Them annoying Powerhouse folk. I'm sick of them!" Tanya said as she stormed off to the bathroom. "I'm not playing, Cassie! They better not say one word!"

Oh God! I thought to myself. *Please don't let nobody say anything else on here.*

I went to my second job, the nursing home I worked at, the next morning. I put in my two weeks being that I would be pretty occupied as head stylist / business owner. OK, Miss CEO! CEO! CEO! I was so ready to start this new journey that awaited me. I had a *sit* to monitor an elder woman. I called her Miss Cookie. She was so sweet, but if she didn't like you, she had the tendency of making you feel small if you crossed her. She gave off Taraji P. Henson's role on *Empire* if you rubbed her the wrong way. I had no worries. We always got along just fine. She was very independent. She did her thing and I did mine. I accompanied Miss Cookie watching her favorite show *The Price Is Right*, when my phone started buzzing with text message notifications. When I looked at my phone, I noticed that it was Marcus. The text read, "Hey. Where are you? I was wondering if we could talk."

I texted back: "At the nursing home. I don't get off until 3 p.m."

Marcus then texted: "Cool, can you come out for a sec? I'm literally around the corner."

I then texted: "I have a 'Sit' right now. I can probably come out for a few minutes but not long."

Marcus texted: "No problem. I'll be over to you in a few."

It was a no-brainer to figure out the reason why Marcus wanted to talk to me. It had everything to do with the salon. I got permission from the nurse covering my shift to take a fifteen-minute break. She approved at the exact moment Marcus called me to let me know he was outside in the parking lot of the nursing home. When I arrived downstairs, he was in the lobby at the door entrance. We greeted each other and then went for a stroll along the roundabout path surrounding the nursing home's lot.

"What's going on?" I asked.

"Nothing much. Just a little upset with you."

"For what?" I sneered.

"Well, you went ahead and got the salon without me. I thought we were going to go into business together?"

"What do you mean you thought we were going into business together? You suggested that, but I never gave you an OK."

"So why take it?"

"From what I remember, Marcus, when you told me about the space, you said you thought of me because you knew I was looking for a space to run my shop. I don't see the problem when you thought this place would be a good fit for me."

"Cassie, I don't understand why you would think that's OK, to just go ahead and take the space and not include me in it!" Marcus exclaimed.

"Are you serious, Marcus? Are you really hearing how you sound? That is like me knowing that you are in need of a car and I see one for sale, offer you it, and then expect to get rides every day! You seeing this as a great fit for me should have been the sole reason to plug me in to this space and not to gain something out of it."

It was a few moments of silence before Marcus responded. He said, "Look, you are right, Cass. I should have looked at this as a way to help you and your business and not as a handout. I just saw this as an opportunity for you to succeed in your business. I wanted to help you more than anything. I just felt like you took that moment from me."

"I didn't see it as that, Marcus. To be honest, I saw it being a foolish decision on my end. It would be more of an emotional decision than anything if I were to be in business with you."

"How is it emotional, Cassie?"

"Because I still have feelings for you!" I shouted back, realizing that those words slipped right out of my mouth. "Look, I gotta get back to work," I said.

"Is it OK if we talk more when you get off?" he asked.

"Sure, but I will be heading to the salon right after work."

"OK, so I'll come back when you get off and I can follow you there. You get off at 3:00 p.m., right?" Marcus asked.

"Yes," I said.

"OK, see you in a couple hours."

Marcus came as promised. When I came outside of the nursing home, he was there. Marcus dropped me to my car and then followed me to the shop. When we got there, I was shocked to see what my mom had done to the place. The décor she surprised me with was out of this world. It was full of warm colors, and it gave such a cozy homebody feeling that it would make my clients feel just like home, just like it felt at my house. But this time, it was a salon and not my home.

Marcus looked around some more with me. He gave a few pointers on where he thought a great admin area would be for ringing out clients. He also talked to me about bookkeeping and things of that nature and how it was imperative that I kept up with it for tax purposes and things like that. Before he left, he asked me to think about his offer to be a business partner. I knew he wanted to be a part of it so badly. I told him I'd think about it. That was short-lived once I presented this proposal to my family when they arrived at the shop. I had everyone meet me there when they got off work. Well, my sisters anyway. I had Tanya working for me just until I was able to handle business on my own and had hired help. The fact that she had a cosmetology license helped a whole lot.

When I told Tanya about the idea of Marcus coming on board at the salon, she was devastated. As you can tell from the encounter of the snobbish remarks from Jada under my Instagram post, Tanya is not one for tolerating bull and will let you know it too. She cried and told me not to do it, and how could I even consider that, with all the church and Marcus himself had me to endure? She was right! I couldn't be in business with him. I didn't trust him.

I texted Marcus that instant and told him that his offer had been declined and if he was a genuine friend and a genuine pastor, he would support my decision and support my business regardless. Marcus told me that he was cool with it and that it wouldn't hinder his support as my pastor or my friend.

Within the next two weeks, I threw a grand opening for the salon. I put out a flyer on social media for people interested in modeling my hairstyles for the "runway" portion of the event. I rounded up ten beautiful girls, and I remember doing each of their hair in a twenty-four-hour time span and began to panic when I had only an hour to get myself ready for the event. Luckily one of my girls from my "best friends" crew came through for me. Her name is Jeanette. She saved the day. She knew my style. Luckily, there was a boutique across the street. She found me this bomb dark-blue glittery fitted dress that hugged my curves in all the right places. She then went to my house, got my underwear, a few things to freshen up. She brought my jewelry and shoes, and I was good to go.

It was a few minutes into the event when Marcus showed up with a few of the church members with the exception of Jermaine. Jermaine came at the start when I was cutting my bow giving access to the shop. They arrived just in time for the modeling segment. It was awesome. Everyone loved the girls' look and hairstyles. Well, all except Jada. Apparently a friend of mine who came to the event overheard Jada talking negatively about the hairstyles. I really didn't understand what her issue was with me, but at that point, I was just sick of her mouth and how she was acting toward me. I didn't bother to address her. It was my moment, and I wasn't going to let her take that from me. Maybe she was upset about the fact that she *suddenly* found interest in hair and cosmetics, and God just happened to open doors for me and used Marcus to do it. Nevertheless, I wasn't going to feed energy to that situation.

After the runway, we gave a toast on God's blessings and success of the salon and my business, and we just mingled the rest of the night. I was sitting in the middle of the salon floor with a few of my friends, and Marcus was also in company. I had caught Marcus staring at me, checking me out. I stared back at him, giving him notice that I caught him gazing. He made conversation with my friends and made flirtatious jokes toward me. It was a fun night. It seemed like Marcus and I were beginning to be in a good space.

Marcus didn't make himself much of a stranger after that night. He came to my salon every single day except Sunday, the only day the shop was closed. I just didn't believe in working on the Lord's day, the Sabbath. A lot of the time, Marcus would work on his sermons and study the Word until I had some free time to entertain him. When we had those moments, we would watch movies and crack jokes.

One particular night after a busy work day, Marcus stayed afterward, as I fixed the salon up, preparing it for the next work day. We enjoyed catching up. It was just like old times. Once, I was preparing to get my things and locked up the shop, Marcus said, "I'm really enjoying myself around you."

"Yeah. Feels like old times, right?" I added.

"Yeah, I miss us like this," he said.

"Me too."

"So why would you leave, Cassie?"

"What do you mean? You broke my trust, Marcus! What was I supposed to do?"

"Stay!"

"Why would I stay, Marcus?" I asked as I grabbed my things and headed toward the door.

Marcus then grabbed me and said, "Because I needed you!" Marcus pulled me to him and we held each other for a second. He looked in my eyes as I did his. Then we kissed.

20

BE AT PEACE WITH ALL MEN

Marcus and I were back at it. We spent a lot of time together. It felt different with us this time. It felt like this time, we were going to be together, be happy, and hopefully get married one day, just as God had said. Most of our time spent was at the shop. It seemed he wanted to be around me all the time, even if it meant that he just watched me do hair. My clients, along with the barbers and their clients next door, started to take notice. People started suspecting that we were together, the church also. I mean, they went from popping in to check up on me to like showing up to the salon almost every day. I remember Marcus would get so mad. He felt like the church was only coming around to pry and figure out whether we were seeing each other or not. We didn't make anything official between us. I always told Marcus that I literally wanted to skip from a genuine and solid friendship to being married. I felt like the pressure that came from having a title would overwhelm us before we arrived at Holy Matrimony. It seemed to work well for Marcus, being that he was a pastor and had to keep his dating life private. I respected and understood that and the role he played in my life. But boy, was it tough. We had to literally act like we were just friends. It seemed like the more we downplayed our relationship, the more everyone saw right through us. Our chemistry was that strong, and it didn't help that we were always getting caught slipping. We became naturals at covering up our shortcomings.

I remember one time I was texting Marcus. I would call him Hot Chocolate because he was my chocolate man. Jermaine happened to be with him that day. He answered Marcus's texts from time to time, and Marcus heard Jermaine shout from the other room, "Hot Chocolate?" So Marcus took the phone and sent me a text saying, "Cassie, Jermaine had my phone and saw your message calling me Hot Chocolate. Text back and make it seem as if it was an accident. I'm going to delete this message."

I then texted back and said, "Oh my gosh, Pastor! I'm so sorry. I meant to text that to someone else. Oh God! I know I'm going to have to hear an earful when I go back to church. Sorry again."

Marcus told me that once he showed the message to Jermaine, Jermaine told him, "Pastor, you better be careful. People already told you she likes you, so you might want to create some distance." It was like a roller coaster, trying to bob and weave all the speculations that came our way. I remember one time Jermaine came to the salon with Marcus. Marcus and I had this thing where we would always clown around and make jokes on one another. Jermaine wasn't very fond of my humor toward Marcus. Jermaine addressed me and told me I needed to watch my mouth, talking to Pastor, or we were going to have a problem. Jermaine and I were so cool. I would have never seen the day he'd flip out on me like that. Jermaine and I joked around a lot ourselves. I didn't think he was serious at that moment until I turned around and caught wind of his demeanor.

I was infuriated. I was so shocked but happy I didn't resort back to how I used to behave in my *unsaved* days, but boy, was I fuming. Marcus saw how heated the moment had become that he grabbed me by the hand and brought me downstairs into the salon basement to calm me down with hugs and kisses. Then, Marcus and I went back upstairs. Jermaine and I made amends even though I felt extremely attacked. Marcus addressed us all in the room and asked, were we all good? Tanya, Trina, and Malcolm were there with us that night. Tanya spoke a few choice words and said, "Honestly, I'm good as long as my sister is good, but I'm not going to be having too much of people feeling like they can check my sister. I know that!"

"I agree," Malcolm said as he chimed in on the conversation. "Cassie is a female and Jermaine needs to watch how he talks to her and I feel like, Pastor, you should have put him in check." I was shocked at the way Malcolm handed both Jermaine and Pastor on a platter. Malcolm and Jermaine were cousins, and Pastor was of course his pastor. It still didn't stop Malcolm from standing up for what was right. He was the man in that room. He didn't hesitate to jump at the chance of standing up for what Marcus clearly shied away from. How could the youngest person and youngest man in the room make such an imbecile out of Jermaine and Marcus? I'll never forget the silence that followed after Malcolm put them both in their place. The consolation only carried me to the highway heading back home with Tanya and Trina.

I was so upset that I needed to get into worship to take the anger away. I had to give it to God. I began to worship in the back seat of my two-door car. My worship was so heightened that Trina pulled over on the highway. I got out of the car and continued to worship. I literally began to cry and worship alongside the highway. As I paced back and forth in this vein, I felt a very familiar hand grab mine. It was Marcus. He noticed me as he was driving on the highway on the way home. He told Tanya and Trina that he'd take me home and for them to just take my car. Marcus put me in the car and held my hand all the way home and said to me, "Just breathe mamas. Just breathe. Everything is going to be OK." I think I fell in love with him a little bit more that night. I felt like he understood all that I'd been through with the church, with him, and with the revelation of knowing that I am his wife. It was nice to know that he had my back as I was going through this. Needless to say, he was the main cause of it all.

Marcus brought me home. He even walked me all the way upstairs and waited until I opened the door to my home to settle in. When I opened the door, Marcus had the chance to see my uncleaned room full of clothes and trash all over. I was super embarrassed. I forgot all about how messy I left my room that week. I wanted to be perfect for Marcus. He was perfect to me. Dang! I couldn't believe I left my room like that.

I spoke to Marcus the next day about all that had taken place. We met up and I shared with him my thoughts. I told him even though I appreciated him for trying to defuse the situation and making sure I got home safe, I was still disappointed that Malcolm stood up for me when he didn't. I told him that Malcolm took on a role he should have played. I think that conversation added a little more to Malcolm's and my relationship as a nuisance to him.

Marcus and I decided to create ways to sneak around in efforts to see each other. We decided to start hanging out at my shop after hours. He'd pack a bag and would spend the night with me, then go home in the wee hours of the morning. Times of temptation would rise between the two of us. My love for God was what kept me from going all the way with Marcus, and the fact that he loved God too made him so understanding of keeping ourselves before marriage.

Marcus and I continued to be in a good space with each other for months. The only time I had moments of apprehension with him was when Jada would come up for the weekends for church. I still never put down my suspicions about Marcus and Jada in regards to her staying with him on the weekend. But I decided to put my suspicions aside and chose to trust him. Even though he made it a point to barely reach out or not at all at those times, I did my best to not let it get to me and trust him and trust that all that was there between them was a *friendship*.

In November that year, it was a shock to us all that Jada's brother was murdered. He was killed in street violence. It was so disheartening, considering that he was innocent. He was a man of great morals and integrity. When I found out the news from Marcus, I was devastated. What hurt me even more was that this stupid vendetta that was going on between me and Jada stood in our way after all this time. Jada was like my big sister. I truly wanted to be there for her as she mourned for her brother. I sent out a text to her the day I heard. I didn't want to call her because I didn't know how she'd receive me. For some reason, she still believed I had something against her. I texted her and said,

Hey, Jada. I'm sorry for your loss. I can't even imagine the pain you must feel right now losing your brother. I just want you to know that I love you and I'm here for you, and if you need me for anything, just know that I am here. Love you, sis. Cassie.

Jada never responded. I was hurt, but still, I did what was in my heart to do. I didn't regret it and I loved Jada regardless. Her feelings for me would never change that. Marcus would keep me abreast of how she was dealing with the loss. It gave me contentment to know that she was handling it OK.

I went out on a limb and went along with a few of the church members to her brother's funeral. Whether Jada received me or not, I showed up. The service was beautiful. Marcus preached a life-changing sermon that day. Nearly eighty people got saved and gave their lives to Christ. I remember worshipping like there was no tomorrow. It always moved me to see souls be won for God. It was a beautiful sight to see. At the repast, we were able to greet Jada. Jada thanked us all for coming out. She hugged and embraced everyone, including me. I thought maybe that would be a great start for our relationship to be repaired. The last thing I would want is for Marcus having to choose between me and his best friend. I definitely was all for us coming together. Not just for Marcus sake, but for Jada and me to get back to the place we once were. I didn't want to rush or force it. I knew when the time was right, God would make it happen.

In December, the opportunity for Jada and me to reconnect presented itself. Marcus was hosting a prayer line. He began to speak on having an *aught against your brother*. Marcus instructed us to make things right with anyone who might have done us wrong or if we had in fact wronged someone. I looked at that as the opportunity to reach out to Jada. I sent her a simple text just saying that I would love to speak to her and clear the air between us. I shared to her that she was always like a big sister to me and I wanted to do whatever I could to get us back in that space. I said that if she was up to it, I'd like for us to meet up for dinner or something so that we could talk. Jada didn't respond *again*.

After my many failed attempts and many days of mourning the fact that Jada and I would never be the same, I decided to bury what we had and let it go. I continued to focus on God, my business, and building my relationship with Marcus.

Soon, doors for ministry began to open. Apparently, I had become of notice to pastors and bishops around the area for all the inspirational words and videos of encouragement I put up on social media. One well-known bishop in the area stopped by my salon and introduced himself and gave me free materials such as books and CDs, to encourage me in ministry. He noticed the calling on my life right away to be a teacher in the Word of God. I remember when Marcus stopped by that day, I showed him what the bishop had given me and the things he spoke over my life. Marcus didn't really have much of a response.

I was asked by another local pastor to be a part of a winter revival service in January. I was asked to preach along with six other evangelists and pastors. I was honored being in a line-up like that in spite of me not having a title or being ordained. It was a door that God had opened in spite of the absence of my credentials. I went forth and preached at the service. It was my very first preaching engagement. It was January 19, 2014. My sermon was called "Now that you are in your *erected position*, it's time for *circumcision*." I talked about how God wanted the people to cut away anything that was preventing them from soaring in their erected (in other words, aroused, established, and set-up) place. It was incredible. The people were truly blessed. I was so excited to share with Marcus how blessed the people were from the encounter. Marcus ignored all my calls and texts that night. I knew that he was upset with me about something. Whenever we were upset with each other, we gave each other the *silent treatment*.

I was so confused on what he could possibly be upset about. My confusion came to a standstill when I discovered, while scrolling down on my timeline of Instagram, that Jada had posted a meme that said, *"There is something really wrong with a person where opportunity questions their loyalty!"* How ironic for her to put that post up soon after I had my preaching engagement. Call me crazy but I couldn't help but believe she was subliminally talking about me. If I was wrong, it was like it wasn't far-fetched from her to throw a little shade my way. I was going to just leave it alone, but I was past the point of *enough is enough*.

I texted Marcus the next day and asked if I could meet with him in person to speak. Marcus had a small office space a few blocks from my shop where he would go to have meetings with the members and get paperwork done for the ministry. He told me to meet him about 12:00 p.m. that day. It was a Monday. Mondays were typically a slow day for my salon, so it was no hassle to meet up. I found my way to his office, and Kim was there also carrying out duties for the church. She and I were cool. She'd support my salon by getting hair services every now and then. Kim escorted me to Marcus's office.

"What's going on? I've been trying to reach you!" I said.

"Thanks, Kim," Marcus said to Kim, motioning her to leave, and she shut the door behind me. "I was upset with what you did, so I refrained from answering your calls." he explained.

"Well, what did I do?" I asked.

"Cassie, you took a whole preaching engagement without asking me as your pastor."

"I didn't know I needed permission! I had no idea."

"How did you not know to ask your pastor to take an engagement? You jumped at the chance of this opportunity. Am I not supposed to question your loyalty?"

"Oh! So that's why Jada put that subliminal on her page about me?"

"What are you talking about, Cassie?" Marcus asked.

"Last night, she put some stupid post up about opportunity questioning loyalty," I answered.

"Cassie, Jada did not put that up toward you. It's probably a post she liked."

"Well, look at the irony in that. The same post you're making reference to right now. Did it ever cross your mind that I had limited church experience? Don't you think instead of feeling a way toward me that you could have called me and explained how things work when taking engagements? I would have understood my error and we could have moved on. I apologize for taking the engagement without your consent, but don't you think as my pastor instead of ignoring me, you could have corrected me in something I'm unfamiliar with?"

"You're right, Cassie. You're right," he said in compassion. "I'm sorry for that. I'll make sure I come to you first instead of assuming next time."

"Thank you. From now on, come to me instead of your little *minions*."

"What are you talking about?"

"Marcus, every time we have an issue between us, I find out from your crew before you. First the salon and now this? I'm tired of Jada always having something to say. She came at me when I got the shop, she came at my girl hairstyles the night of the grand opening, and now she has something to say about my engagement? I'm sick of it."

"Listen to me, Cassie. I'm sorry, OK? I'll do better next time," Marcus said. Then there was a knock at the door. "Yes?"

"Pastor, your twelve thirty appointment is here," Kim yelled out to Marcus behind the closed door to his office.

"OK, I'll be with them in a sec."

"Well, I'll let you get to your meeting."

"OK, I'll meet you over at the shop later, OK?"

"OK," I said.

"I'll see you later," Marcus said as he gave me a hug. I left and went to the shop.

Marcus never came to the shop afterward like he had promised. He texted me and let me know he was super busy with meetings and would be tied up for a few days. I stayed in communication with him over the phone. We shared brief phone calls and small conversations through text. The next time I was around Marcus was at Bible study that Thursday.

Of course, God used him mightily. Bible study was awesome, definitely one for the books. After Bible study, Marcus came up to me and gave me a high five. I got myself together to leave church for the night to head home.

Desmond stopped me on my way out and gave me a hug, and then said, "Hey, Cassie? Jada wants to meet with you in the office."

"OK," I said, wondering why she wanted to meet. I then followed Desmond to the office room. There were two other girls in the room, Direnda and Destiny. I figured it was about praise and worship because all who were in the room were girls from the praise and worship team. After a few moments passed, Jada came into the room to speak to us.

"Hey, ladies," Jada said as she addressed us.

"Hey," we said in unison.

"OK, so this meeting was called for me and Cassie," Jada said as she looked at me. "Cassie, I have the other girls here so no one can leave this room saying that anything took place that hasn't taken place."

"OK. That's no problem," I agreed.

"Great. Let's dive right in. Cassie, I feel that this was a long time coming for us to have this meeting that is long overdue. My issue with you is I don't understand why you would think that anything I put on my page would have anything to do with you."

"Well, for starters, Jada, Marcus shared with me that you told him that I don't like you." Jada had this puzzled look on her face the moment those words came out of my mouth. I then continued and said, "I don't understand why you would tell him that, considering how close we were. I looked at you as a big sister and shared with you more than I would share to Pastor or anyone else at this church. I even reached out to you to make amends. Did you not receive my text messages?" I asked. Jada nodded her head, implying yes as her answer. I then asked, "Why didn't you respond?" Jada grew silent. I couldn't take it anymore. I just broke down.

"I don't want to do this anymore!" I said. "This is not how church is supposed to be. I didn't come here for that. I came here for a family to worship God with and to build a relationship with. I miss my big sister. I don't want to keep fighting like this," I cried, wiping tears from my eyes.

"Cassie is right!" cried out Direnda. "Church shouldn't be like this. Let's come together and put this all behind us."

I then asked the girls if we could all pray. I did this heartfelt prayer about togetherness and unity. I also prayed against the devil for trying to create division among us. After I ended the prayer, we gave each other hugs. I gave Jada a hug. I embraced her wholeheartedly. But I noticed how stiff her body became when I put my arms around her. It was like she froze, like she was so cold to the idea of me even touching her. I knew in that moment that she wanted nothing to do with me. I should have known that she felt that way when she didn't answer why she never reached out to me.

I was upset with Marcus. I realized that I was set up. Everyone knew about that meeting but me. It was an attempt to sidetrack me, to set me up. Why would Marcus do that without even telling me? Me! The woman he is supposed to be seeing. I felt like it was all wrong. I felt that the proper way of handling it was him being there himself, front and center as a pastor. He should have been present, especially when he was the one who told me all that she said about me supposedly not liking her.

When I got home, I went to look on my Instagram page. I chose to believe that in spite of Jada's coldness toward me, the petty feud we had toward each other was water under the bridge. I went to search her name just to show her some love and tell her how happy I was that we could now move forward. When I went to search for her, I couldn't find her anywhere. I was blocked! It was official. She wanted nothing to do with me. I cried my last tear with Jada. I tried so many times. It was clear that she was the one in dislike. It was time I accepted that. I texted Marcus that night before I went to bed. I wrote:

> Marcus, I was set up by you. I felt like that was foul. You approved of a meeting being called on me and you didn't tell me about it, nor did you sit in on it as our pastor? I think that we should call it quits between us. SENT.

I put my phone down on my nightstand, and before I could get undressed, I received a message back from Marcus. He texted back "Okay." Just "Okay"? Seriously? Maybe it was time for me to accept that Marcus didn't care much to have anything to do with me either.

21

WHOSOEVER DENIES ME
IN FRONT OF MEN . . .

"Cassie, maybe it is time for you to let Marcus go!" Tanya said, handing me tissue to wipe my tears. I had Tanya and Trina come over to tend to my broken heart.

"Tanya is right, Cassie. You probably heard God wrong. Maybe it's best that you let go, and if it's meant to be, it *will* be," Trina added.

"Guys, I know what God told me! He told me that Marcus was my husband."

"Then what is taking him so long to marry you? Why would God put you through this?" Tanya asked.

"I don't know. All I know is that I refuse to not believe what he spoke to me. I know what he told me," I explained.

"Cassie, I don't think this revelation is from God. Only the devil will put you through this. God loves you too much to put you through this," Trina said, trying to reason with me.

"Trina, I know God's voice. I just need to be left alone. Excuse me," I said as I made my way to the bathroom. I overheard Tanya and Trina talking about me that night.

"I don't know what else to do. She is not letting up on this revelation. It's getting out of hand, Trina."

"Tanya, Cassie will be fine. She will get through this. God will show her. Don't worry. She will come to her senses eventually."

God, what is going on? I thought to myself. *Am I not hearing you correctly? Is this not you? Show me, Lord, if I got it wrong. Everyone is starting to think I am crazy! Show me, Lord. Is he the one for me?*

I had a headache the next day. I had a busy schedule at the shop. But I couldn't allow how crappy I was feeling to stop me from carrying out my day. Tanya and Trina decided to come along with me to the shop. Tanya didn't really have many appointments that day. She told me that she would hop in if I needed her help. But I think Tanya and Trina were less concerned about my appointments and more concerned about my mental status.

A woman named Hattie was my first appointment for the day. She was in town visiting family. She was from Houston, Texas. She came across my salon on the Internet and saw my work and set up an appointment to get her hair done.

"Hey, I'm Hattie. I'm here for my ten o'clock. I'm looking for *Cassay*," she said in her Southern accent.

"Hi. That's me. Come on in, get comfy, and take a seat in my chair."

"Girl, you do some great work. The only style I get is a full head, long hair with bangs. I don't like that cone look at the top. I see your work so I know you are gonna hook it up."

"Yes, I am, Hattie. I am going to take good care of you."

"*Hey now*," Hattie said in excitement. The girls and I laughed along with her. We just loved her little accent.

"Trina, do me a favor? Can you find a sermon for us to watch and put it on the TV?" I asked.

"Got it, Cass."

"Oh! OK, y'all some churchgoing sistas. All right now," Hattie said.

"Yes, we love the Lord—that's for sure," I added.

"That's awesome. I think I want to go this weekend before I head back home. What church do you go to?"

"We go to the Powerhouse. I can give you the information before you go."

"OK, great. Whew. I'm so glad I met you ladies. I can feel the presence of God in this place. God has anointed you, young lady, to do some hair and win some souls. *Hey now!*"

I chuckled. "Thanks, Miss Hattie."

"Hey, I'm just calling it like it is. What's your pastor's name?" Hattie asked.

"Pastor Marcus Boyd," I told her.

"All right now. Is he single?" she asked.

"Yes, he is." I answered.

"Hmm," she said. Then Hattie turned around to me in the middle of me sectioning her hair, preparing to braid it for her sew-in. She said, "Honey, I don't fake the front like I'm *holier than thou*. But God just told me to tell you that your *pastor is your husband*!"

Trina and Tanya looked at each other in utter shock and then looked at me. I cried and said, "I told y'all! I know what God told me!"

"Wow! That's crazy," Tanya said. "We was just talking about this last night, ma'am."

"Cassie, sorry we doubted. We thought you were going crazy," Trina explained.

"You all had this conversation already?" Hattie asked.

"Yes. I have been struggling with this *revelation*. With all that I have endured, I thought that maybe I was wrong," I cried.

"You ain't wrong, honey. That man is *your husband*. What's his favorite color?"

"I don't know. I never asked him. He wears black a lot and wears it well," I said.

"Text him now and ask him."

"I can't. I cut him off. I broke it off with him."

"Don't matter! Text him and ask what his favorite color is."

I texted Marcus and asked what his favorite color was. Marcus must have been waiting by the phone because he texted back right away.

"He said red and black," I said to Hattie.

"OK. Here is what you do. Find yourself a nice black-and-red dress, and you wear that to church this Sunday. I'm coming along too. I want to praise the Lord and see this man of God."

"Wait, what?" I said, concerned that she would put us on blast to the church.

"Don't worry, darlin'. I already did my part. I will be there to praise the Lord and observe," Hattie explained.

"Thank you, Miss Hattie."

"No problem, honey. You just go get you a nice red-and-black dress now, and you wear it on Sunday."

That Sunday, I did exactly what Hattie told me. Hattie came to church like she said she would. Trina and I took Hattie out to eat afterward. She said she liked the church a lot. She thought Marcus was a well-put-together man and God had great things in store for his ministry. I didn't really know and still don't know the significance of wearing a red-and-black dress, but I do know one thing: with the exception of Marcus preaching, he didn't take his eyes off me.

We were back at it in no time. We spoke about how we felt about the meeting with Jada. I found out that Marcus was the one who told Jada not to respond to me when I reached out to make amends. He said it was because Jada was still mourning over the death of her brother. I didn't want to put any more effort than I already had trying to repair what was lost between us. I just dropped the issue with her as a whole. I figured if Jada wanted me to be in her life, she would welcome me with open arms. Until then, I decided to move on from that and focus on Marcus and me. We were in a good place, for now, that is.

One Sunday after service, Marcus and I were cracking jokes to each other among the other members. I remember leaning into him to hug him in a cuddly way. I felt myself melt in his arms. Marcus interrupted my comfortableness by nudging me off him, reminding me that we were in front of the church members. I immediately straightened out and shot him a little smirk, indicating that I understood why he did that.

It was still winter. A snowstorm was heading upstate our way. I wanted to invite Marcus over to spend the night at the shop like we always did, at least once or twice every two weeks. I figured we could order some pizza and watch some movies together. I wanted to stay at the salon that night, knowing that I had to be to the salon in the morning anyway. I didn't want my car snowed in to prevent me from being there. I figured Marcus could keep me company. So I sent him a text:

"Hey, Marcus."

"Great evening, Cassie. How are you?"

"Good so far, how about you?"

"I'm great. Is there anything you need right now?"

"No, I'm fine." I wrote back.

"Okay. Great. I'll speak to you later."

"Are you going to bed early or something?"

"No! It's just that I don't speak to my members past a certain hour!"

Wait! Did I read that correctly? I wrote back, "SINCE WHEN?! YOU KNOW WHAT . . . SAY NO MORE!"

Did he really try to address me as his member? Who was Marcus around? Who was he fronting for? Who was he around at nine o'clock at night?

Marcus called my phone nonstop that night. That was it! I was through! I listened to a sermon from T. D. Jakes on my Apple TV and went to sleep. Marcus was going to see how much of a member I was.

I woke up about 8:00 a.m. the next day. I had about twenty missed calls from Marcus since 6:00 a.m. I ignored every single one. He wanted me as a member; he got me as a member. Around 8:45 a.m., I heard the door open to the other side. It was Paris getting the barbershop ready for the day. I then heard someone come in after him and say, "Hey, Paris." *Shoot! It was Marcus.* "Is there anybody in the hair salon right now?" he asked.

"I'm not sure. It's dark over there, so I don't think Cassie got in yet," Paris said to Marcus.

"OK, cool. I'll just get my hair cut and wait until she gets here."

I didn't have a client until twelve o'clock. Marcus was going to be waiting for hours to see me. I didn't make a peep. Not a sound. I wanted him to get his hair done and then *leave!* Next thing I knew, about a half hour later, I heard a bunch of weights being used downstairs in the basement. The barbers also had a section down in the basement to work out in. I remember going down there one day. I caught Mahdi working out. He was using the pull-up bar. Oh my gosh, that boy was so fine. *OK, back to the story before I get accused of lusting again.* I knew Marcus was down there working out because when we would work out in the morning, we would either go to Planet Fitness or we'd work out in the shop's basement. Marcus had no idea I was in the shop. And I didn't care either!

It was ten minutes to 12:00 p.m. when my client came. His name was Clark. Clark had been coming to me about a month. I was able to sneak to the bathroom to freshen up a bit, brush my teeth, and wipe my face. I always had an overnight bag handy just in case I was stuck there. I started twisting Clark's locks. I couldn't get my mind off how much Marcus upset me. I decided to speak to Clark about it to get his opinion. Clark felt like Marcus was seeing someone else and texted me that night in front of *whoever* he was with to act like we were not seeing each other. In the middle of our conversation, Marcus barged in from the back door of the salon. He then grabbed me from behind and held me close to him.

"Hey, Cassie," he whispered in my ear, as if what he did never happened.

"Marcus, get off me! I'm your *member*, right?"

"Cassie, I didn't mean it like that. Desmond had my phone. He texted that!"

"Bye, Pastor!" I said, struggling to get his hands off me.

"Cassie, are you serious?"

"I'm dead serious. I'm tired of you trying to play me. I'm your member from now on!" I yelled.

"Oh my gosh, man," Marcus said, taking a sharp exhale. Marcus had let go of holding me. He started to head out of the door. Then he turned around and took a seat in my waiting area across from me.

"Cassie? Cassie? Cassie, really? You're really doing this? Cassie?"

"Yesssssssss, Pastor?"

"Yo, stop playing with me!" Marcus said as he laughed.

"I'm dead serious, Marcus!" I said, holding back my laugh even though I was serious.

Marcus waited around that entire day, client after client. I would not budge. But he didn't give up. Giving up wasn't in Marcus's nature. He would wait me out until I gave in. I finally had a break about 5:00 p.m. Marcus came up to me, got on his knees, and said, "Cassie. Look at me. I'm sorry. Please forgive me. I care about you a lot. I never want to hurt you. Desmond had my phone. Believe me."

I felt in my heart that Marcus wasn't being honest with me. Well, at least I questioned it. He waited around for me, for hours. Maybe he was telling the truth. So I put aside my doubts. I decided to trust him. I did. I believed him.

Marcus and I continued to fight and make up. That became the norm for us. Most of our fights stemmed from him either constantly hurling insults at me or him denying me one minute then embracing me the next. It didn't matter what company we kept around us; all of a sudden, he began to belittle me on how I looked and even mock me when people asked about the nature of our relationship.

He told me that he made fun of me a lot because he really liked me. He gave me an example on little boys using this method as a way of expressing how they felt about girls. It was to pick on them. I thought it was very immature. It annoyed me so much that I would find myself cutting him off. Every time I did, he chased and hounded me down. He wouldn't take no for an answer. He refused to let me walk away. And what's worse, I refused to let him go.

No matter what fights we had, we tried our best to put on a face for the church. There were times when my emotions would get the best of me and it would show as he tried to engage with me. One time, Whitney came to church with me. During the greeting song, he went up to me as I was sitting with Whitney in the pew. I happened to be off duty that day from praise and worship. He came up to me to try and shake my hand. I put my head down and refused to acknowledge him. I was upset with Marcus yet again. I was over the back and forth. I was so mad at him. I was done with pretending. I was done with him making me feel less than. I was done with him denying me.

22

HOW CAN TWO WALK EXCEPT THEY AGREE

This went on for an entire year. At that point, I would question my relationship with Marcus. Marcus started sharing with me that he was unsure about whether God wanted me to be his wife. I was baffled because he seemed to be sure of this when he shared with Toni that he had a glimpse of *revelation* about us. Marcus became less and less consistent. He wouldn't come to the salon as much. He didn't take me out on dates with him as much as he used to. He would make plans to hang with me and never show. But whenever I so much as fixed my mouth to tell him I was done with him, he did anything and everything to wheel me back in.

In August that year, I had turned twenty-six years old. I threw this big party, inviting my family and friends. I also invited a few people from the church that I was close with, like Destiny and Jermaine. Jermaine and I were back on good terms. Of course, I extended the invitation to Marcus. Marcus had already built a bond with my family. Marcus practically begged my mother to run the children's church at Powerhouse. He asked Paradise to be a part of the ushering board. He also became really close to Tanya. Tanya was really into music as Marcus was. That was his avenue to connect to her. My sister Ramara, on the other hand, fed Marcus with a long spoon. She wasn't too fond of him at all. Marcus was already well acquainted with my family, but I really wanted him to come hang out with my family and friends as they celebrated my birthday with me.

I had my birthday celebration at Andy's bar that night. Everyone that I had invited came out, everyone except Marcus. I was really upset. My friends were too. Jeanette had no hesitation expressing how she felt.

"I'm not feeling Marcus at all, like where is he at?"

"I have no idea," I said. "Probably held up at church or something."

"Well, when do you think he will be here? Today I'm supposed to be celebrating my man's birthday too. I was trying to meet him but I can't stay too long," Jackie said. Jackie was a part of my best-friends crew too.

"He's a mad cool dude, but I don't know why he is taking so long to show up on your birthday," Jeanette said. Jeanette takes birthdays *very* seriously.

During the mixer, I noticed that Marcus left me a voicemail. I assumed that I had bad service and his calls didn't go through. He left a voicemail saying, "Hey, Cassie. This is Pastor Boyd calling. Just want to wish you a very special happy birthday. I pray that God gives you many more years to come. I pray blessings overtake your life, in Jesus' name. God bless!"

Seriously? Not only did he not show up but he left a very generic birthday message on my voicemail? I was so disappointed. Marcus didn't care. He didn't show; he never came. Holidays, events, milestones, preaching engagements, it didn't matter. Marcus didn't show up. He stopped showing up for me.

When I got to the shop the next day, I caught my sister Tanya up on how Marcus didn't show up to my birthday dinner. She had to leave a little early and couldn't stay. Just as I was in the middle of telling her how upset I was, Marcus walked in.

"Hey, hey, ladies. How are y'all doing this morning?" Marcus asked.

"We're good, Pastor," Tanya replied. I ignored Marcus. I continued to tidy up the salon. I got annoyed by his conversation with Tanya. He really came in the salon like everything was sweet and nothing happened, like he just didn't stand me up and not show at my birthday party. Well, if he wanted to pretend nothing happened, I was going to pretend he was not in the room.

Shortly after conversing with Tanya, Marcus came up to me.

"Hey, Cassie, can we talk?" Marcus asked.

"Sure," I said as I walked out the back door and down to the basement. That was the area Marcus and I settled our feuds whenever I had company.

"Are you mad at me?" he asked.

"Why would I not be mad at you?"

"I'm sorry I got tied up doing some things."

"You know what, Marcus, it doesn't even matter anymore. I don't care. Do what you want from this point on."

"Cassie, I was busy. I'm sorry."

"You're always busy when it comes to me. This is my birthday we are talking about. That wasn't important enough to you? You never show up for me. This is the problem I have with you. I always show up. You never do!"

"I'm sorry, Cassie. Please forgive me. I'll do better next time. I promise."

I started to cry. "There won't be a next time, Marcus. It's over. I'm done!"

"Cassie, please don't do this."

"You did this! This is not what you want, Marcus. You wasted my time enough."

"Cassie, I'm sorry. I really am," Marcus said as his voice began to crack.

"I think it's best we just move on and go our separate ways."

"I love you."

"I love you too. But you don't love me the way that I love you."

"Cassie, please. Don't do this."

"You have five minutes until you have to get on the prayer line," I reminded Marcus. Marcus had recently started a prayer line at noon for the church and others who had barriers that prevented them from coming to church.

"Cassie, can you just pray for us, please?"

"We don't have time to pray, Marcus."

"Cassie, I am not getting on that prayer line until you pray for us!"

I prayed. I prayed that God would get the glory out of us. I prayed that God would restore us to what he saw fit. I asked God to heal my heart and help me to forgive Marcus and to make it easy for him to get on the prayer line to give the people what he had instilled Marcus to give to them. I then ended the prayer with an amen.

Tanya had called me from upstairs. She let me know that Toni was here to take me out for my birthday as a surprise. I decided to go with her, but before I left Marcus, I said, "I love you, Marcus. I just wish you knew how much I do."

I never forgot the look on Marcus's face when I said those words to him. It was as if he knew he had lost me for good. I was tired. I was fed up. I needed to clear my mind of it all. What better way to do that than have a day out on the town with Toni?

I spent the whole day with Toni. She brought one of her other friends along, so I invited Trina out with us as well. We had a blast. She treated us to Lake George. We dined out and took a ride on a speedboat. We swam a bit as well. It was about 5:00 p.m. that day when we headed back home. I had Toni drop me off at the shop after she brought Trina back home.

When I went inside the shop, the salon was decorated with a bunch of birthday party decorations. My mom Dakota always did little cute things like that for me to make me feel special for my birthday. I was excited and happy my mother took the time out to put a smile on my face. She and I had grown so close since I had been saved. When I scanned the room, I realized that Marcus was on the couch. He had this defeated look on his face that looked as if he hoped I didn't kick him out.

"Umm, Cassie. Can I see you in the back really quick?" my mom asked. I followed behind her. "Marcus has been here all day. He didn't want to leave. He told me he will wait until you get back. He's been here for hours. Go talk to him, sweetie. You can tell he's really sorry."

"OK, Mom."

"OK, sweetie. I love you."

"Love you too, Mommy."

My mother and I went back to the salon floor. It was such an awkward silence in the room. It was clear that Marcus knew my mom had talked to me on his behalf.

"Cassie, I invited some of my daycare kids by to celebrate your birthday with us."

"OK, Mom. That's fine. I need to go home and change. I'm wet and icky from swimming in the lake."

"Are you going home to change? I'll take you," Marcus said.

"Yes. That's a good idea, Cassie. Pastor, take her home to get freshened up. Everything will be ready by then," Dakota agreed.

Marcus and I headed out of the shop and walked to his black 2005 Altima. He opened the door to the passenger side so I could get in. In the passenger-side seat, I noticed a birthday bag with my name on it.

"Marcus? What is this?" I asked as I looked at him with a smile.

"Hold on! Hold on! Don't open it yet," Marcus said in excitement. "Wait until I get in the car first."

"Oh gosh. You're so extra." I laughed.

"OK, so first off, Cassie, I want to start by saying that what I got you isn't all that extravagant. But I felt like it was something you really need. But before you open that gift, I would like you to open the card I bought you."

"OK," I said in curiosity. When I opened the card envelope, I took out the card. On the cover was a picture of an old man pushing a car that seemed to be broken down.

"I wanted to get you a card that symbolizes our relationship. The man symbolizes you and the car reminds me of our relationship. No matter how much our relationship struggles or break down, you always keep us going."

The words he wrote were pretty nice. He just summed up how much my birthday means to him as well as our friendship. It seemed pretty platonic, what he wrote in the card. I could tell he was writing tactfully in the event the card ended up in someone else's hands. It didn't matter to me. I knew what was shared between us. I then pulled out the gift he bought for me. It was a Steve Madden wallet from Macy's. We laughed. Marcus used to always make fun about my wallet. He felt I was in desperate need of a new one. He was right. We were good again, but of course, it didn't last. Still the same ups and downs that troubled our relationship found their way to us again.

Marcus's birthday came around in the fall of October. I set up the shop with balloons and party decorations. I also bought him a birthday cake and put together an area where he could just relax for the day and whatever food he wanted to order out was on me. I thought it would be easy to get him to come. I had recently hired him as a consultant for the salon. I figured I'd finally give him a chance, considering how much he kept getting on my case about hiring him. But nope. He sent me a text saying he couldn't make it. I insisted that he come and told him that he was mandated to come because I was super busy that day and I needed him to help me with some paperwork. When he showed up, I greeted him with a surprise. Marcus took one look at the room, didn't acknowledge anything I did. He just took a seat on the couch. Apparently he wasn't feeling too good, but a thank you wouldn't hurt. My client was even offended. She said, "Wow, and he's a pastor? What a jerk!"

Marcus couldn't seem to get anything on any holiday right, for that matter. He even went missing on Thanksgiving and Christmas, with not even so much as a call or text wishing me happy holidays. I know! Stupid, right? Why didn't I just walk away for good?

I'd call Marcus out on his inconsistencies all the time. No matter how hard I tried to cut him off. I couldn't. He popped up everywhere. He would even start having fits of rage when I would try to end things with him. He never hit me though. He would just grab me and force a kiss on me, or if we'd argue in the car, he'd bang the steering wheel. He eventually started yelling at me. Like who was this guy that God said was mine?

Marcus told me the reason he would act out toward me. He told me that Veronica had told him all that I shared to her about Marcus. I told him it was true. What was I supposed to do? I had no one to confide in about Marcus. My family and friends' feelings toward him wore thin. One time, my mom actually kicked him out of her house. She felt like Marcus was trying to turn me against my family and was trying to use the shop as a tool to do just that. Considering that Veronica cared for him like a brother, using her as an outlet seemed befitting.

Marcus was also opposed to my *calling*. He expressed that he didn't want a *preacher* as his wife. I told Marcus that if he didn't want that, then he didn't want me. I knew that was what God was calling me to. I didn't get why that was an issue for him. Wouldn't a pastor want a woman by his side doing ministry with him? I was so confused. Why would God tell me this if I was not Marcus's ideal wife? Who I was and what I was called to be were not who he wanted. I felt alone holding on to this *revelation*, holding on to Marcus, holding on to *us*. But there was no agreement between us. How could the two of us walk together in life and in purpose if we couldn't even agree?

23

RESIST THE DEVIL
AND HE WILL FLEE

If it wasn't enough of Marcus fighting, going back and forth on this *revelation* God gave me, everyone else around us seemed to see things between us clearly. I had my one-year anniversary at the salon. I took pictures with everyone in attendance. I had the pictures developed so that I would make a collage on the salon wall. Paris would always come to my side of the shop, both him and Mahdi. Mahdi would always come over to crack jokes and might even get his hair washed, here and there, to keep his waves fresh. But Paris's time spent with us was different. Paris caught wind of me preaching, and he would come across a lot of my inspirational videos of me teaching and encouraging people in the Lord. I came to find out Paris was saved as well. We spoke all the time about the Word and revelation from God and sharing testimonies and such. He and I grew really close. We had like this bro-and-sis type bond.

I remember one instance when I was talking to Paris as I normally would in our down time at the shop, I was in the middle of sharing to him a *word* the Lord had given me. Paris seemed to be a little distracted by something that had his attention behind me. I noticed him going in and out of focus. Still, I continued to share the word. The next thing I knew, Paris stopped me in midsentence: "Yo, Cass? Why does it look like you and Marcus are married in this picture?"

"What?" I asked.

"You and Marcus look married! Ahahaha," Paris said as he was arrested by laughter.

"What are you talking about? The shop anniversary photos? How? We are in a group photo!" I said.

"I don't know! That's the crazy part. Even though y'all are in a group photo, it's like everyone around y'all in this pic don't exist. I just see y'all being married, Cass! I don't know why I see that for y'all."

Here we go again! I thought to myself. Not only was Paris potentially seeing this possibly in the Spirit between Marcus and me, what was worse was Marcus walked right inside the shop directly after Paris's comment.

"Hey, hey?" Marcus said as we walked in and put his briefcase and Bible down on the couch. "Paris, are you ready for me?" Marcus asked, seeing if Paris was ready to give him a haircut.

"Yeah, I'm ready. I was just telling Cass that y'all look like y'all are married in this picture."

"What picture, where?" Marcus asked.

"Right here in this group picture," Paris explained as we walked over and pointed toward the pic he made reference to.

"How did you gather that off a group pic?" Marcus asked.

"That's the crazy part. I don't know. That's all I see when I see y'all in this pic."

"Let me guess, Cassie made you say that, right?" Marcus asked, implying that I encouraged Paris's preconceptions.

"Are you serious? Why would I make him say that? Paris, your client is waiting for you. Go cut his hair," I said, extremely irritated by Marcus's insinuations.

It greatly upset me that Marcus downplayed everything that was brought to his attention about us. I mean, wasn't he the one who told Toni initially that he believed that God was telling him that I was his wife through his mom? Did he not confirm that to me also? Now you'd think the whole idea of us being with each other was too impossible a thought for him to conceptualize.

After Marcus had got his hair cut by Paris, he came back in the room and tried to engage with me as usual. But I wasn't about to sweep under the rug the comments he made to Paris. He looked around the room to see if the coast was clear and then he started for a hug and kiss. I rejected him.

"What's the problem now, Cass?" he asked.

"Marcus, I don't want to do this anymore."

"Do what?"

"This! Us! I'm done playing games."

"What are you talking about, Cassie? How am I playing games?"

"The game of you one minute saying I'm the one and then acting like I'm not the next."

"Well, I'm not going to sit here and act like I know for sure if you are or not!"

"So go pray and fast and do whatever you gotta do to find out!" I screamed.

"I've been doing that. What have you been thinking I have been doing this whole time?"

"Playing games, Marcus! It don't take that long to figure out if this is something God wants for you!" I said. I took a deep breath and then said to him, "Marcus, I don't want to see you again until you know if this is what God wants for you."

"What do you mean you don't want to see me?"

"Just go figure it out! You know what you have to do to get the clarity you need. Being around me is not getting us anywhere. If anything, you are making me feel that by the time you get the reassurance you need, I'm going to be over it and done with you."

"See, Cassie, this is what I am talking about. You make me feel like all you care about is the *revelation*. Do you even like me for *me*?"

"What kind of question is that, Marcus? Of course I like you, and sometimes I hate the fact that I love you!"

"But you only love me based on this *revelation* you got from God. Would you even be dealing with me if God never told you?"

"No, I wouldn't!"

"Exactly, Cassie, that's my point. Sometimes I feel like if it wasn't for God, you probably wouldn't even like me. You wouldn't even be attracted to me. I want you to like me and want me, whether God told you I am your husband or not. I don't feel wanted by you."

"Marcus, I'm sorry but I can't lie. When I got saved, I dropped everything. I dropped every desire I had in my old life. I made room for what God wants for me. I gave God a clean slate to put in place what he wants and desires for me. And you were one of the things God revealed to me. I grew to love you from that. It wasn't my intention to make you feel unwanted. But outside of God, I wouldn't have thought to look your way. My focus was on God, and him alone. You just happen to be the man God revealed to me for my life. Until you fast, Marcus, you'll never understand this."

"So you are saying that you don't want me around until I hear from God?"

"Yes. That's exactly what I'm saying."

"OK, Cassie. Remember you said it."

Marcus gathered his things with not so much as a goodbye. It was apparent that he was upset with me. But come on! How long would you keep a person around that keeps having you in question where you stand and no progress is being made?

I spent the rest of the day working my feelings away. I wasn't sure if I drove Marcus away for good or not. I wanted him to take a stand! Man up! Make a decision! I remember when I was finishing up with a client, Mahdi walked in. He came in and sat on the couch, put his headphones in his ears like he normally would. He was either on Facebook or listening to music. That was his everyday routine when he caught a break from cutting hair. He was so fine. My goodness.

He had a girlfriend though. I wasn't one of those to entertain someone that was already taken. I'm never that girl. But being that Mahdi had a girl, I figured I could get a little advice from him.

"Hey, Mahdi."

"Sup!"

"I have a question. Need a little advice."

"You don't got Paris to talk to you today?" he asked. Mahdi was so shady.

"I am not trying to talk to you now that Paris is not available, Mahdi."

"Yeah, OK," Mahdi said as he put one of his earplugs back in his ear, after he pulled it out to hear what I had to say.

I then sat next to him and tapped his shoulder and asked, "You got a girlfriend, right?"

"Yeah, why?"

"How do you guys overcome your arguments when you have them?"

"I don't speak on my personal life," Mahdi said.

"OK," I said. I got up and walked away. I guessed I wouldn't be asking him for advice anymore.

When I got home, all I could think about was how I pushed Marcus away. I wondered if I acted off impulse. Was I quick to quit? Would he walk away now after all the back and forth? Was he at home right now trying to seek the Lord about us? So many questions ran through my mind. I had to remind myself that what God has for me is for me. Neither Marcus nor I nor anyone, for that matter, could stop that. I went to bed with God's peace, knowing and standing on that very thought: *What God has for me is for me!*

Going into work the next day, I pulled in the parking lot. Marcus's car was already there. What was he doing here? Either God spoke to him about us or he just didn't take what I said to him seriously. When I walked toward the salon, Marcus met me at the doorway.

"What are you doing here?" I asked.

"I needed to see you."

"Did you hear from God yet?"

"No."

"So why did you come here?" I asked, even though I badly wanted him to.

"I can't say that God told me anything, Cassie. All I know is that I can't stay away."

"Well, what are you trying to do, Marcus?"

"Can we just take our time and figure this out together? I just can't not be around you."

"Well, what do you expect from me while you figure it out?"

"Cassie, just be patient with me. Please? Trust me that I am doing everything to get the answers I need."

I was confused. I didn't know what to do. I knew what my heart wanted, but my mind wasn't up for the challenge. My heart and mind needed to be in the same place in order to move effectively in my feelings for Marcus. I told him that we could just see how things played out. I didn't want to push him away, but I didn't want to make him feel comfortable being in limbo with me either. The good thing at that time was that I had a planned trip to Atlanta to visit Trina. Trina had recently moved to Decatur and found a great home church. They were having a women's retreat for that weekend. Trina had convinced me to go. It was timely for me and very needed to take a break from my everyday life and perhaps even Marcus. I needed to clear my head. I needed this trip for clarity. I told Marcus that I would be away that weekend, and because he was a consultant for the shop, I trusted that he had the ability to stay on top of things and he would step in while I was away. I had two new girls working for me: Dina and Myra. My sister Tanya no longer worked with us. She had moved away that year as well: Houston, Texas.

The women's retreat was amazing. I met so many women from all different walks of life, so many prolific teachers and preachers of the Gospel. There was not a topic we didn't cover. From relationships to purpose, callings, and discovering your God-given identity, we received so much insight from mighty women of God. They had this segment called Real Talk, where the ladies who hosted spoke in-depth about a lot about trauma and challenges in their lives and how God had delivered them from it all and how they discovered their purposes through them. That was probably the most life-changing thing that took place for me out of the entire trip; well, at least that's what I thought.

The last night of the retreat, Trina's pastor brought the event home. He was the only male preacher and the last speaker of the women's retreat. The service didn't take place at the church like the others. We traveled to fellowship with another church close by and merged with their church service. The building we went to was *huge*! It was like this big ole warehouse. The crazy part about it was the building matched Marcus's vision of what he wanted for Powerhouse. I took so many pictures so that I could share them with Marcus to keep him inspired. When I entered the building, I could tell that they had literally just moved in. The edifice was so spacious. The little that they brought in from their previous church filled maybe 5 percent of the building. The boundaries in there seemed limitless. During the service, the pastor of the church and his First Lady shared their testimony about how they came across such a huge property. It was nothing short of a blessing. Between giving their testimony and the way they executed the operations of church services, I was encouraged to jot down a couple of notes to bring back to Marcus to better the Powerhouse Ministry. I mean, even the way they handled tithes and offering made you feel like it was the best thing you could ever partake in, not only to be a blessing to your church but also a greater blessing to yourself. I was ecstatic. I couldn't wait to go back home to share all that I learned to my pastor and our church.

When the service came to a close, Trina introduced me to a lot of her church acquaintances. She had built some really strong bonds with people since she moved out to Atlanta. Her new friends were a perfect fit. They reminded me of being back at home. Trina introduced me to her pastors as well. They were well-known pastors. It's interesting that Trina and I were at a women's conference in Atlanta prior to her moving there. Trina's First Lady/co-pastor happened to be one of the speakers. I was so drawn to her spiritually before she even walked on the stage and preached. I had no idea why. I just knew that when I saw her, my spirit leaped as John the Baptist leaped in the womb of his mother Elizabeth when he came in contact with Jesus, who was in the womb of his mother Mary. I'd never felt that way before. All I knew is as I looked at her, I immediately saw myself. I came to find out she was a pastor and a wife with five children. I was in utter shock when she shared this information. I knew God was calling me to be a pastor and to marry a pastor, and God shared to me through Johnson early on in my new life of being a Christian that I would have a few kids of my own. I wanted five. Would you believe that without Marcus even knowing how many kids I wanted, he desired five kids as well? This just added one more to the many confirmations I had from God concerning him.

It was pretty cool to meet Trina's pastors. They asked me what I did for a living and asked about my relationship with God. They thought I had a *sweet* spirit. Before I left, Trina asked for the man of God to pray for me before I headed back home. I remember the four of us formed a circle holding hands as he prayed. He prayed this: "Father, we bless you on today for this woman of God. We pray that you bless her as she made the sacrifice to travel all the way to Atlanta to get a word from you. Father God, we ask that . . . hmmm . . . Yes, Lord . . . Thank you, Holy Ghost . . . Hallelujah . . . Yes, God! That's why she came, God. She came for *clarity.* Woman of God, there is an *evil spirit* around you. This spirit is around you almost every day."

I could not believe what I was hearing. I prayed to God about Marcus for clarity with us. I prayed that I would know what to make of why Marcus was at a standstill but was always around and not wanting to leave my side. The moment the man of God said this, I *knew* he was talking about Marcus. I knew in that moment, God was revealing to me through his prophet that Marcus was being used by an evil spirit.

"I blow that *evil spirit* away from her right now *in the name of Jesus*! Flee!" He continued. "And it is so! In Jesus' name . . . Amen and amen!"

"Thank you," I said in gratitude as I gave both pastors a hug.

"Anytime, young lady. The Lord is with you. You have *nothing* to fear. Go in peace."

I walked away with Trina as I cried profusely. I was so confused. All I kept asking myself was, Why was Marcus after me? Why did he hate me so badly? Why did he have bad intentions with me? What did I ever do to him?

I was so heartbroken. I had all these notes to better the ministry. I couldn't help but look for ways I can make the church better. I brought so many people to the church left and right. God had used me mightily as a *soul-winner*. I couldn't understand why he was after me. It was time for me to let go of him. I had to get rid of him once and for all, for good. I had to resist him. He was being used by the *devil*, by the enemy. Resisting him was the only way he would *flee*.

24

THE SPIRIT SEARCHES
ALL THINGS

When I got back home, I went straight to my salon. My mother Dakota surprised me by redecorating the shop. It was so pretty. She had a soft yellow-and-lavender color scheme going on. The change was just in time for the spring season, which happened to be a few weeks away.

"Mommy, you are so sweet."

"Oh, girl, please, I love doing things like this. It's no bother to me at all."

"Aw, thank you, Mommy, I love it."

"Anytime, baby. So how was your trip? How'd the women's retreat go?"

"It was interesting. It went pretty well. I had a great time," I said. I decided not to tell my mom about what Trina's pastor said about Marcus. I didn't want to add to her disapproval of him. "How was it in the shop?"

"It was pretty quiet when you left. Not a lot of people came to get their hair done. You know how your clients are. They always want you," she said as she chuckled. "I did book you up for the remainder of this week, so be prepared for the overflow."

"I'm going to make sure I get a lot of rest for that," I said. "Marcus came by at all?" I asked.

"No. Actually he didn't. He hasn't stopped by once since you've been gone. I just figured he took a break as well because you weren't here."

He was supposed to be here to help you guys out, I thought to myself. I should have known he disappeared while I was away. He didn't so much as give me a call while I was out of town.

"Yeah, maybe he did. He has a lot to deal with, regarding the church. He probably needs the rest," I said. "OK, Mommy, I'm going. See you tomorrow."

I gave my mommy a huge hug and kiss and went home. *Why would Marcus not help out at the shop when he promised to do just that?* I guess it didn't matter anyway. I got my Word. I got my clarity. It was time to get rid of this man, this *evil spirit*, this Judas of mine.

I went to work the next day. I got there earlier than anticipated. I wasn't able to sleep much. The man of God's words about Marcus playing in my head made sleep a distant reality. When I got to the salon, I locked the doors. I knew that Marcus would be popping by as if he were here the entire weekend and pretending that he was just *oh so excited* to see me. Now that I knew it was all fluff, I was prepared to disregard his flattery. Before you knew it, as I guessed it best, Marcus was at my door.

"Cassie! It's me! Open up!" Marcus yelled. I let him in. "Cassie, you're back!" he said in excitement as he attempted to embrace me. I walked away before his arms could reach me.

"We need to talk."

"What did I do now, Cassie?" he asked. "What are you upset with me about this time?"

"I don't understand why you keep looking at me as your enemy. Why do you hate me so much?"

"What are you talking about? Why would I hate you?"

"When I went to the retreat, I asked God for clarity about you. Trina's pastor prayed over me and confirmed to me that I came for clarity."

"OK, so what happened?"

"He told me that there is an *evil spirit* around me, and I know that *spirit* is *you!*"

"Cassie, are you serious? How do you know for sure that it's me? Why wouldn't it be Malcolm?"

"Because I didn't ask God for clarity about Malcolm, I asked about clarity for you."

"Who is this pastor? See, this is why I don't like you going anywhere. I don't like when you go to these church functions because you always come back with something to come against us," Marcus explained.

"Well, I don't know. All I know is what I prayed, and that's what I was told."

"I don't understand. Why would he say that about me? I'm not even upset with the man of God. I still love him. I don't wish any harm on him. I pray God continues to bless him. I don't take it personal. But just know I'm not here to come against you, Cassie."

I was confused. I mean the way Marcus talked in integrity and responded even after being accused of operating with an *evil spirit*. It made me think; maybe it wasn't Marcus. Maybe the prophet had it wrong, or maybe he was right but it wasn't about Marcus.

"What is his name on Instagram?" Marcus asked. When I gave him the information, he looked the pastor up. He came across a clip of the pastor preaching, and he was blown away. "Wow! He is amazing. Powerful preacher."

What? He is affirming the very man that said he's operating with an evil spirit? I thought to myself. I was so confused. I was taken aback by how Marcus handled the situation after he was accused of moving a certain way with me. He was raving about the pastor. *God, did I receive it wrong? Was I deceived?*

Marcus never stopped coming around me. He still continued to come by the shop. Even though he still worked, he found excuses to come around outside that obligation. Before you knew it, Marcus was back in my good graces. I decided to disregard what Trina's pastor said to me. After all, he did say that he blew the *evil spirit* away. Maybe it stopped having a hold on Marcus.

The signs given to me pertaining to Marcus being my husband never stopped. One time, Marcus and I helped this young teen mom in need who was fighting for visitation to see her kids that her foster parents had custody of. The young lady started going to the church. She gravitated to Pastor because she looked at him as her spiritual father, and she gravitated toward me as well. Marcus decided it would be best for him and me to go to her court appearance together. When we met her foster parents, they were pastors also. The first lady asked, was I Marcus's wife? I thought it was odd for her to ask, considering that I didn't have a ring on my finger, nor did Marcus. We also didn't come off like we were seeing each other. It was another time when Marcus received a voice message from another married couple who were pastors. Marcus told me that the couple took a liking to him, and he wanted me to listen to the voicemail that the First Lady left on his phone. He wanted to hear it for the first time with me. The lady invited him to speak at a church service, and she ended the message by saying, "By the way, bring your wife."

I remember Marcus wanted me to go with him shopping. He was looking for a tuxedo. We happened to run into some familiar faces and they asked us, "Are you guys shopping for a tux for y'all wedding?" We always assured them that we weren't together. Still, I would chuckle inside just seeing how every time we were together lately, someone always made reference to me being his wife or asked about a *wedding*. I remember an old client came in to get her hair done and asked, "How's your husband doing? I haven't seen him the past couple of times I've been here." I always found myself telling people, "He is my pastor."

Marcus would always say that I was reading into the signs too much. He always made jokes about me saying something was a sign from God when it wasn't. He'd always think that things were just coincidences. It always annoyed me when he said things like that. It just seemed no matter the signs that took place around us, he seemed to be totally unbothered by them. After a while, I started to act unaware of all the things that were happening around us and with us regarding marriage. I just jotted them down instead. It didn't help that Marcus was marrying a couple right around that time.

There was a young lady named Katherine. She used to go to the Powerhouse. She left because she met her soon-to-be husband. They were in the beginning stages of starting their own ministry. She was also a very loyal client of mine. Kat got her hair done by me faithfully. Whether she had an appointment or found herself popping up, she was always down for the *slay*. Marcus and I were just finished at the shop; we were watching a movie. I was lying down with my legs comfortably across his lap. Kat had popped up and looked through the window to see if I was still there at the shop. We immediately separated and went to different corners of the couch, frightened about whether or not she had seen us enjoying each other's company. Luckily, she couldn't see through the tinted windows.

I got Katherine and her bridesmaids all dolled up. She and the girls had put on their gowns and were ready to start down the aisle for the wedding to commence. Katherine had a snagged piece of fabric on her dress.

"Oh no, my dress ripped," she said, a little bummed.

"It's nothing to worry about, Kat. It's just a small piece," I said.

"Can you cut it off for me?" she asked.

"No problem," I said. I grabbed my kit of scissors out of my hair travel bag, and I cut the small piece of garment off her dress.

"Oh, that's not bad. It's just a small piece. I can't even tell something is missing," Kat said, relieved.

"I told you so. OK. Go! God bless you and the union you are about to enter in with your husband and God."

"Thanks, Cass," Katherine said as she hiked her dress up and started to head into the doors of the sanctuary.

I stood there in awe and watched Katherine as she walked down the aisle, entering marital bliss. I stood in a daze. She was beautiful. I was so happy for her. I continued to watch her as I still had the torn garment from her dress. I smiled, watching her take every step until she reached her husband. I then looked at the garment I had in my hand that I cut off her dress. Then I heard a voice say, "If I can just touch the hem of his garment, I will be made whole."

"I hear you, Lord. I hear you," I whispered softly to myself.

"By the power vested in me, I now pronounce you man and wife! You may now kiss your bride!"

25

THE LAST SHALL BE FIRST

I was so encouraged after Katherine's wedding. The fact that God spoke to me using the scripture of the woman with the issue of blood and how she touched the hem of Jesus's garment believing that she would be made whole and God acted on her belief was mind-boggling. I believe the faith I had about being Marcus's wife was as of that woman, and I too would be made whole. I was pondering the thought of Marcus and me getting married. I saw it, the wedding and all. Then suddenly, I was arrested in my spirit about a song, a particular song: "At Last" by Etta James. God had put that song in my spirit as a wedding song for Marcus and me. I thought to myself, *Perfect*. It fit us. It fit our love story. After all this time and all that we went through, I would be able to finally say, "At last."

I loved being in those moments when I would daydream about the day God's promise would manifest. Most of the time, all I had were glimpses of confirmations to hold on to. But reality will always try to find a way to pull me out of la-la land. Marcus was still telling me he didn't get revelation yet. I would ask him if he had fasted and sought God as he said he would. He told me all the demands at church didn't permit him the time. Meanwhile, I dealt with subliminal comments from members at the church. One night after Bible study, the praise and worship leader Direnda decided to bring up marriage, among me and other members that were a part of the rehearsal that took place. She put me on the spot and asked, "So do you guys think that God made a specific mate for you?" She asked this question but looked directly at me for an answer. I knew in my heart it was a setup, considering that I had looked around at everyone else as they looked to me for a response.

"I definitely believe that God has my husband tailor made for me," I said in all boldness.

"So you believe that God has a specific mate for everyone?" she said, testing me again.

"I didn't say everyone, I just said I know he has a man specifically designed for me," I shot back. I remember thinking to myself: *What is this? Was Marcus telling them what he and I talked about and what we shared? Surely he wouldn't do the same thing he did last time. No! I don't think he's that stupid.*

It didn't help that Marcus was still in limbo. I was so over it. How was it that God was telling me all these things and Marcus didn't receive even one word from the Lord? Either he really was not in the right posture to hear from God or God had already revealed it to him and he was dismissing it. I just wanted God to show him already, even if it was out in the open. For heaven's sakes, embarrass him if that's what it takes. I had been patient long enough. I felt like Marcus was stringing me along. He was like a dangling treat to a pup. I was that pup, waiting to have what had been lingering over my head far too long. When would I get this break? When would I receive my *breakthrough*?

We were now in the month of May, in the year 2015. Marcus came into the shop, and he was elated to share to me what he had in store for the church.

"Cassie, guess what? I have great news."

"What's up?" I asked.

"So you know how I am putting together a spring revival, right?"

"Yes."

"You know how we were looking to lock in this woman pastor I was telling you about?"

"Yeah, what about it?"

"It's official! She accepted our offer to be a speaker."

"That's great, Marcus," I said,

"That's great? That's your response? Do you know who Prophetess Pam Vinette is?"

"No."

"Cassie, she is a *beast* in the prophetic. Anything that woman says out of her mouth comes to pass."

"Really?"

"Yes. I know if *that* woman says something out of her mouth, I know it's all truth!"

I hope she says something to you so that you know I am your wife, I thought to myself.

"And the fact that she is going to preach at *my church*? I can't believe it. This is too good to be true. I have the best leaders in the world, man! They were able to get Prophetess Pam Vinette," Marcus said as he walked away. "May 18th can't come soon enough. *Whew! Hallelujah! Whew! Thank you, Jesus!* You're going to see how powerful the woman of God is, Cassie. I'm telling you, just wait!"

I wasted no time. I told my sister Tanya about this woman Marcus was raving about. Tanya happened to be in town for the month of May. She came to visit and to get the rest of her things she left behind to settle in Houston permanently.

"Girl, I'm telling you. You gotta be there!"

"Marcus said she's that good, huh?"

"Tanya, *yes*! I believe him too. I pray she says something to me about Marcus. We can't keep going on like this."

"Well, maybe she'll say something about my boo also," Tanya said. She had gotten reconnected recently with her first love James, who had also moved to Houston.

"Maybe so, girl. I feel it. I pray God uses her so that Marcus can know once and for all."

I literally counted the weeks. I counted the days. Finally, May 18 was here. I was in such great expectation to meet this lady and have her to speak to me. I had invited Paris along also. Apparently, Marcus had been raving about this woman to Paris too. Paris had some things God was dealing with him with, about working with young boys.

"Y'all ready?" I asked Tanya and my cousin Tay Tay. Tay Tay is my favorite little cousin. He was about nineteen at the time. He had the mind of a twelve-year-old. He had ADHD. He was also super hyper. But he is my everything. I love him. He loves church and loves Marcus. Marcus and I kept our dating life a secret from Tay Tay. As far as we were concerned, Marcus was his pastor. He adored Marcus. I didn't want anything Marcus and I had going on to hinder his innocent thoughts about Marcus. But Marcus made himself very questionable in Tay Tay's eyes when it came to our feelings for each other. I was mad at Marcus one time because he went out of town to the city with Jada, and he acted like he couldn't talk to me around her. He told me that he was going to Junior's, so I told him I wanted a piece of cheesecake from there. Marcus purchased a piece of cheesecake from the Cheesecake Factory instead. As his way of apologizing, he fed it to me, and Tay Tay caught him in the act. Tay Tay shouted, "Aww, shoot, Pastor is feeling Cassie."

Marcus said to him, "Shut up, Tay Tay! You better not tell anybody either!"

"Yeah, we're ready," Tanya answered. "You think she's going to say something to us?" she asked.

"Tanya, there is no doubt in my mind. That lady is going to speak to me!"

"Aye! Don't really care what the f*** these n****s think. Aye! I got deep pockets, I swear my sh**'s on sink. Aye—"

"Hey! Tay Tay! Are you serious right now?" I said as I snatched his headphones from his ears.

"Oh, my bad, cuz!" Tay Tay said as he shielded himself from a potential blow to the chest.

"No Fetty Wap for you today, buddy. If it's not gospel or about church, I don't want to hear it!"

"All right, gosh! You don't have to yell all the time. Dang."

"Don't start, Tay!"

"I'm not. Gosh! Can we leave already? I'm ready for Monday Night Raw," he said. That was the name of the event at the church that night. Tay Tay always acted up whenever he was impatient. I knew just what to do to pick him up.

"Hold on, Tay," I said as I grabbed my phone and started to record him. "You ready for what?" I asked.

"I'm ready for Monday Night Raw!"

"Let's get it," I said.

"Show us you're ready . . . Show us that you're ready aye . . . Show us you're ready . . . Show us that you're ready . . . Aye . . . Huh . . . huh . . . huh . . . huh . . . Aye . . . Huh . . . huh . . . huh . . . Aye!" Tanya and I chanted as Tay Tay danced to our made-up song. We had him doing that all month, up until the night of the revival.

"OK, y'all, let's go. I'm not trying to be late," I said. "We still gotta pick up Paris, and we need to get there in time for good seats. So c'mon."

When we got to Powerhouse, it was packed. I guess Pamela Vinette was a very popular woman. We were lucky enough to find some great seats. We found ourselves in the fifth pew on the left-hand side. Church was in an uproar. The praise and worship segment never disappoints. *Again*, I was off duty. I was able to be all eyes and ears. I had great expectations that I was going to get prophesied to, that night.

Finally, Pamela Vinette was at the pulpit. She ministered with such grace and elegance. I remember being moved by her sermon that night, but for the life of me, I can't remember what she talked about. C'mon now, don't act like you didn't ever leave a church service and someone asked you, "Hey, how was church?" and you said, "It was the bomb!" and then they asked, "What was it about?" and you had not a clue. Yes! It be like that sometimes. Yet still you feel so refreshed and recharged. Your spirit was *satisfied*. That was how the service was to me. It was good. Maybe part of the reason I didn't remember was because I had my mind on one thing and *one thing only*, and that was to get prophesied to by Pam Vinette.

The moment finally arrived. Prophetess Vinette began to work the floor, prophesying to people left and right. This woman, that man, this boy, that girl, she was working the prophetic. She didn't come to play. God had an agenda for his people, and Vinette was in place to fulfill it.

"Young man with the X X X shirt on, come here," she said. Pam had called out my little cousin Tay Tay. She continued, "What's your name, son?"

"Tay Tay."

"Tay Tay, I can see you doing something with poetry. God is going to use you in the area of poetry. That is what he called you to do. You need to stop listening to that hip-hop music. That's going to get you into trouble. That's not you."

"I tell him every time," I whispered to Tanya and my friend Netty. She was a client of mine as well. I invited her out to the Powerhouse a couple of times. She finally made it to one of our services.

"Do you understand, son?" Vinette asked.

"Yes, ma'am," Tay Tay responded. Tay Tay started heading back to our pew. Marcus looked back at me, and we chuckled privately at the matter. He was well aware of the many times I had put Tay Tay in his place behind the music he'd listen to.

"You right there in the blue shirt . . . Yes . . . Make your way down here," Vinette said. She was addressing Paris. Paris and Tay Tay walked past each other simultaneously. Tay Tay plopped himself in the seat next to Netty. Apparently, he had an attitude about the music Vinette told him to refrain from listening to.

"Told you, Tay Tay," I said.

"I know, Cassie. Dang! You always gotta embarrass me. Gosh!"

"Shh. Don't start, Tay Tay," Tanya said, shooting him a death stare.

"You are truly a man of God, son," she said to Paris. "God is going to use you to start a program dealing with young men. You will be a great mentor to them. It's going to be a success. You will have great influence. Be patient! The Lord makes everything perfect in its time."

Paris started heading back to our pew. He and Marcus threw a head nod at each other. They were both in cahoots. Starting a boys' group was something they had been discussing and putting in the making for quite some time now.

Pam Vinette had moved on and began to minister and prophesy to other people in the service. Once she was finished, she made an altar call. She asked anyone that needed prayer to come down to the altar.

"You coming?" Tanya asked.

"No. I'm going to wait," I said.

"OK, I'ma go," she said. "Excuse me, y'all, excuse me."

Was I supposed to go? Was that supposed to be the time I go, and maybe then, she'll prophesy to me? I thought. *No! You know what you asked God. She's going to call you out. I trust you, Lord.*

Pamela began to pray over everyone. Not a single person was left out at that altar. She made sure she got to everybody. Then she reached Tanya. Tanya then lifted her hands.

"So come lay down . . . the burdens you have carried . . . for in the sanctuary, deliverance is *here*," she sang. "Your heart is taking your mind to places it shouldn't go."

"C'mon. That's right!" Marcus shouted. He was in the loop of Tanya's feelings about James.

"God is going to repair and mend that relationship," Pam stated. "So come lay down . . . the burden you have carried . . . for in the sanctuary, God is here." She continued to sing.

The service finally reached benediction. Vinette had told everyone to stand up so that she could put a prayer in the atmosphere to bless us before we left. She said a few remarks and honored Marcus for inviting her to preach. I then locked eyes on her. I didn't take my eyes off her. She continued to talk, but she kept looking back at me. I started to pray: *Please, Lord. Don't let her leave without speaking to me. She can't leave, God. She has to talk to me. Marcus needs to know this once and for all. Please, God, I'm begging you. Don't let her leave. Please, God! I love you! You mean the world to me! I just need to know! I need Marcus to know all that you have been telling me. Please, Lord, please!*

"I'm sorry, I'm trying to close out, but I can't shake you off me. You in the red," Pam said as she pointed at me. "You right there!"

"Me?" I asked. I was so shocked that she called me out. I had to make sure I was the one in red that she was referring to.

"Yes, you! You are so beautiful. Come here," she said.

I walked down the aisle. It seemed as though the place became still, like it was just her and me. Everyone else around was a blur. Right before I reached her, I walked past the row Marcus was in and I remember saying out loud, "Oh boy!" I knew she was going to say something to me that would give me the answers that I needed from God once and for all.

"Woman of God, the Lord told me to tell you . . . *At last! My love has come along . . . at last.*"

Immediately, I began to *jump*, *scream*, and *shout*. The next thing I knew, I took off and I began to run around the church. I couldn't contain myself. My sister Paradise tried to hand me a prayer shawl. I snatched it from her and began to twirl it around as I ran around the church. I heard my sister Tanya crying out, "Oh my God! Oh my God!"

I couldn't believe it. She was singing the wedding song that God had put in my spirit for Marcus and me for our wedding day.

"I told y'all! I told y'all! I know what's up! I know what's up!" I shouted. I gave Pam a high five and all. I was so excited! I knew what God had told me!

"OK, calm down, honey. Let me say this. Don't you choose. You let God choose. You have an *at last*! Now you can shout," she said as she chuckled with the rest of the congregation. They must have thought I was too excited to get married. But what they did not know was that God confirmed to me what he had told me about Marcus three years ago.

When service was over, I was still pacing back and forth, up and down the altar. Marcus's sister Jessica came up to me and said, "God bless you, sis. You deserve it!" But she had no idea that this was about her brother and me.

"Good luck. Marriage ain't what it's cracked up to be," Sister Evette said as she walked past me. I'm assuming she wasn't too fond of married life.

I made my way outside. Once I gathered myself, I met up with Tanya, Paris, Netty, Paradise, and Tay Tay.

"Cassie, this is crazy!" Paris said. "We been talking about this! You should have seen Marcus's face. Ahahahaha!" Paris laughed.

"For real? How did he look?" I asked.

"Like he saw a ghost. Ahahahaha!" Paris laughed again. I swear he has the best laugh ever.

"Yeah, I went up to him after church and patted him on his back and was like *Hey, bro!*" Paradise said.

"Ain't no denying it now! If that ain't enough revelation for him, I don't know what to tell him," Tanya said.

I couldn't believe it. God showed up. He showed out, just as I asked. It was better than what I asked. Marcus couldn't deny it anymore. I just couldn't believe it. God let it be known. I will someday have an "at last."

26

WE KNOW IN PART . . .
WE PROPHESY IN PART

I couldn't believe it. The Lord really heard my cry. He really had Pam Vinette speak to me. Marcus avoided me for a good three days. I was confused. I didn't know why he didn't bother to call or anything. I talked to Tanya about it. She said, "Maybe he is in shock. Give him the benefit of the doubt." I took her advice. I gave him his space. I figured he'd come around when he was ready. It was weird though. I thought after that, he'd come running to me. Instead he did the total opposite.

The following Monday was Memorial Day. We had another service to go to. That day concluded our last day of revival. Tanya and I still excited about the word we received last service. We figured we could take a quick trip to the local David's Bridal before going home to get ready for the service.

"Hey, ladies. Welcome to David's Bridal. Who is getting married?"

"She is!" Tanya said as she pointed to me.

"OK, congratulations! I am Kim, your sales associate today. I'm going to give you a form to fill out."

"Well, I wasn't planning on trying anything on. I was just hoping to look around at some wedding dresses if that's OK."

"Oh sure, not a problem. It's just our policy here, just in case you decide that you like something and may want to try it on, we can assist you with that."

"OK, sure," I said with my hand out to receive the form. "Do you have a pen?"

"Sure do," Kim said as she handed me the clipboard with the form along with a pen attached.

Hmmm. Name of bride . . . Name of groom? Wedding date? Dress alterations ready by?

"Oh, don't worry about putting down all that info. Just your name, address, phone number or email address is fine," Kim explained.

"OK, whew! I was getting a little overwhelmed there," I said jokingly.

"OK. Perfect! You are more than welcome to take a look at the dresses. If you need any assistance, you can come grab me, and I'll be right over."

"Thanks, Kim," I said.

"Yeah, thanks. Come on, girl. Let's look at these dresses," Tanya said as she took my hand, leading the way to the dresses.

I started looking at the dresses. They were beautiful! As I was looking, I kept chuckling to myself about all the times Marcus would jokingly get on his knee and ask to marry me. I remember a time Marcus fake proposed to me in Wendy's on the lobby floor. He always did stuff like that to annoy me and sing love songs to me in the process. I told him he better not even think to propose to me at no fast-food joint! Then I thought about all the times he talked about how he wanted this *huge* wedding. He told me that his spiritual mentor he was very close with since he was ten had put aside a lot of money for his wedding. I didn't care about that stuff. I told Marcus I was more invested in the marriage than I was the wedding. I was fine with eloping and maybe having a dope reception. I didn't care. I loved him. I didn't care about the extra stuff.

"Ooh, this is nice!" I yelled.

"Let me see," Tanya said, looking at the dress I had in my hand. "Cassie, that is so nice. That's a nice mermaid fit too. It would look nice with your curves."

"I like it a lot. Should I try it on?"

"Yes! Try it!"

"OK. Let's do it! Excuse me! Kim!" Tanya yelled across the room. When she caught Kim's attention, she signaled her to come over to us.

"You ladies found anything?"

"Yes, I would like to try on this dress," I said.

"No problem. I'll take that for you. You can follow me."

Tanya and I followed her to the dressing rooms. She pointed me to the dressing room that wasn't occupied. I tried on the dress and I loved it! So did Tanya and Kim. After I prayed and rang their infamous bell as a gesture for blessings for all brides, I took off my dress and handed it to Kim so that she could put it on file for me.

"Just so you know, sweetie. The dress you chose is on sale. We had a special that was running all month, and today is the last day to take advantage."

"Oh wow! Is it possible to get a price check on it?"

"Sure. Meet me up front, and we will get the price for you. You can make a down payment as well. You don't have to purchase it in full."

"OK, great," I said.

OK, God, I only have $150 on me to spare. If you want me to put money down *on this dress today, let it be in my budget. I ask nothing but your will to be done in Jesus' name . . .*

"OK, so in order to take advantage of this deal, you would need to put down $148.65."

"Let's do it!" I said.

"Awesome. Cash or card?"

"Cash!" I said.

Tanya and I rushed home that day after paying a visit to David's Bridal. It was the final night of revival, and after the previous service, we were not trying to miss it. The guest speaker that night didn't show up. Marcus hired a friend of his, Pastor Homes, as the speaker to conclude the revival. I don't know who the original speaker was, but I was sure glad he didn't show up because Pastor Homes tore that place up with the Word.

When service concluded, I greeted a few of the members and then left. Marcus was still keeping his distance from me. I didn't get it! A word that came forth that was supposed to bring us closer did the exact opposite. I didn't go out of my way to greet Marcus either. I remember going home that night feeling so defeated, wondering why I put a down payment on a wedding dress.

Before I went to bed, I decided to look for a sermon. I was so disappointed and downcast that I knew the only way to get out of this pit I was in was for God to speak to me. I looked on YouTube, and I came across a woman by the name of Janet Floyd. I immediately clicked on the video because the topic of her sermon grabbed my attention. The title was "My Word Did This." Janet Floyd was talking about the story with Joseph and his brothers. Joseph told his brother about a dream the Lord gave him. As a result of that, the brothers grew jealous and hated him for it and threw him in a pit. Joseph's brothers sold him into slavery, and from then on, he went through a series of obstacles as a result of the trouble his brothers caused him. Janet Floyd, after breaking down the story of Joseph, made a point to say, "*The reason why you are in what you are in and going through what you are going through is not because of trouble. It's because of your prophesy. Your word did this!*"

In that moment, it clicked. What I was going through clicked for me. What I was going through was because of the prophecy. Janet let it be known that whenever the *devil* is giving you hell, it's because there is a Word over your life. I knew what God told me was true. I just had to hold on and get through this. This Word the *devil* was fighting me on was coming to pass. It was only a matter of time that, like Joseph, I'd be promoted.

The very next day, I was back in high spirits. I was at the shop, knocking out every hairstyle I had for the day. I was grounded. I was empowered by the message God brought to me that night. I had no worry in the world, and I operated as such that entire day. The day went so smoothly. I was in such a good mood that I even hung out with Mahdi in my downtime. Yes, Mahdi! Can you believe it? Me and his mean self were taking *selfies* and all.

"Wait! We gotta take that picture again. That is mad busted!"

"What are you talking about, shawty? You look fine," Mahdi said as he laughed.

"Uh-uh, Mahdi. We gotta take that again. Come on! *Please?*"

"Aight. One more and then I'm done."

"All right, bet," I said as we snapped another picture. "See, that's better."

"You're right, shawty."

"OK, now a silly one," I requested.

"See, I knew you were gonna do that stupid shi—"

"Uh-uh. Watch your mouth."

"I ain't even say it though."

"But you were going to."

"Whatever."

"*Exactly.* Now silly face," I said as I put on my silly face and he did the same. "Ahaha. I'm saving this one," I said as I ran away from Mahdi so that he couldn't take my phone and try to delete it. Mahdi and I became pretty close *surprisingly.* I didn't think it would be possible considering how cold and standoffish he was. He was almost as cool as I was with Paris. But Mahdi and I played around a lot more than anything.

"Hold up, Cassie! Your shoe is untied. You're playing around too much, and you're about to catch a body," Mahdi said. That was his way of saying I was about to fall.

"My shoes are tied. What are you talking about?"

"Not your front ones. The laces you have in the back."

"Oh," I said, remembering that with these particular boots, I had shoestrings on the back of them also.

"Let me see," Mahdi said as he motioned for me to walk over to him as he was sitting on the couch. I turned around to where the heel of my foot was facing him so that he could tie my lace for me. "Aight. You good!" he said in his slang.

"Thanks, Mahdi," I said as I smiled.

"You good," he said.

"What's going on? How y'all doing?" Marcus said as he entered the shop.

"Oh hey," I said, startled and at the same time feeling extremely awkward that he walked in as Mahdi still had his hand on my shoe.

"What's up, Mahdi? How are you?"

"Sup," Mahdi said back as he got up from the couch and headed toward the door to go back next door to the barbershop. Silence stood still in the room until Mahdi made his exit and closed the door.

"You think that's OK, for me to walk in the room with your foot up on him like that?" Marcus asked.

"He was only tying my shoe, Marcus."

"I know, Cassie. I know you well enough to know that you wouldn't be doing anything you shouldn't be doing with anyone. I'm just making a point that it don't look right for me to walk in and see that," Marcus explained.

"I get it, but it was nothing, Marcus," I assured him. Even though Mahdi was very handsome, I didn't see him as anything more than a friend. I had eyes for Marcus and him *only*.

"How are you doing though?" Marcus asked.

"I'm doing well. Can't complain. You?"

"I'm doing good," Marcus said. The room grew silent again.

Then I said, "How come you've been avoiding me?"

"I just needed some space. Some time to think."

"For what?"

"I don't know. I just can't believe what Pam Vinette said the other night."

"I tried to tell you. I know what I heard."

"This is so crazy, Cass," Marcus said, still trying to process what took place on that night of revival. "Cass?"

"Yes."

"What if God told you that to see if he could trust you but that's not what he actually meant?"

"What do you mean, Marcus?" I asked, trying to make out his thoughts.

"OK. For instance, you know how God told Abraham to offer his son Isaac as a sacrifice, right?"

"Yes," I said.

"And you know how Abraham went to do what God said and then God stopped him and told him not to lay a hand on that boy? And then God told him that now he knows he can trust Abraham and then he sent him an animal to sacrifice instead?"

"What are you getting at, Marcus? What are you trying to say?" I asked, extremely annoyed at the point that he was trying to make.

"What if God only told you that about me to see if he can trust you but don't intend for it to be what he told you."

"You know what, Marcus, if that's what you think, then that's fine."

"Cassie, why are you getting mad? I'm only asking a question!"

"I'm just annoyed by you at this point. You second-guess everything with us, which is exactly why I wanted you to stay away until you get *revelation!*"

"Why are you getting frustrated with me? I'm only trying to understand. I'm only asking, what if God told you this to test you?"

"I don't think God would play with my feelings like that. He has been giving me the same revelation straight for three years now. I think if he was *playing* with me, he would have told me 'psych' a long time ago."

"So you don't think it's possible at all?"

"What are you saying right now, Marcus?"

"Oh my gosh! Forget it, Cassie!"

"What do you want me to do? Change my answer! I already told you no! That woman sang what is supposed to be *our* wedding song. Why would God have her sing to me a wedding song that he put on my heart for you and intend it for another man? You think God would do that? He is not the author of confusion, Marcus! You know the Word! Besides, I asked God to confirm what he told me through the woman *you* said is *so* used by God, and he did! I don't know what else you're looking for! I don't know what else you want from me!"

When I finished that statement, Marcus didn't respond. We didn't speak for a few moments. I was super exhausted about this whole thing. Every time I turned around, Marcus was fighting with me about this revelation. I didn't get it at all. It was causing us so many issues. I couldn't take it. I couldn't stand it. I didn't understand. What more could God do? What more could he say? How much more could he keep revealing to me what Marcus was clearly blind to? Why would he stick around? Why wouldn't he just walk away?

"Cassie, I'm sorry. I'm just trying to understand. That's all! I'm not trying to upset you."

"But you are. You are trying to force me to make sense out of what only God can get you to understand. I really feel like if you got in his presence like I told you to about me, he would reveal to you what he has already told me."

"You're right. I'm going to do my best to make time to hear from him about us. I promise," Marcus said. "Can I get a hug?"

I walked over to Marcus and hugged him. As much as I wanted to believe that he would do what it took to get in God's presence about us, I just didn't. It was clear that Marcus had other things going on in his life, things that were more of a priority than seeking the Lord about us. And those other things, I believed wholeheartedly, had everything to do with another woman in his life. It had to be someone else. It had to be someone else in his life that made it so hard for him to see about us. It was only a matter of time that God would reveal to me who *she* was.

27

ARE YOU THE ONE OR SHALL I LOOK FOR ANOTHER?

In the month of June, I was made aware that Adore Cutz had just expanded. Kevin, the owner, had opened a new location down the street. I was happy that my two favorite barbers Paris and Mahdi were going to stay at the shop next door. Kevin had invited us to come and check out the new barbershop. They were having food and drinks there, a couple of close friends and family, and even the mayor, Kathy Sheehan, would be present as well. I called up Marcus to tell him about the event to invite him. He didn't answer or return any of my calls. I figured since I found out last minute, he probably was unaware as well.

I was running a little late. I had a few clients that I had to take care of before going. My mom made it over there before me. She went with a barber named Chris who also worked next door from us. Who would have known that this person she befriended would become my mom's future husband, my stepdaddy. My mother called me to see where I was at.

"Hello? Cassie, where are you?"

"I'm just finishing up. I'm heading there now," I said.

"OK. I'm here with Chris. Let me know when you're outside."

"OK, Mommy."

"Marcus is here too. He's here with the young lady that always works with him at the church."

"Oh, really," I said, wondering if this was the reason he was dodging my calls. "OK, Mom. Thanks. See you soon."

I went to pick up Tanya before I went to the church. She was leaving that weekend. I wanted to spend as much time as possible with her before she moved.

When we got to the new barbershop, I went inside, and sure enough, I saw Marcus and Jada in line, trying to greet the Mayor. Jada touched the lower part of Marcus's back and whispered something in his ear. I'm assuming she was telling him to greet the mayor because they started walking over to her. Kevin, Marcus, and Mayor Sheehan all prepared to take a photo together. As I walked past, Marcus noticed me. I continued to move about in the party. I figured he shouldn't have any problem ignoring me in this party like he did my phone calls.

As I was conversing and eating some refreshments with my family, Marcus came over to greet us. I acted like he didn't exist. Marcus then pulled up a chair right next to me and sat down as his way of demanding attention from me.

"You can't speak?" Marcus asked.

"Oh, you can now? I thought the same when you ignored my phone calls."

"I couldn't answer. I was in here with all this loud music and chatter."

"Whatever, Marcus."

"Why are you so stubborn, Cassie? Miss Dakota, why is your daughter so stubborn?" Marcus asked my mom.

"Don't put me in it, Marcus. I have nothing to do with it," my mother said jokingly.

Marcus then put his hand on my upper thigh and said, "You're really gonna act like this right now?"

When Marcus grabbed my thigh, I looked up to see where Jada was. I noticed that she was in clear view of Marcus and me. When she noticed that I looked at her, she put her head down.

"I'm about to leave. I'm going to call you in a few, all right?" Marcus asked as he squeezed my inner thigh.

"OK," I said.

Marcus got up from his seat and walked over to Jada. It looked like he asked her, was she ready to go? Jada shook her head yes and then Marcus walked toward the door. Jada then looked at me and then walked off behind him. I thought to myself, *Maybe I'm tripping. Maybe they are just friends. If they were more, I don't see why she'd allow him to be engaging with me like that in front of her.*

After seeing that, the most I could suspect is that she liked him but he didn't feel the same for her. But if not her, then who? Who would he be dealing with besides me? Marcus was becoming more and more inconsistent. I started being more and more intolerant of him and found every reason to push him away. I felt like I was being taken advantage of. Marcus even stopped coming to work at the shop like he was supposed to. The only time I saw him was when he'd come by Saturdays to pick up his money. I had him on an under-the-table salary, so no matter whether he came or not, I still paid him. Marcus would tell me that he had these preaching engagements to go to, none of which he invited me to. I felt I was being robbed, and I wasn't blind to that fact. After a month or so of going through this, I decided to fast.

I fasted and prayed for a day. I prayed that God would put it on Marcus's heart to quit. I repented that I allowed Marcus to work with me when I knew in my heart that God wasn't leading him and me to work together. However, it was hard for me to take matters into my own hands by firing him. I knew this was the only income Marcus was getting consistently. Sure, he was getting income from the church, but it wasn't much. I didn't want to be the reason he struggled to make ends meet as the man I saw a future with and, more importantly, my pastor. The day I fasted just so happened to be a slow day at the shop. I remember lying down on the couch and praying to God. Then someone opened the door and walked in the shop. It was *Marcus*.

"Hey, Cassie. Can I talk to you?"

"Sure," I said. Marcus made his way to sit down next to me on the couch.

"Look, I came by because I need to say something that has been really bothering me."

"OK. What's going on?" I asked, concerned.

"Cassie, God has been dealing with me all morning. I just came over here to tell you that I am sorry. I should have never asked to be a part of the salon. I should have never taken money from you. I should have only supported you as a pastor and as a friend and someone I am getting to know on a deeper level. I feel like it's getting in the way of who we are to each other. With that being said, I don't want any more money from you. I want to be here to support you with the way that I should have from the beginning."

Wow! In less than a day, God had answered my prayer. "Thank you, Marcus! That really means a lot."

"I'm glad," Marcus said. "Cassie, I just want to be there for you with no strings attached."

I was so happy God had answered my prayers. The Lord knew it was hard for me to drop the ball on Marcus. Now that he stepped in and made things right, I was able to move forward with him outside of mixing business with pleasure.

Things started looking up for Marcus and me since he quit at the shop. Because I was so used to the back and forth of us being cool one minute and at odds the next, I learned to soak up every moment we had together when things were great. Some moments were too great, so great that I almost put aside my *vow* to God to save myself for marriage. I wanted Marcus so bad in that way, and he wanted me. Before you knew it, we were back at it, making out yet again at the shop. Then he asked, "Do you still have those condoms here?"

A man from the local clinic would come to both the barbershop side and my salon side to pass out free condoms. My mom would stash them away for whatever reason whenever they came. I guess Marcus paid much attention to that.

"Yes. It's in the black cabinet over there by the wall."

Marcus walked over to the black cabinet. When he opened it, sure enough, Marcus found the stash of condoms in the midst of salon products we had in stock. He grabbed one and shut the cabinet and then turned around and attempted to walk toward me. But immediately he noticed the unsure look on my face. I could feel the paleness over my face that was screaming, *I don't want to do this!*

"You don't want to, huh, Cassie?" Marcus asked. "We don't have to. We can wait if you're not comfortable."

I looked down to the floor and said, "I want to wait." I was afraid that Marcus would be upset that I denied him yet again after years of not being intimate with him.

Marcus walked over toward me and lifted my head up. "Then we will wait," he said as he hugged me. "You are worth waiting for, Cassie."

I was relieved of timidity in that moment. If I'd ever hesitated, believing that Marcus didn't care about me, I was sure in that moment just how much he did. Marcus came over to me and embraced me as he planted a kiss on my forehead. I'll never forget how safe I felt that day. It didn't matter the number of ups and downs, Marcus always remained a true gentlemen as he respected my decision to wait.

July came rolling in just as fast as June came and left. After service one Sunday, Marcus had asked all the leaders and church members to meet. At the time, I stepped down from leadership. Between the shop and being fully present at church, it was too much for me to handle. Pastor told us that the church was facing foreclosure. We had until the end of the month to come up with a certain amount of money in order to keep the building. Moved by the thought of us losing our church, I made arrangements to do whatever I could to help in any way to keep the church in our possession. I had plans of going to New York City on Independence Day for the first time. I wanted to experience the fireworks out there. But I felt that canceling my plans and doing what I could for the church was most important to me.

My best friend Whitney and I came up with an Independence Day sale. I put in motion a 20 percent off sale on all hair services as she cooked hot dogs and hamburger meals to sell. I informed Marcus about the sale we came up with and had him collect all monies from the clients. I let him keep all proceeds, and I paid the two girls that worked for me from my savings. Between that and what the other leaders and members were able to round up, we were able to keep the church. Hallelujah! God is so *good!* We were able to save our church. Little did I know, in a few short weeks, I myself would be facing something similar.

Two weeks later, I had a client who came to me for the first time who wanted a touch-up on his dreads. In the middle of doing his hair, we started talking about Jesus. I always found a way to talk about God to my clients. Anytime there was a segue about Christianity, I would hop in and share my testimony. I'll never forget. I was in the middle of telling the middle-aged man how I had gave my life to Christ. I told him how God had opened so many doors for me, and my shop was one of them. He was completely blown away by my testimony. In the middle of our conversation, two Caucasian men walked in.

"Hello, are you the owner?" one of the gentlemen asked.

"Yes, I am. Can I help you?"

"Yes. If you don't mind, can you step out here to talk? I would hate for this information to be disclosed in front of your client."

"Sure, no problem. One moment," I said. "Excuse me for a moment," I said to the client as I walked over to the two gentlemen. I then closed the door behind me.

"What's going on?" I asked.

"Sorry to barge in like this. We are sorry to inform you, but this building is under foreclosure. The owner Kevin wasn't able to keep up with the payments of the building. You have until the 31st of August 2015 to evacuate the premises."

"OK. Thanks, gentlemen," I said as I reached out to shake their hands.

"We are really sorry to inform you of this."

"Oh, it's all right. If God made a way before, he will do it again."

"Wow!" the other gentleman said. "I have never seen such great faith."

"Well, sir, that's what happens when you serve a great God!"

"Wow. Good luck to you, ma'am. I wish you all the best."

"God bless you," I said as I shook their hands and returned to my client.

"Everything all right?" the client asked.

"Yes. Apparently we have to move. The building is under foreclosure," I said.

"Oh wow. I'm so sorry about that," he said with compassion.

"Oh, that's OK. When God closes a door, that means another one opens."

"Wow, miss! I'm honored to be in your presence. You have such great faith."

"Aww, thanks. OK, now let's get back into this testimony," I said as I continued to share my story.

For some reason, I was not worried. I trusted God! I've seen God move in ways that were unimaginable, especially with my salon. I knew God had nothing but greater in store for me. After I was done at the shop, I called Marcus to let him know the news about the shop. I knew that he had my back and that he was the perfect person to confide in that would boost my faith even more. Not only was he the man I loved, he was also my pastor. But when I told Marcus, he said to me, "Well, I'm glad it served its purpose!" I was devastated at his response. I couldn't believe that was his response. When his church was at stake, I jumped at the chance to help out. I raised $1,300 in one day to save the church. I didn't expect any of it back, but a *"Don't worry, I got your back"* or an *"I'll help you look for a new place"* or better yet, *"Trust God, Cassie! He'll make a way"* would have sufficed. Instead, I got *"I'm glad it served its purpose!"*

That same night, I searched on Albany's Craigslist to find a place for rent. After going through a couple of listings, I found a really nice space that was in a great location. From the looks of the building in the picture, it looked like a Laundromat. There was a showing for it at 5:30 p.m. the next day, which was a Wednesday. Wednesday was the salon's sale day. I ran a "$50 off" sale every Wednesday, and my schedule was full. I remember praying to God that night. I prayed, *God, if it's in your will for me to see the building, then you will free up my schedule. If it isn't, then you have something else greater.*

I woke up bright and early that Wednesday. I didn't want anything I did on my end to push by my schedule to prevent me from making it to see the building, in the event God allowed me to go. Everyone seemed to make it for their appointments, so the option to see the place was slim to none. Marcus came by around 4:30 p.m. Apparently, he had an appointment that I had no idea about. When he finished getting his hair cut, he came over to my salon.

"Hey, hey!" he said.

"Hey," I said giving back a dry greeting, still disappointed about his response to my salon being in foreclosure.

"How are y'all doing today?" he asked me and my other hairstylist Dina.

"Good," Dina answered. "You?"

"I'm great! I'm getting ready to go to Barbados tonight. I'm so excited! Can't wait," he said.

"Barbados?" I asked. "I didn't know you were going out of town?"

"Yeah. I'm leaving tonight. Kim's brother is getting married and I'm his best man," Marcus said.

"Best man?" I asked, curious to know how Kim's brother and Marcus were so close that he would consider Marcus to be his best man.

"Yes. *Best man.*"

"Yeah, OK," I said, not being able to help how odd I felt in that moment. I then looked at the clock. It was 5:15 p.m. I had a five o'clock appointment scheduled for a weave installation, but the client never showed up. I had a fifteen-minute grace period for clients to come before I canceled their appointments. When I realized that my client wasn't coming, I cut my conversation with Marcus short.

"OK, well, enjoy your trip," I said as I gathered my things. "Dina, you ready to go?"

"Yes. Ready when you are."

"OK, ladies. Enjoy the rest of your day," Marcus said as he left the shop.

Why in the world was Marcus going all the way out to Barbados to attend the wedding of a groom he barely even knew, and be his best man, at that? He barely spoke to Kim and her mother, Evangelist Ashley, let alone Kim's brother. Anyway, that is neither here nor there. I had a space to look at, and I wasn't about to strain myself to figure out why the man I was seeing, who tells me when my salon is being foreclosed on, *"I'm glad it served its purpose,"* was going to Barbados for a groom he barely knew. I had other things far more important to focus on, like looking at a potential space to house my salon.

We got to the new building just in time to see the place. Dina and I discovered once we walked up the ramp that the *so-called* Laundromat turned out to be a hair salon. The owner of the salon was a woman by the name of Laura. She was in the middle of expanding her salon and found a place bigger to house her vision. She was leaving the space and was looking for someone to buy her furniture and equipment and possibly rent the salon. I happened to be looking for a new space, and I also needed furniture and equipment because the only thing that belonged to me was the kit of tools I came with. She had stations, sinks, décor; everything I needed, she had. I knew in that moment that God had opened up another door. This door was *mine.* She had other candidates in place to take over the salon and her equipment, so she didn't make any promises. I filled out the application in faith and handed it to her and put it in God's hands.

I prayed that same night about the shop once I came home from looking at the place. I couldn't sleep because I was so excited about it and I just really believed that God was going to give me the space and the equipment that came with it. It was so *beautiful!* Even Dina loved it. We had to get that space. I got off work about 7:00 p.m. that day. When I was on my way home, I felt extremely led by the Holy Spirit to go to the salon that I hoped to acquire. When I got there, I was led to get out and pray. I walked up and down the ramp, praying over the building. People who were walking past thought I was crazy. I was praying and reciting scriptures like *"Father, you said you will give me houses I did not build"* and *"You will never withhold anything good from me"* and *"Seek ye first the kingdom of God and his righteousness and all these things shall be added unto you."* I prayed until the Holy Ghost let up. I just believed that my prayers would put me in this woman's mind, to have me in mind for the salon.

Sure enough, that Friday morning, the next day, I woke up to a missed call from Laura. She left a voicemail for me to give her a call. When I called her, she said, *"Cassie, I don't know why, but I feel like I'm supposed to give you the shop and the equipment with it. Is there any way we can meet up, work out a payment plan for the equipment, and close the deal?"*

I was ecstatic. I met with Laura that morning and worked out payment arrangements for the equipment. She also put in a good word for me to the owners of the building. With Laura advocating for me, I was able to rent the space as well.

157

I would never forget that day. Not only did I get the keys to my new shop, it was also the same day I finished paying the last payment on my wedding dress. I was finally able to bring it home.

After all that running around, I made it to the shop just in time for my twelve o'clock appointment.

"How did it go?" Dina asked.

"We got the keys," I said as I dangled the keys in my hand.

"Oh my gosh, Cassie! You have to tell me everything."

"I will. First, let's knock out these appointments, and we will go out to eat. I'll tell you all about it. Any calls?" I asked.

"Yes. There were a few clients that made appointments. A woman named Keisha for this Saturday at 1:00 p.m. Your client Nay Nay also booked for Saturday at 3:00 p.m. Claire also called with an itinerary for her wedding party for Sunday and also a woman named Kim, inquiring about an appointment not this upcoming Wednesday, but the following week, August 5th."

"Kim?"

"Yes. She said she goes to your church."

"Oh, OK. She hasn't booked with me in years," I said, remembering the times I did her hair when I worked with Toni. "Book her for whatever is available," I said. *I wonder what makes her want to come to me after all these years.*

28

THE LORD HAS NOT CHOSEN THESE

Marcus got back in town the following Wednesday from his trip to Barbados. I knew he was going to be so shocked to find out that while he was away, I had already found a new spot. When he came inside the salon, I told him to sit down and that I had something to show him.

"What is it?" Marcus asked.

"Hold on," I said as I walked to the reception desk to get the folder that had my new lease enclosed.

"You finally got your own place!" Marcus shouted in sheer excitement.

"No. It's the lease to my new shop," I explained.

"Oh," Marcus said as his excitement deflated.

"That's it?" I asked. "Just 'Oh'?"

"I just thought it was for your own apartment—that's all."

"I'm not in a rush to move," I shot at him.

No matter how long I've dealt with this man, he never gets happy about anything I achieve. But when it comes to him, it's innate in me to leap for joy. It just wasn't the same energy both ways. I even got a new car that same day before going to work. Everyone in the salon and a few of the barbers, Mahdi and Paris, were even hyped about my new car. Marcus just walked right past it and left the salon.

That same week, we moved out of my old shop and into my new one. We were settled in by the time the month of August crept in. I had taken clients that day. I mean, it's not like we had much to move. It was an early birthday present to myself. I threw a birthday get-together and all. All my family and friends were there, even some of my clients. Marcus showed up too. I guess he learned from last year. He took me out to eat and all. He even treated my best friend Whitney. Her mom and I shared the same birthday. Whitney's mom passed a couple years back. I thought it was sweet of Marcus to invite her along. At my birthday party, Marcus gave such a great speech about how great a woman I am. He made reference to the Scripture, in Proverbs 31:10, which states, *"Who can find a virtuous woman? For her price is far above rubies."* I remember Jeanette, one of my besties, pulled out her phone and started recording. She thought Marcus was going to propose. Marcus ran from the camera and chuckled as Jermaine said, "Pastor is not finishing his speech until all recording stops!" He was always doing the most to prove he was in Marcus's corner.

A couple days later, Kim came to the shop for her hair appointment. Even though I didn't see much of her at the shop, Kim and I were always cool. After a while, even her mom grew on me too. I would call her Mama Ashley.

"Hey, girl," I said when Kim walked in the salon. "It's been a while."

"Hey, Cassie. I know, girl. I usually go to my hairstylist I go to all the time, but I wanted a bob again, and you hooked my bob up for my birthday that time."

"Yes! I remember, girl. You were *slayed!"* I said. We both laughed as she took a seat in my salon chair.

"It's so nice in here," Kim said.

"Thank you. I love it!"

"You're welcome."

"OK. So refresh my memory. You want a layer bob with a deep swoop bang, right?"

"Almost. I'm going to switch it up a bit," she said as we laughed. "I want a bob with layers like you did the last time, but instead of the swoop, I want a blunt-cut bang," she explained.

"OK, cool. Let's get started."

I put on a movie for Kim and me to watch as I did her hair. We made small talk. She was going to school still and discussing what she wanted to do next once she graduated. I told her how I graduated with my associate's degree in seminary but I had to stop once I got the salon. It was hard for me to continue school and run my salon at the same time. Then she asked, "So are you seeing someone special?"

"Yes, I am," I said.

"Who?" she asked.

"A guy I have been seeing for a while now."

"Oh, OK. Is it serious?" Kim asked.

"We are getting there. I know he's my husband. God revealed it to me," I said, confiding in her.

"Really?"

"Yes. It's funny because at the revival, the prophet that spoke to me, she was actually singing our wedding song and he was there."

"Oh wow," Kim said. "Was he there?"

"Yes, he was, girl. Paul was so shocked when she sang it too," I said, being quick on my feet, lying about Marcus's name.

Kim was a member of the church. I wanted to conceal Marcus's identity, like he would have wanted me to. An awkward silence covered the room. Then I asked, "What about you? Are you seeing anyone?"

"Yes, I am. I met this guy in the airport."

"Oh, that's cool. What happened?"

"Nothing really. We introduced ourselves, and we've been talking ever since."

"Oh, that's sweet."

"Yeah. We are just taking it slow."

"Of course, and whatever is meant to be will be."

"*Exactly*," Kim agreed.

Sunday service was on an all-time high that week. The church went crazy. Many souls were saved, recommitments to Christ were made, and lives were changed. Even though this particular service needed to be noted for all the good that happened in the Lord's house, there was another event that took place that stood out to me. Marcus called people up before service was over, for prayer. After praying for a couple of people, Marcus reached the point of praying for this one particular girl. Her name was Nilani. A church sister, Dria, invited her. They worked together. Nilani was *very* beautiful. And for some reason, I felt in my heart that she was someone I could see Marcus falling head over heels for. Nilani was everything that describes Marcus's type. I knew that if she joined the church, *revelation* as I knew it regarding Marcus and me would be over!

"I need everyone to lift their hands!" Marcus commanded. "I need everyone to pray for . . . What's your name, sis?"

"Nilani," she said in such a sweet voice.

"I need you all to *touch and agree* with me as I pray for Nilani. God has opened a door for her to take a job down in Virginia. We are going to pray for traveling mercies and great success as she takes such a great leap of faith, Amen?"

"Amen," we all said in unison. "*Thank you, Jesus,*" I whispered to myself in a state of relief.

My relief was short-lived when I came to church the following week and noticed that Nilani was at the Powerhouse. During the announcements, Marcus had shared to the congregation that Nilani decided to stay after all. He told us that God had spoken to Nilani about her turning down the new position in Virginia to stay and help build the ministry. I was completely devastated. I knew in that moment, I might as well have kissed Marcus *goodbye*. In Christian *spirit,* I embraced Nilani and welcomed her into our church family. She seemed like a very sweet young lady. Such a pure spirit she had. So quiet, so meek. She was *nothing* like me. As Nilani became more of a familiar face in the church, I would catch Marcus's eyes just gazing upon her. He was smitten by her presence. It broke my heart to see the way he would look at her; it was the same way he used to look at me.

One weekend, we went down to Brooklyn to an out-of-town preaching engagement Marcus had. He had me catch a ride with the older church women. Marcus always assigned me to travel with the older women of the church. Not that I had a problem with them, he just never had me with the young people. I always wondered why. We all went to a nearby pizza shop to grab food. When we were all in line, Marcus said, "Oh, I just love my church. I need to get you all in a picture. Everyone stand still."

We all posed for the picture. When Marcus finished taking the picture, he looked up and fixed his eyes on Nilani. Before we went home, Marcus whispered something to Nilani and then I watched them go over to Marcus's mother Liz. He introduced them to each other, and he was in awe as Nilani and his mother conversed. My heart was shattering as I took in every moment Marcus and Nilani interacted. I remember going to church the very next day, I cried nearly the whole service, hoping everyone thought I was just in the *Spirit.* My sister Paradise and my best friend Whitney consoled me as much as they could.

I finally had my first encounter with Nilani when she actually approached me. We were in the middle of the church's infamous welcome song. In passing, we noticed each other, and she said, "Hi, pretty girl," Nilani said as she greeted me.

"Oh, stop it, girl! You are the pretty one," I said, playfully redirecting her compliment to who I believe the pretty girl *really* was.

"Whatever!" Nilani shot back, with all playfulness out the window.

I didn't know what happened. All I know was in that moment, Nilani wasn't too fond of me. It was so weird because Nilani went above and beyond to befriend my best friend Whitney. She always talked to Whitney about them going out on outings together. She even went out of her way to befriend Whitney on all her social media sites. After a while, Nilani asked me to follow her on IG and Facebook. She started selling hair extensions and caught wind that I had a salon. In spite of her inconsistencies toward me, being hot and cold, I followed her in hopes of supporting, as I would anyone else in church. When I went to look her up, she blocked me. I knew she blocked me because I couldn't find her, but when Whitney looked for her, she was found just fine. I couldn't read her at all. One minute, she was cool, and then the next, she wanted no part of me.

Nilani even stood up for me at one point. We had an activity in our church meeting, and we all had to put an anonymous note in a bowl about what we like about someone else in the church. When a note toward me came up, it said, *"Cassie . . . Never mind!"* Nilani went in on the anonymous person on my behalf. I even told her "Thank you" and how much I appreciated her for what she did and all. But then she came at me during Sunday school. It was hosted by Evangelist Ashley. We were talking about how you know you are hearing from God. I gave a few pointers, and once I finished, Nilani interjected by saying, *"How can a person hear from God about someone being their husband, but God didn't tell the man?"* The fact that I didn't bring that up at all only proved to me that conversations were had about me, and Marcus putting his head down after her statement proved it.

Marcus *and* Nilani were moving *funny* toward me. They had the nerve to call me in Marcus's office to offer me another *leadership* position. My spirit picked up foolery the moment they pitched me this request. I remember looking at him, then her, and then back at him again as he held his hand up for a high five. I smiled, hit Marcus's hand, then left. I saw right through them. I knew something was up.

I was drained. I wasn't even sad anymore. I was just over it. It's been the same thing, the same song and dance, over and over and over again! I was giving up. The weight of this *revelation* about being Marcus's wife was too much of a cross to bear. After a while, it got to the point that my spirit was faint. I was weakened to the point that no sermon preached or heard could suffice with how downtrodden I felt. Then I was able to catch a break; a glimpse of light began to appear. I found out that a very prolific preacher who was well known was coming to preach at a local church. I happened to get off earlier that day to make it to the engagement. I needed something fresh. I needed to hear someone fresh. I needed God to have something be released in my hearing that would put me back on track with what God revealed to me about Marcus. That was my *exact* prayer, going to this church event.

I went alone, just me, myself, and I. It felt good to go to a church where nobody knew me, a place where I wouldn't be judged or have people trying to figure me out. That was short-lived when Kim and Nilani walked in. Kim then noticed me and whispered to Nilani as she pointed my way. They were more interested in the two empty chairs next to me than they were in seeing me. Kim and Nilani made their way over and sat next to me as they greeted me with a *dry* hi.

Marcus, soon after, walked in, with Jermaine as his armor bearer for the night following suit. They were walking down the aisle of the church to the front with the clergy. *Just great!* I thought to myself.

"Excuse me!" a woman said in front of me. Her name was Karen. I knew of her because I went to school with her son and she also went to my sister Ramara's church.

"Yes?" I asked.

"Come here," Karen said as she motioned me to lean in closer to her. I followed her instructions and did as she asked. *"You see that man of God right there?"* she shouted as she pointed at Marcus.

"Yesssssss," I said very long and low, hoping she didn't say anything crazy while both Kim and Nilani were sitting *right* next to me.

"The Lord told me to tell you . . . that's . . . your . . . *husband*! Hmmm. That's what he said," Karen said as she rocked back and forth in her seat, shouting, "Whoo . . . Thank you, *Jesus! Hallelujah!"*

I couldn't believe what I heard. I was frozen. Not only did God confirm what I asked him to confirm to me, he also made sure it was given to me in the presence of Nilani and Kim. *Oh my God! Did they hear? I hope they didn't!* I thought to myself. I was so afraid to look over at them to see if they caught wind of what Karen said.

"Yes, Lord! That is *your husband!"* Karen continued to say.

"Hey, may I talk to you for a second?" I asked her.

"Sure," she said as she followed me out of the sanctuary.

I had Miss Karen follow me to the women's bathroom. I checked all bathroom stalls to make sure nobody was in there. Then I shut the door behind us.

"Are you OK, sweetie?"

"No," I said. I began to cry profusely.

"Oh my God! What's the matter, sweetheart?" Karen asked.

"What you told me," I said.

"Honey, I'm sorry. I just had to tell you what the Lord told me. The Lord told me to tell you that young man is your husband," she explained.

"You didn't say anything wrong," I assured her. "God revealed this to me years ago. Since 2011."

"The Lord told me too. I remember when he came to preach at my church a few years back. God used him in a mighty way. I started talking to the Lord as the man of God preached, Marcus Boyd. I said to the Lord, *'Lord? He's gonna need a wife by his side. A good wife.'* And then I saw you. Then God confirmed to me that it was *you.* I saw this light coming from you. That's when I said to the Lord, *'Hmmm. I see what you are doing, Lord.'"*

"Thank you, Jesus!" I said as I cried tears of joy. It's funny because she was not the only person who saw *light* on me. I had a client come to me and say she was so afraid to get her hair done by me and afraid to be around me. She saw light beaming from me. That was nothing shy of God's light, and I wasn't worthy of that. I then hugged Miss Karen. "God used you to answer my prayer."

"God is so good, isn't he?"

"Yes, he is!" I agreed.

"OK now. Let's go back into the sanctuary. We don't want to miss all that good preaching," she said as we chuckled.

"Oh, Miss Karen? Just one more thing?"

"Yes, sweetie?"

"The girls that are sitting next to me, they go to my church. Can we not speak on what you told me around them?" I asked.

"No problem," Karen said.

"Thanks," I said.

"Anytime. Now, are you ready to go back out there?" she asked.

"Yes. I'm ready."

29

TOUCH NOT MY ANOINTING AND DO MY PROPHET NO HARM

The way God used Karen *that* church service gave me such reassurance that God was in fact behind what he had revealed to me. But for the life of me, I still didn't understand why everything God made so clear to me was *still* such a blur for Marcus. I found myself, once *again*, back in the same spiral of thoughts. Luckily for me, those very thoughts started to subside when shop duties began to call.

It was the beginning of October of 2015. I was entering my second year of having an established salon. In the middle of preparations the night before my anniversary party, I was surprised by a visitor.

"Hey, Cassie?"

"Oh my gosh! Mahdi! How are you?" I said as I ran over to Mahdi for a hug.

"I'm good. So you are here now?"

"Yeah, this is my new spot."

"Oh, that's what's up! It's really nice in here."

"Thank you. How about you? Where are you *at*?"

"I'm working at a barbershop on Central Avenue now. I am booth renting and cutting there."

"Oh, OK. What's up with Paris?"

"I heard he's working out of his home, doing a few heads here and there."

"Oh, OK. Dang yo! I really miss y'all."

"I miss y'all too. I'll be around now that I know where you're at. I'll come check you."

"Yes, definitely," I said.

"Aiight. Well, it was good seeing you."

"You too. Actually, I'm having my second year anniversary party at the shop tomorrow. You should come."

"OK. Cool. I'll stop by when I get off."

"Great," I said. "See you then."

The anniversary party was epic. We had an even better turnout this year. Many more clients showed up, family and loved ones attended, and Marcus came through with a few of the church members. Marcus played the stranger card toward me. It was typical when the church came around. He snuck in ways to engage with me, *here* and *there*, just to show me that he was giving me some attention. I could still tell that he was still very off toward me. As much as I was moved by the confirmation I received by Miss Karen at the last church event, I still was extremely annoyed about Marcus's behavior toward me and the lack thereof. I caught him in moments where he would be all in Nilani's face. I was far off, so he didn't peep that I noticed. I couldn't believe him. How dare he flirt with another woman in *my* salon?

I was over it. I decided to enjoy my night and my party. I took pictures with everyone that night. I took more photos with Jermaine than anybody. For some reason, Jermaine was adamant about having our photos together to be picture perfect. Once I took a group photo with everyone, the church family left right along with Marcus. That was when all the fun began. We danced and partied all night long. *Relax, saints!* I kept it cute. I didn't do anything that the Lord would frown upon. Later on at the party, I was in the middle of the dance floor talking to Whitney and Dina. We had a quick moment discussing how the party went, and we were going over a couple of ideas to better the shop by taking it to the next level. After the cookout and Independence Day sale, I realized that Whitney would be an asset to the shop. It would eventually become a one-stop shop. Whitney had recently launched her boutique, and as she was also a great team player, she was a perfect addition to the salon. As we were wrapping up our discussion, I felt someone tap me on the shoulder. It was Mahdi.

"Hey! You came!" I said as I hugged him. I was so glad to see him.

"Told you I'd be here, *shawty.*"

"Aww, so sweet. Make yourself comfortable."

"OK, cool. I also bought a bottle of wine."

"Aww, Mahdi. You didn't have to," I said. Even though I wasn't much of a drinker, the gesture was nice. "You can actually put it over there by the refreshment table."

"OK, cool."

"Aww. Thanks for coming. It means a lot to me."

"Anytime, *shawty,*" Mahdi said. Mahdi and I gave each other a hug and attempted to kiss each other on the cheek. Somehow in that attempt, we locked lips. I remember in that moment I was shocked that happened by accident, but at the same time, I felt something in that little kiss. I walked over to Whitney and Dina.

"Guys?" I said.

"Yes?" they answered.

"I kissed Mahdi."

"You kissed Mahdi?"

"Yeah. It was by accident, but I think I liked it," I said. We all burst out laughing.

"Are you saying that you are crushing on Mahdi?" Whitney asked.

"Right, 'cause Mahdi is cute, and Marcus is still playing around," Dina said.

"No. Mahdi and I are just friends. It was just a little kiss, and it was an accident. It's not that serious."

A couple of days after the anniversary, I got a call from Jermaine. He asked me for a ride home from work. I'd help him out every now and then, whenever he had a hard time getting around.

"Hey, Maine!" I said, pulling up as I noticed him in front of Hannaford Plaza.

"Cassieeeee."

"What's up? How was work?" I asked.

"It was cool. Glad I'm off though."

"I bet," I said.

"So I got to tell you something," Jermaine said as he shot his eyes my way.

"What's up?" I asked.

"I'm kinda hesitant to tell you."

"Why? Just tell me," I said.

"So I had a dream about you."

"About *me*?" I asked. "What was it about?"

"I had a dream that you and I were messing around and . . . we *slept* together."

"What?" I said as I laughed. "Maine, *seriously?*" I asked, wondering why he would dream such a thing.

"Weird, right?"

"Yes, that's *super* weird." I laughed at the thought of looking at Jermaine in that way. Jermaine wasn't a bad-looking guy. At one point, I felt he was more attractive than Marcus. Back then, we were much younger. Marcus was just our mentor at the time, and I was not even the least bit attracted to Marcus.

Changing the subject, Jermaine asked, "So have you decided if you are going to be officially on board with being a leader again at the ministry?"

"I'm not sure yet, still thinking about it," I said. This had been an ongoing conversation with Jermaine, once I told him that Marcus wanted me back in leadership. I left leadership because it became too much committing to that and the salon.

"I don't want to commit myself as a leader, especially with how much the salon is taking off. To be quite honest, I don't really feel like I fit in anyway," I said.

"Cassie, are you serious? You fit right in. We need you at the ministry. Sometimes I get frustrated when you feel like that. We got your back, Cass! I got your back."

"I know you do, Maine," I said as I thought to myself, *It's not you that I'm worried about.*

"You should seriously consider being on board." He pushed.

"I'll think about it."

"OK," he said. "Now that we are done talking about that, how 'bout that dream though?"

I looked over at him with a "you must be crazy" expression on my face as he looked over with an expression insinuating he was *joking.* We just burst out laughing. Jermaine was always being silly.

After a week or so of pondering about joining the leadership team at the church again, I let Marcus know that I accepted his offer. He was so excited and, at the same time, hoping that I wouldn't leave *again* behind us bumping heads in our personal lives. I told him that he didn't have anything to worry about and I was all in for the ministry. I meant that wholeheartedly because little did he know, my feelings for him started to fade. Marcus was becoming more and more distant, and I was getting used to the scene. He even started being inconsiderate and rude toward me. I knew that Nilani played a major part in that because he always found ways to compare me to her all the time. He even went as far as saying I wasn't the prettiest girl in church anymore, now that she showed up. He tried to dress it up with humor like he was joking. I grew more and more annoyed with him, and he became less and less attractive to me. So *yes!* It was easy for me to commit to the church, and Marcus made it that way.

Between the shop and assignments from leadership, I stayed very busy. Jermaine started to come around a lot more. He'd come by the shop, helping me by either proofreading my assignments for the ministry or helping to clean the shop. He'd sweep floors, wipe down stations, and even take out the trash. I would call him my garbage man just to be silly.

After I spent a short amount of time with Jermaine, he finally came out and told me that he liked me. Little did he know the feelings were mutual. There were ways about him that I loved because he reminded me so much of Marcus. The difference was, Jermaine was a *true* gentleman. He always made me feel special in the smallest ways. He was so genuine. He had always been. Jermaine and I started hanging out. We would go to the movies or hang out and watch movies together as friends. But things began to spark between us in a different way. One day, Jermaine invited me over to his house. After much hesitation, I paid him a visit. We watched the hip-hop era *Carmen* starring Beyoncé Knowles. It was our favorite movie to watch together. Jermaine and I recited that movie all the time, from start to finish. It was fun to hang out with Jermaine that night.

"I had so much fun tonight, Maine. It felt really good to not think about the shop or anything else. I needed this," I said.

"Yeah, me too," Jermaine agreed.

"I should probably head out."

"OK, I'll walk you out."

"Great," I said. I grabbed my leather jacket off of the armrest of the couch. I headed toward the door as Jermaine followed behind me.

"Cassie, how much do you weigh?" Jermaine asked.

"What?" I said as I laughed. "What kind of question is that, Jermaine?"

"I'm just curious," he said as he laughed.

"A woman never tells her weight," I shot back.

"I bet I can pick you up."

"I bet you can't." I laughed, looking at how slim he was.

"Seriously. Let me try."

I took a quick look at him. Then I placed my jacket on the floor next to me. "Come on, let's see whatcha got," I said, putting all my weight down as I stiffened my body and planted my feet solidly on the floor, making it hard for him to achieve his task. Before you knew it, Jermaine scooped me right up.

"Ahh!" I shouted in laughter as I was in shock that he completed the task.

"I knew I could." He laughed.

"All right. Now put me down!" I playfully demanded.

Then Jermaine put me down. He still had his arms around my waist and I had mine around his neck. Jermaine then leaned in for a kiss.

I pulled back and said, "I have to go."

"You don't want to kiss me?"

"I do. Believe me, I do. But I can't."

"Why not?" Jermaine asked.

"What about Kamilla?" I asked.

"We're not together anymore."

"I know. But what if you guys get back together? I don't want to be the rebound girl," I said as I thought that he could possibly be that to Marcus and me. I cared about Jermaine a lot. I wouldn't want that for him if Marcus and I truly became what God said. They were like brothers. I couldn't do that!

"You would never be that, Cassie. I'm into you and *only you*!"

Those words hit me. That was the difference between Jermaine and Marcus.

Jermaine looked at me as the only one. Meanwhile, my gut told me that I was an option for Marcus. I gazed into Jermaine's eyes and saw the sincerity behind his words. Right there, in that moment, we *kissed.*

I continued to hang with Jermaine. It was easy with him. He and I would laugh and joke all the time, even more now than ever. We would even go to the leadership meetings and would just be having all types of inside jokes that we didn't even have to speak on. We would catch things going on in the room and just be cracking up. One particular weekly meeting at the church, Marcus brought up a particular topic, *relationships.*

"I know a lot of us in this room want to be married. With that being said, I'm going to go around the room and ask everyone if they are ready for marriage and if the answer is yes, I want you to explain why you think you are ready. We're going to start with . . . Nilani."

"Yes?" Nilani asked with a squeaky voice and all smitten.

"Are you ready for marriage, and if so, why."

"I just feel I'm ready because I want to spend the rest of my life with someone I can do life with and . . ."

Blah, Blah, Blah! I thought to myself. They could have done this on their own time. I'm sure they hang out enough together. *Next!*

"Very good answer, Nilani," Marcus said, all googly-eyed. Marcus continued, "Kim?"

After Marcus grilled everyone in the meeting, *especially* the girls as if he was on the show *The Bachelor,* narrowing down which of us women would be his bride, he finally changed the subject by going to the next activity.

"OK now. I'm going to have our new assistant director take over from here." Nilani fulfilled the role of pastor's assistant now that Jada was no longer a part of the church.

"Thank you, Pastor," Nilani said flirtatiously. "Now we are going to pick from the bowl and read every note that was written anonymously from you guys about your peers."

"OK," we all said, unenthused.

"Don't show too much excitement," Nilani said as she rolled her eyes. "Kim, you are appreciated in all that you do for the ministry, thank you. Aww, so sweet." Kim gave a quick smile as she looked around the room. "Brian, you are the best Usher Board director that anyone could ever ask for. Aww, yes, you are, Brian." Brother Brian gave a dignified head nod. "Cassie, I love how determined and dedicated to God you are, even when you're under tremendous pressure. That was nice, Cassie, right?"

"Better than last time," I mumbled under my breath, remembering how someone wrote in a last note for me, "Cassie . . . uh . . . never mind," trying to be funny, as everyone chuckled and Marcus just sat there. Surprisingly, Nilani didn't. I did thank her for *checking* it when it happened though.

"What was that?" Nilani asked.

"Sure," I said.

"Great," she added. "Moving on," Nilani said as she continued with the affirmation activity. I looked over at Jermaine. I noticed he smiled in a sly way. I knew he wrote that note, considering how much I disciplined myself not to go past a making-out session with him.

When the weekend came around, Jermaine and I made plans to hang out. That night, I decided to stay over. I enjoyed his company. I enjoyed his warm embrace. I felt safe with him. It was never a struggle to fall asleep. Quite frankly, I had the best sleeping episodes at his house than any other place. This night, however, didn't go as planned. It was about 4:00 a.m. I woke up because my legs were burning *so* bad. I felt like my legs were on *fire*! I picked up my phone that was next to me on my bed and turned on my phone's flashlight. When I looked at my legs, I was completely breaking out. Hives everywhere! The bumps on me were the size of mosquito bites.

"Maine! Maine!"

"*What?*" he said, jumping out of the pullout bed from the couch we were lying on.

"My legs are burning! They are on fire!"

"Let me see," he said, taking my phone to use my flashlight. "Oh my gosh, Cassie!"

"It looks bad?" I asked in concern.

"It looks like mosquito bites."

"That's what I thought," I said.

"Are you allergic to anything? Did you use a different detergent or fabric softener or something?"

"No," I said.

"Oh my gosh. Let me give you a warm wet rag or something. Hold on. Stay there!" Jermaine said as he went to get one. After he wrung the water out of a rag from the kitchen sink, he brought it over to me.

"Here, put this on your legs," he said as he handed the rag to me. I started dabbing it on my legs. Still no relief.

"Is it working?" he asked.

"No," I said. "Maybe I should go home. I probably need to soak in the bath or something."

"Are you sure, Cassie? It's like 4:00 a.m.! Maybe you should wait until the sunrise. I don't feel comfortable with you leaving my house so late."

"I'll be fine," I said, pulling up my pants over my boy shorts.

"OK. Please call me when you get home."

"OK," I said as he gave me a kiss.

I ran to my car from Jermaine's complex. It was dark and cold outside. I got in my car and didn't even wait for it to warm up.

I blew it home! The whole ride, my legs were burning. I had no idea why. What could I have touched? What could I have eaten? What was I allergic to? I tried to retrace the whole day, up until the point of my legs burning. *Nothing!* I finally pulled up to my house. I opened the door quietly, trying to avoid waking up my sisters, who were sound asleep. I turned the lights on. I took my jacket off. I removed my shirt and then I hesitated before pulling down my pants. I was afraid of what I might see on my legs. Finally, I coached myself through. I counted. One . . . two . . . three! I pulled my pants down. *What? Nothing? Gone! No hives! No bumps! Nothing!* "What the heck is going on?" I whispered. Then immediately after, a thought came to mind. A thought God sent to sound the alarm: "*Touch not my anointing, do my prophet no harm.*"

Frozen by that thought, I stood still in my room. I became fearful because God stepped in. *Why? Because of the revelation! Because of Marcus.* It was right there, in that moment, that the fling between Jermaine and me was *over!*

30

THOU ANOINTS MY HEAD WITH OIL, MY CUP OVERFLOWS

Jermaine continued to reach out to me. He would text me most of the time. I remember one night where Jermaine sent a video of his empty bed and then put the camera on him as he wore a sad face, indicating that he wanted me to keep him company. Even though I'd dodge Jermaine's attempts to see me, he wasn't the type to just pop up like Marcus. If I didn't give him permission to come by, he wouldn't. When we did speak, I kept my conversations very brief with him. I blamed it on me being busy at the shop. I couldn't tell him why I had to officially cut him off. I mean, come on. How crazy would that sound? Marcus and I were so secretive and Jermaine was under the impression that Marcus told him *everything*. He wouldn't have believed me and probably would have run and told Marcus. Not only that, if I were to tell him what happened the night I broke out in hives, how it completely disappeared when I got home and how God checked me by word of Scripture, Jermaine would think I was crazy for sure.

At one point, I thought Jermaine could have told Marcus about him and me. I knew Jermaine was really into me and would possibly want to share that with Marcus and get some advice. Marcus suddenly coming back around gave me that impression. Another crazy thing took place. Shortly after that incident happened at Jermaine's house, Marcus shared to me that he had a dream that the men in the church were caressing me and it was as if I looked at him for help, and he did nothing to stop it. He said he felt guilty that he had the power to do something about it, but didn't. Even though I thought, *Duh! You allowed so many attacks toward me and did nothing*, I wondered if God was showing him indirectly what happened with Jermaine and me.

Marcus started back with his pop-up routine again. He'd come to the shop unannounced, *again*. Marcus called himself flirting with me to get in good with me, *again*. He'd even made nice with my employees and close friends. After Marcus checked in on me a few times, I figured that Jermaine didn't share to him anything. Marcus wasn't the type to hold on to information too long. From knowing him all these years and how he was never able to hold water for nothing, I knew if Jermaine told him anything, he would have definitely spilled the beans by now.

"What's going on, what's going on?" Marcus said as he entered the shop like he was Obama himself.

"Hey," Dina and I said in unison.

"How are you doing, Cassie?"

"Good," I said.

"How is it today?"

"Busy," I said, continuing to keep my answers short with him.

"That's always good," Marcus replied. "Well, I wanted to stop in and check on you and to also see if you were interested in preaching for one of our *five-minute exhortations* that are taking place next Sunday?"

I was shocked he was finally giving me permission to preach after all these years. Any other time, Marcus would either fight against me for doing it or show little to no support. How 'bout it for a pastor, huh? I responded, "Sure, I'd love to." I was excited but curious as to why he would approve of me preaching at his church.

"Perfect. I can let Evangelist Ashley know and have her fill you in on the details. She said that during her consecration period, the Lord had revealed to her that you should minister next Sunday," Marcus said.

Well, there was my answer. I knew he didn't think of me preaching on his own. I was shocked that Evangelist Ashley thought of me. She did mention it to me at our last Sunday service, and she told me she would get back to me once Marcus approved. We came a long way, considering her false accusations of me being lustful didn't get in the way of her knowing that I am truly called by God to preach.

"OK, sounds great," I said.

"OK, I'll catch you guys later. And, Miss?" Marcus said, addressing the client I had in my chair. "The woman who's doing your hair said the service is free."

"Ahahaha!" I laughed in the most condescending way.

"Later, y'all," Marcus said, making his way out of the salon.

"Bye," I said, relieved that he didn't choose to stay long and made a quick exit. Needless to say, I was super excited to preach. As soon as I left the salon for the night, I went right to work and began studying the Word of God. I went into consecration that entire week. I wanted to make sure that I was pure and heard from God crystal clear. I wanted the message to be accurate, relevant, and from God *himself.*

The day finally came. It was *finally* time to preach in my home church, among my church family and loved ones. More than anything, I wanted it to be all of God and none of me. Now, I am naturally a nervous wreck. I am always one to never draw attention on myself. Imagine what I felt like when the Lord revealed to me my calling. I am always anxious right before a preaching engagement. My first preaching engagement, I was so afraid to go up to preach. I prayed all the way up until the pastor of that church announced me to come up. I remember God said to me a brief moment before, "Cassie, take the shoes off your feet! The ground that you are standing on is holy ground." In that moment, the Lord reminded me that I cannot do this in *him* and operating as *me* at the same time. I had to literally put aside my self-doubt, my fears, my anxiety, and totally trust and lean on him. When I tell you I preached the house down, I mean the Lord used me so well that the church went up in worship for an hour or so. And if you have ever been in a Black church before, then you know exactly what I'm talking about. From then on, every time I go up to preach I take my shoes off. That was my way of reverencing God, my way of allowing him to totally use me. And it was going to be the same here, at the Powerhouse.

Praise and worship was up first. My girl Trina went off on the mic. That girl always sang your way out of something. That was my girl. Direnda was amazing too. She had the sweetest voice. Her worship was so pure. And I can't forget about Jermaine. He has a voice on him too. I'm glad we were able to remain cool even though I ended things between us. Finally, Marcus was up at the pulpit. He gave a few announcements about our weekly meetings for leadership. Then he talked about our Thanksgiving Drive service that was coming up in a few weeks. After that, he collected tithes and offering, and before you knew it, it was about that time. Marcus introduced me as the speaker.

"Without further ado, let's welcome our speaker to the mic: Sister Cassie!" Marcus exclaimed as he extended the mic out toward me to retrieve it. The church began to clap and cheer as I made my way to the pulpit.

"C'mon, give God some praise! I said give God some praise. C'mon! You can sit and be cute all you want to. But last time I checked, *cute* didn't make me better! Last time I checked, *cute* didn't keep me in my right mind! *Hallelujah, Jesus!* But it's at the name of Jesus that every knee shall bow and every tongue must confess that Jesus Christ is the Lord. C'mon and give God some praise!" I shouted as the church continued to praise God. "I want to thank God, who is the head of my life. I also would like to thank our pastor, Pastor Marcus Carter James Boyd. Let's thank God for our pastor. Hallelujah . . . hallelujah. Without further ado, let's get into the Word. My reading is from Psalm 23:5 and it reads: 'Thou preparest a table before me, in the presence of my enemies. You anoint my head with oil and my cup overflows.' The topic of my sermon is 'You Have Been Anointed!'"

As I was preaching, I noticed everyone was glued to me, all attention on me. The saints were soaking up every word. Some were screaming, some were shouting, some were crying, others were praising. I couldn't help but notice how much God was using me. It was such a beautiful sight to see. I wouldn't have traded that moment for the world. They were hungry for God, hungry for fresh revelation, and hungry for the Word. I was born to do this. This was nothing short of God's glory. I knew all of heaven was smiling down on us. I knew God was proud of me.

"When the insects get into the ears of the sheep, it kills the sheep. But because of the oil, the insect cannot get to the head. If it cannot get to the head, it cannot get to the eyes. If it cannot get to the eyes, it cannot get to the ears. If it cannot get to the ears, it cannot plant itself in the ears because you have been anointed! I want you to look at your neighbor and say, 'Neighbor? Give God some praise for the *slide off*!' The enemy is about to slide off! *Hallelujah, Jesus! Hallelujah, God!*" I concluded and I handed back the mic to Marcus. As I walked back to my seat, I couldn't help but join the worshipers in the room. The message was so impactful, so loaded, and so empowering that even Marcus added a few words.

"Hallelujah! You need to know that devil is sliding off! Give God glory because you know he's sliding off! Hallelujah! Hallelujah! Not only does your anointing destroy yokes, your anointing frustrates your haters!

"Whoo!" the saints shouted.

Marcus continued, "Because when they come into your vicinity and your purview, everything that they tried to do that used to work before the *anointing*, now that you have the *anointing*, they don't have an impact anymore! Now that you have the *anointing*, it does not faze you anymore!"

"Yes!" I agreed.

Marcus continued, "Now that you have the *anointing*, it does not bother you anymore. And God said to David, not only will I anoint you, I'll have you experience an overflow. Not only will God give you the power that was so powerful what *she* just said. Not only will God give you the power to repel every demonic force, not only will God give you the power to repel every gossiper, not only will God give you the power to repel the adversary, but because you had to deal with them, I'm going to cause your life to overflow. Because the devil thought it could break you, not only did it not break you, it positioned you for an overflow. Look at your neighbor and say, 'This is my time—'"

"This is my time!" I shouted along with the congregation.

"For an *overflow*!" Marcus continued.

"For an overflow!"

"Amen! You may be seated in the presence of the Lord.

Once we got settled, Marcus went in his sermon for Sunday's service. Of course, he did well. He never disappoints. Marcus preached for a good fifteen minutes. Afterward, he did the altar call. Some received salvation, others joined the church, and the rest went up for prayer. When the last person received prayer, Marcus dismissed the church.

I began to gather my belongings and started to make my way toward the door to leave the church. A small line of church members began to form in front of me. The first person to approach me was Desmond.

"Powerful message today, sis!"

"Aww, I appreciate it, Des. I was so nervous."

"I couldn't tell. You were in your element."

"Thanks," I said.

Then Nilani came up. "Great job, Cassie. I needed that. You have no idea." She was really moved by it. I remember seeing her cry when I was done preaching and back at my seat.

"I'm so glad you were blessed," I said, humbled that she would share that with me.

Next up was Miss Waters. "Exceptional job, Cassie. I recorded everything. I'll be sure to send it to you, and I'll be watching it again."

"Yes, please send me a copy. That would be great."

"My spiritual daughter, I knew you could do it. I knew God would use you."

"Aww, Mama Ashley. Thank you for believing in me," I thanked her.

Lastly, Jermaine came up. "Young Cass?"

"My Maine man!" I shot right back at him.

"You killed it."

"To God be *all* the glory," I said as I gave him a hug.

So much love was shared to me. It felt good to know that the people I've been in church with all these years believed in me. They saw how much it means to me to preach God's word. I couldn't wait to hear what Marcus thought. I was in great expectation. Only Marcus knew how much I struggled with timidity and anxiety. I knew he'd call me as soon as he got home from church.

Three days went by. No sign of Marcus. Not a call or text. Nothing. I didn't expect that. Not from him. Not from my pastor. I was so confused. Why would he not reach out, being that he was the one who approved and asked me to preach? I didn't understand why he didn't reach out. Maybe he was busy? Maybe he had more important things to do besides give me a report of my performance. Finally, Thursday showed up. I received a call from Marcus. I thought I would have to wait to hear from him at Bible study that night. He wouldn't have been able to avoid me then.

"Hey, Pastor?" I said in the most formal way.

"Hey, Cassie. How are you?" he said in a very shallow way. It was like he was forcing himself to talk to me. It seemed like he didn't wanna call.

"Are you OK?" I asked. "You seem a bit down."

"Yes, I'm fine," Marcus said unconvincingly. "I'm calling you to discuss how you did Sunday."

"OK," I said as my smile grew from ear to ear. I was so excited to hear his perspective.

"I think it was very disrespectful to preach without shoes on your feet. When someone asks you to preach, you don't do it with shoes off." He snarled.

I jumped back from the phone, startled at his comment. I swear I'm always doing something wrong. "Pastor, I'm sorry. That is what I do every time I preach. I was never told it was wrong. I didn't know until now. I apologize. That's just my way of reminding myself that I am on God's territory and that I am on holy ground. It's just a subconscious reminder to myself—that's all," I said, feeling extremely disappointed.

"Yes! Well, it was very disrespectful. The next thing is that you were talking *way too fast*. Even Kim said that and kept yelling to you to slow down."

"OK," I said, feeling super defeated.

"Lastly, your sermon was good. However, one would suggest you got it from YouTube," Marcus said as he grilled me.

"Pastor, I would *never* take someone else's work and make it my own. I studied really hard. Everything I preach comes from the heart. It comes from God."

"Well, I feel like I've heard it from somewhere before. Anyway, besides that, you did *pretty* good."

"Thanks, Pastor," I said, holding back tears.

"See you tonight at Bible study, *right*?"

"Yes," I said, rolling my eyes. "I'll be there."

"Great! See you then," Marcus said as he hung up.

I burst into tears. I could never win with him. I was never good enough. Either everyone lied to me, or he didn't give me the credit I deserved. Like *really*? I mean, I'm not against constructive criticism and I know I'm not perfect and probably not the best, but for Marcus to go as far as to say I stole my sermon from YouTube? I had never been so insulted in my life. How could I be under someone that was hell-bent on breaking me down, first in my love life, now in ministry? How could I continue to follow this man as my pastor?

It was slow at work the next day. I decided to go check out Paris at the new barbershop he was now working at. I needed someone unbiased that I could talk to. Because Paris was cool with me and Marcus, I knew he'd be the perfect person to confide in.

"What? You got it from YouTube? He said that to you?"

"Yes, he did."

"Aw, come on, Marcus! You got to do better, my man," Paris said. "Do you have the video of you preaching?"

"Yes, Paradise recorded it for me," I explained.

"Let me see it. I want to see for myself how you did."

"Please be honest," I said, passing him my phone.

"OK," he said. Paris plugged my AUX cord to my phone so that we could listen to it from my car radio.

"Ooh!" he said as he listened to a part that he could relate to. "Wow! Uh-huh!" he continued. I patiently waited as I watched him listen to the sermon. I kept my composure in eager anticipation to hear his opinion about my preaching.

"Cassie, what? That was dope. I wish I was there. I mean, how did you compare the enemy to an insect and how the same way the insect can get inside the sheep's ear to destroy them is the same way the enemy tries to get into our ear to destroy us? That's crazy! And I love how you broke down how the oil the shepherd uses on the sheep stops the insects from destroying the sheep, and you killed that whole breakdown on the word *overflow*."

"Really? You liked it?" I asked as I smiled shyly.

"Yes, Cass. You always crush it! I mean, even your 'Word of the day' you put up every week. Truth be told, Cassie, I think Marcus is intimidated by you," Paris said.

"It's crazy you say that because that's what my friends think," I added.

"I just feel like he was reaching about you talking fast. Like, so what? I heard every word you said. Then he's talking about you are disrespecting him by taking your shoes off? I feel like he was finding reason to nullify how you did. Then the whole YouTube shot. Cassie, I watch sermons all the time and I've heard many people preach from the Scripture and I ain't ever heard nothing like that before!" Paris explained.

"I don't know. I just don't get it."

"I don't either. I never see anyone go hard for him like you do. If he looked at you as someone building with you, you guys could be a force."

"Well, I don't know if I can continue going there if he comes against me, every single time I preach."

"You have to do what's best for you, Cassie. If being there isn't working for you, maybe it's time for you to leave."

"Maybe you're right. On another note, how has it been here at your new place of work? You like it better down here?" I asked.

"Yeah. It's cool."

"That's good. Mahdi stopped by to see us at our new spot."

"Oh yeah?" Paris asked.

"Yeah. He actually lives right down the street from us. I really miss y'all being next door."

"I know, right? We were like family."

"Right. It's not the same. We have to see each other more."

"I know," said Paris.

"You know what? Let's all get together this Saturday. We can meet at my shop and watch movies. I'll order food."

"This Saturday is no good, Cass. I go see my son this weekend. I won't be back from the city until Monday."

"How about next Saturday, then?"

"Next Saturday is good. I can do that," Paris agreed.

"OK, cool. I'm going to tell Mahdi too."

"Sounds good. All right, Cass. Let me get back to work. I have to get ready for my next cut. My boy should be here any minute."

"OK. Thanks, Paris."

"Anytime. You know you're li'l sis. Later."

"Later."

31

THIS MAN RECEIVES SINNERS AND EATS WITH THEM

It was the Saturday before Thanksgiving of that year. I was on my last client that just so happened to be my crazy cousin Keisha. She was always so fun to be around, never a dull moment when she came to the salon.

"Yes, Cass. That's what I am talking about. You slayed this and I look *good*, OK?" Keisha said as she looked in the mirror and stroked the long extended-weave ponytail she so badly wanted me to do for her.

"You are a mess, Keisha," I said as I laughed at her once she began to dance around the room. Keisha was definitely *feeling herself.*

"Thank you so much, cousin."

"No problem," I said. "That will be *sixty dollars*," I said as I extended my hand toward her in an effort to retrieve some money.

"Cass, can I give you *thirty* today and get you the rest in two weeks?"

"C'mon, Keisha! You do this all the time. I got bills to pay just like you."

"I know, but I only got a couple of dollars to my name and I gotta make sure Jah Jah is good."

"Whatever," I said, waiting to take her *thirty dollars*. She knew bringing up her son would have me cut her a break. She knew he was my favorite little guy.

"Thanks, big cuz," Keisha said, handing me the money as she gave me a side hug.

"Hmmm," I said.

"What's going on, y'all?" Paris said as he swung open the door of the salon and made his way in.

"Hey, Paris! You made it," I said as I walked over to him and gave him a hug.

"You know I was coming through," he said as he scoped the place. "It looks really nice in here, Cassie. I like the new spot."

"Really?" I asked. "Thank you. I love it too."

"What's going on, Keisha?" Paris said.

"Hey. What y'all got planned tonight?" Keisha asked, looking like she felt a way about not being invited.

"Oh, we're just ordering food and watching a movie. Mahdi is supposed to be on his way too."

"Oh well, I'm staying. I want to see Mahdi's *fine a***," Keisha said.

"Here you go, Keisha!" I said, laughing at her.

"Yeah, you're always talking about you're going to *scoop* Mahdi and all that. You better have that *same* energy when he walks in too," Paris said, indicating that he was tired of her talking about liking Mahdi but never approaching him.

"I am! Watch! The next time I see him, I'm going to say, 'Hey, Mahdi, do you want to be my next *baby zaddyyyy*?'"

"What's up, y'all?" Mahdi said as he entered the salon, right when Keisha just finished her statement. Keisha's eyes widened. Embarrassed that Mahdi could have potentially heard what she said, Keisha walked to the miniature couch to sit down and said, "Hi."

"Ahahahahahaha!" Paris laughed, realizing that Keisha was not as bold as she portrayed herself to be once Mahdi came in the room.

"Hey, Mahdi. How are you?" I said, greeting him with a hug, hoping that I could disguise the awkwardness Keisha was feeling.

"Hey, Keisha? What's up with you? How's your brother doing?" Mahdi asked.

"Tay Tay is doing good," Keisha said, very short with timidity.

"That's good," Mahdi said. "What are we ordering to eat? I'm starving."

"I figured we can order pizza and wings and watch the Kevin Hart stand-up *Laugh at My Pain*. I heard it was good."

"Yeah, it's funny as hell," said Mahdi.

"I didn't see it before," Paris said. "How about you, Miss *Zaddyyyyyyyyy*?" Paris said to Keisha, still teasing her about Mahdi.

"Shut up, Paris," Keisha said, rolling her eyes.

"All right, y'all chill," I said, laughing at Paris mimicking Keisha.

Chilling with all of them was cool. It felt good to not think about work, church, or Marcus. I was surprised he didn't pop in that night. But I had so much fun between watching the stand-up comedy and talking and laughing and catching up with Paris and Mahdi that I didn't even take to heart Marcus not stopping by. I wanted to keep up with my weekend links with Paris and Mahdi just to keep in touch, so I planned another gathering for us in the following week. I invited Keisha too. But this time, only Keisha and Mahdi showed. Paris couldn't make it and had to cancel with us last minute. Mahdi, Keisha, and I decided to go out to eat at Fridays. After chilling together the weekend before, Keisha started warming up to Mahdi. She was getting comfortable flirting with him. She kept throwing flirtatious remarks across the table to Mahdi, the side he and I were sitting at. Keisha then asked Mahdi to take a picture of her.

"Yes, Mahdi. Get my good side," she said, positioning herself to take a photo.

"Oh. That's your good side? Aight bet," Mahdi said as he took Keisha's phone to take a photo. Mahdi held the phone up as he flipped the camera around toward him and me. He took photos of us as Keisha thought he was taking some of her. It was hilarious. She didn't catch on until she received her phone back. Then Keisha noticed *our* photos. When Keisha's facial expression dropped from a smile, Mahdi and I laughed hysterically. We always did silly stuff together that only he and I found funny. It was just like old times, back at the other shop—nothing short of jokes and silly photos.

Before you knew it, it went from all of us getting together, to Mahdi and me hanging out by ourselves. We talked to each other every day. We talked about everything. Mahdi told me he broke up with his girl. I told him how I was seeing someone that I was really into for a long time, but things didn't work out between us. I didn't let him know that it was Marcus I was talking about. Funny story, Mahdi told me one time, when he and I were hanging out, that he was originally Marcus's barber. He said that Marcus started going to Paris because Mahdi would be late all the time. He mentioned Marcus because Mahdi was showing me his music. He loved to rap. As he was showing me, it was one particular song he wanted me to hear. Mahdi went to an email he sent to Marcus. He sent music to Marcus before. Mahdi told me that Marcus was fond of his music as well. As I got to know more and more about Mahdi, I started to catch feelings for him. It wasn't long after that he confessed his feelings for me too.

Mahdi and I got to the point where we saw each other every single day. Because he lived down the street, whenever I was too tired and didn't feel like driving home, I'd stay the night at his house. I let Mahdi know early on that I was saving myself for marriage. He respected it. He always assured me that he didn't want to do anything that I was not ready for. He was so sweet. It was smooth and perfect between us. But as perfect as we were, one thing always hung over my head about us, and that thing was, Mahdi was not *saved*. After a few discussions with him on the topic, seeing how he would confess over and over again that he didn't believe in Jesus Christ and believed it was a man-made religion, I told Mahdi that this would never work. I needed the man in my life to believe in Jesus Christ. Mahdi not believing didn't cut it for me. But with all my attempts to walk away, I still chose to get to know him more and more. I mean, he never judged me. So why judge him? If he respected my beliefs, then maybe I should respect his, *right*?

At this time, the month of December came rolling in. It had been a few weeks since Mahdi and I hit it off. Everything was great. The more I got to know him, the more I appreciated who he was. Even though Mahdi wasn't a *believer*, he acted more like a Christian than most. I went to Bible study one particular night. I felt so good. I couldn't wait to hear the Word. But this night was not the norm for me. What I thought would be a good night of Marcus bringing forth the Word turned out to be a night of conviction.

"Do not be unequally yoked with unbelievers! For the Bible says, what partnership has righteousness and lawlessness? Or what fellowship has light with darkness?" Marcus shouted.

It was crazy. Normally when the Word is being preached, I'd be praising and shouting away. But I'm not going to lie. I was playing *Silence of the Lamb* that night.

"Some of y'all are in relationships you know God don't approve of. Whether it's an associate, a friend, or a lover, it is time for you to close the chapter on that relationship. I don't know who this is for, but the Lord says, 'It is time for you to un-fellow that fellow.'" Marcus continued as if God wasn't lighting up my behind enough.

Whew! I couldn't wait to get out of there. I never felt so uncomfortable in my life. Don't it seem like whenever you go to church and the pastor preaches, it's almost as if they have been following you all week? They just so happen to preach on something you were going through or a part of! But I knew God was behind it. Nothing is hidden from him. He sees and knows all. It was time for me to face the music.

I made plans to see Mahdi that night. I told him earlier in the day that I would come to see him after Bible study before I made my way home. Driving over to him, I began to ponder on the message Marcus preached. I wrestled back and forth in my mind about whether or not I should end things with Mahdi. On one end, I was rehashing the Scripture about being unequally yoked. But on the other end, I thought about the scripture where Jesus sat among *sinners*. He even stayed at Zacchaeus' house at the time Jesus was carrying out his purpose in ministry. For those who know the Word, we know that Zacchaeus was a money-grabbing tax collector. What do we say to that? After moments of scripture battling with myself, I went right to my go-to, prayer:

> Dear Lord, you know I absolutely love you with my whole heart. My whole being is to please you. Lord, I'm struggling right now. I'm not sure if you want me to end things with Mahdi or not. When I meet with him tonight, please give me a sign. Show me a sign that I know it's you letting me know whether or not I should walk away. In Jesus name I pray, Amen.

When I arrived in front of Mahdi's house, he was already on his way out the door to come see me. He must have been looking out the window as I was pulling up, so I didn't need to call him.

"Hey, beautiful," Mahdi said as he got in the car. Mahdi leaned over and hugged me as he planted a kiss on my cheek. "I missed you all day today. How was Bible study?"

"It was *interesting*," I said.

"Oh, OK," he said. I was glad he didn't ask what it was about.

"How about you? How was your day?" I asked, switching the subject.

"It was good. Did a couple cuts and that's about it. I couldn't wait to see you though."

"Is that right?" I asked; right when we were suddenly interrupted by a couple of knocks on my driver-side window.

"Yes, officer?" I asked as I rolled my car window down.

"What's your name, miss?" the first officer asked.

"Cassie," I said, wondering why he was approaching us.

"Cassie what?" he asked.

"Cassie Parker," I said.

"License and registration, please."

"Sure," I said, reaching slowly for my glove compartment.

"What's your name, boy?" the officer asked Mahdi.

"I don't have to give you my name. What is the reason you are pulling us over? Better yet, come over to a parked car and asking us our names?"

"Well, you look suspicious."

"Why do I look suspicious, officer? Because I'm Black?" Mahdi shot back.

"We were just chasing a young man who fit your description. Now what is your name, *boy*?"

"Unless you got a warrant, I'm not giving you my name!" said Mahdi.

"Hey, sir. We are just trying to do our job. Just understand," said the second officer.

"No! I over-stand! I don't understand! I over-stand! I over-stand that every time y'all see a Black man, he looks suspicious. How do I look suspicious coming outside of my house to see my girl who is parked in front of my house? So like I said, officers, if you don't have a warrant, then I'm not giving you my name!"

"Babe, please just calm down," I said, trying to stop the situation from escalating.

"Cassie, no! I'm sick of these crackers, man. Every time I turn around, I'm getting pulled over, stopped, or harassed by cops. It's every single day! I'm so sick of these *crackers*!"

"All right, that's it! Out of the car!" the first officer said to Mahdi as he walked over to the passenger-side door.

"Man, I'm not getting out of nothing!"

"I said get out, boy!" the first officer said as he opened the passenger door and yanked Mahdi out of the car, throwing him to the ground face down. The officer then put his knee in Mahdi's back as he grabbed both Mahdi's arms in an effort to put handcuffs on him. Then officer two pulled out his gun and shouted, "Freeze!"

"Ah! You're hurting me, man! Get off of me!"

"Shut the f*** up!" the first officer shouted. "Put your hands behind your back now!"

"All right! All right!" Mahdi said as he stopped resisting and did as the officer asked. "Can you get off now?!"

"I said, shut the f*** up!" the first officer said as he continued to press his knee in Mahdi's back.

"You're hurting him! Officer, *please, I'm begging you! Get off of him.*"

"He should have listened the first time!" the second officer replied. Meanwhile, the first one ignored my pleading. I then ran up the stairs and knocked on Mahdi's front door for his roommate Dante.

"*D! D! Open up!*" I shouted. I waited about five seconds before he opened the door.

"What's going on?"

"They are trying to arrest Mahdi!" I yelled.

"For what?"

"I don't know! We were just sitting in the car and the cops dragged him out!" I shouted, crying hysterically, hoping it wouldn't be another incident like the movie *Fruitvale Station.* After the first officer successfully put handcuffs on Mahdi, he walked over toward the house, where Dante and I were on the porch.

"Good evening. Does this gentleman live with you?" the officer asked.

"Yes. He lives here. Why, what's up? Why y'all got him down on the ground like that?"

"*Hey!* I'm the one doing the questions here. He said his license is inside. You want to grab it for us?"

"No, sir. And unless you have a search warrant, you won't be coming in here to get it either!" Dante said, getting smart with the officer.

"What's your name, boy?"

"Why? So I can be down on the ground next to him?" Dante said, pointing at Mahdi. "I'm not telling you nothing unless my lawyer is present."

"Trying to be a smart a**, huh? All right! Well, we're taking ya homeboy downtown. He won't be released until he sees the judge. C'mon, Clark!" the officer said to his partner.

"*What? Y'all are really taking him in?*" I asked. The officers didn't even bother to respond. They just grabbed Mahdi off the ground and started walking him toward the police car.

"I gotchu, bro!" Dante yelled out. "I'll be down there in the morning."

"These f***ing crackers, man!" Mahdi yelled back as he was getting in the back seat of the police car. "Cass, go home! I'm good! I'll call you tomorrow as soon as I get out!"

I stood there on their porch as I watched them drive off. *Dang, Lord! That was one heck of a sign!*

I made sure I got to the courthouse early. I wanted to make sure I was there to see what type of charges the officers were trying to pin on Mahdi. The judge dismissed the case and let Mahdi go. He said they didn't have good enough grounds to hold him. Mahdi walked out without having to pay a fine.

"Good looking, bro!" Mahdi said to Dante as he made his way to us. Dante and I were sitting in the back, right next to the double doors. Mahdi decided to have me drop him off to his place and told Dante that he'd see him back at the house. When Mahdi and I got in the car, he tried to make small talk.

"Crazy what happened last night, right? F***ing *crackers*!" he said, shaking his head. "You OK though?"

"I've had better days," I said as I chuckled.

"How do you feel about what happened?" Mahdi asked.

"Well, I feel like you definitely didn't make the situation any better."

"What do you mean?" he asked as he was baffled about my response. "What was I supposed to do?"

"I feel like you didn't do anything to defuse the situation? What if they shot you, Mahdi? What about your family? What about your daughter?" I asked. I knew I could get through to him by bringing up his daughter. I knew how much she meant to him. "I just feel like you lack self-control, Mahdi. You could have handled that *way* better than you did."

"Cassie! You don't know what it's like to get harassed every day by cops because you're a *Black man*. I'm stopped every time I leave the house damn near!" Mahdi explained. Then he took a deep breath to keep his composure. "I don't know, man. I was just fed up last night. I'm sorry. I don't know how else I was supposed to handle that." We arrived at Mahdi's house a few moments later. He lived surprisingly close to the courthouse. "I'll talk to you later, Cassie." Mahdi said as he got out of the car. I drove off when he went inside his home.

Is this your sign, Lord? Was I being too harsh? Was I supposed to be upset for him standing up for himself? Is this your way of escape for me? I didn't know what to think. I didn't know what to make of all that had happened. The only thing I could do at that point was call my big sister Tanya. I needed her advice and needed to hear what she had to say about engaging any further with Mahdi. What I should have considered was that I was asking for an opinion from someone that is *so* pro-Black.

"Absolutely *not*, Cassie! Don't you stop talking to that man because of racist cops!" Tanya screamed. I think she was more upset about the racist cops than the matter at hand.

"Tanya, you don't understand. I prayed to God about a sign on whether or not to leave him alone, and all of this happened. What if this was God's way of showing me?"

"Cassie, you think God showed you a sign by having this guy stand up for himself and what's *right*? Don't you know how much our *Black* men have to go through being harassed by racist police on a daily basis?"

"I get it. I just feel like him calling them crackers and flipping out and being angry didn't make the situation any better."

"Cassie, even *Jesus* flipped tables! I think you should cut the man some slack. To cut him off because of that would be kind of foul."

I thought to myself: *Maybe Tanya's right. Maybe I should brush this whole situation off and give him another chance. Hopefully, nothing like this ever happens again.* But those thoughts were short-lived when my stylist Dina came to work later on at the shop.

"Cassie, I have to tell you something," Dina said, rushing to her station to set her purse and the rest of her belongings down.

"What happened?"

"You can't tell Mahdi, all right?"

"OK. What's up?"

"So Mahdi just called me and told me that his ex-girlfriend's father came to his shop and tried to rush him!"

"*What?*"

"Yes, sis! And he and the rest of the barbers in the shop jumped the ex's dad and some dude he came with."

Welp! So much for wishful thinking . . .

32

HIS BLOOD WILL I REQUIRE AT THINE HANDS

I decided to keep things going with Mahdi and me. I didn't penalize him for fighting his ex's father and uncle. I mean, as saved as I am, I know how difficult it is to *turn the other cheek*. I just didn't think it would be fair to cut him off behind sticking up for and protecting himself when I threw a few blows in my past life to do the same. Things were great with us. I made sure I never crossed boundaries with him by going *all the way* even when it would get tempting at times. I believe it was God's word that kept me from falling. Not so much the Word that is written in Scripture, but the word that continued to be a lingering thought in my mind about Marcus and him being the one *God chose for me*. What made it more difficult to drop the ideal all in all was that Marcus continued to stick around. His seldom pop-ups weren't so seldom anymore. He suddenly started coming around to visit at the shop again. He'd come a couple times in a week. I'm not going to lie, every time he walked through the door, my heart skipped a beat. There was no denying how I felt for him. Still, I refused to let my feelings for Marcus get in the way of getting to know Mahdi. Things with Mahdi were just so *easy*. He never kept me wondering or in question about me being the only one.

That confidence in Mahdi was short-lived when Mahdi and I took a picture together. I posted our selfie on my Instagram page. In all of five minutes, his ex shared a post on her page of Mahdi texting her with a caption saying, "Can her man please stay out my inbox!" The message insinuated his desire to sleep with her again. I was extremely upset. As far as me, even though I had strong feelings lingering for Marcus and I knew there was no way Mahdi was completely over his ex after being separated from her about a month or so, I didn't act on my feelings. But *clearly*, he had.

I didn't hesitate to check Mahdi about the post I saw. I told him that if he couldn't prove otherwise, we were done. Mahdi immediately responded with all confidence and told me he could prove it to me and asked that I come over after I was done at the shop. When I arrived, Mahdi gave me his phone. He freely let me peruse *all* through the messages between him and his ex. The message she put up was before Mahdi and I even started hanging out. It also showed her starting that particular conversation and her popping up on him at his job and how he eluded her by jumping in a cab and pulling off. With all the information he showed me, I was impressed by him for not retaliating by exposing her and what really took place. That not only showed me the maturity and integrity in him, it also showed what I thought he lacked the most: *self-control.* As happy as I was about Mahdi living up to him *proving himself,* I felt like he was truly ready to commit to me and I was just so unsure. I needed God to show me! Really show me! *Should I pursue Mahdi or Marcus?*

I struggled with which way to go for another month or so. But my routine stayed the same. I kept hanging out with Mahdi as Marcus continued to stop by. Marcus made it easy to continue to see Mahdi. Even though he stuck around, he never went out of his way to suggest we hang out more outside the shop. Maybe I didn't make it any easier for him to do so by keeping my distance. I wasn't about to get sucked up in the revolving door with him again. But still, I didn't know what to do. I had no answers. But all that changed when the church had another revival service.

We had a three-night revival the first week of March. Kim thought it would be a good idea and brought it to Marcus's attention. It couldn't have come quick enough. Lord knew I needed a recharge. I noticed that both Nilani and Jada stopped coming to church. Jada moved back to her hometown, and I assumed Nilani was visiting her family back in Virginia. I wondered if Nilani not being in church anymore was the reason behind Marcus coming back around all of a sudden. I didn't think too much of it. That was up until Nilani started becoming extra friendly on social media. I just so happened to check my Instagram. Nilani liked the selfie I had of Mahdi and me. She was liking *this.* She was liking *that.* She liked at least five pictures of mine until she asked to follow my page. It was clear that she had unblocked me. I accepted her request. I started looking on her page as well and noticed she had started a winery business. I liked the picture of a business event she had and I commented. I asked her why she didn't tell me about her event and how I would have come to support. She told me how she disconnected from the entire church and how she believed nobody liked her in the church and wanted nothing to do with her anymore. I was saddened by that. I knew she wasn't fond of me, which I never really had a clue as to why. All I knew is that what I was not going to allow her to feel is that I had anything against her. I told her that I was sorry for all that she had gone through at the church, even though I had not a clue why she had left and what she went through. I told her at the end of the day, she is a *soul.* She is a *believer!* I hated that she felt alone especially when I knew she made the sacrifice to move upstate just to help build the church. I gave her my number and told her if she needed me for anything, to give me a call.

I went to revival that night. The guest speaker was on *fire!* I didn't get to catch all that the man had preached because I had filled in as an usher and helped my sister Paradise with all the demands of that. But what I did catch was *good.* I can't really tell you the specifics because I don't remember. However, I do remember how I felt that night after hearing the sermon. I knew that it was time to end things with Mahdi. I felt God was leading me toward that decision. I had to be honest with myself. We were like night and day, *literally.* We were not the same. We didn't believe in the same things. I was called! I was chosen! How would that work being with someone who didn't *believe?*

Once service ended, Paradise and I cleaned up. We decided afterward to go to dinner at Friday's. I made the decision once I settled down at the restaurant, I'd call Mahdi and end things with him.

"You know what you're going to say?" Paradise asked.

"No! I'm so nervous."

"I think you are doing the right thing. You have to follow your heart. You have to follow God. You always tell me that."

"I know. I have to practice what I preach. It's time to take my own advice," I said as I pulled out my phone to call Mahdi. I took a deep breath and dialed Mahdi's number. It went straight to voicemail.

"*Well?*" Paradise asked.

"It just went to voicemail," I said. Knowing Mahdi, he fell asleep with the phone in his hand and it died. That happened so many times when I would stay over with him. "I'll try again a little later," I said as I walked over to a nearby outlet to plug my phone up to charge. Not even two minutes on the charger, my phone began to ring.

"Oh boy!" I said, looking at Paradise in shock. "That has to be Mahdi."

"Take your time. Don't rush into it right away."

"OK," I said. When I walked over to the phone, I couldn't believe my eyes. It wasn't Mahdi calling, it was *Marcus.*

"It's *Pastor!*" I said.

"*Pastor?*" she asked. Then I answered.

"Hey, Pastor," I said as formally as I knew how.

"Hey, Cassie! What's going on?"

"Nothing much. Is everything OK?" I asked. I was shocked. It was so long since he had called me this late. I figured I must have done something wrong as

I was filling in as an usher. Marcus hadn't called me this late since the time we had been dating.

"Why would you think something is wrong?" he asked.

"Oh. I just thought I probably forgot something ushering tonight," I explained.

"Oh no. You're fine. I was just saying *hey*."

"Oh. *Hey!*" I said feeling extremely awkward.

"What are you doing?" he asked.

"Nothing much. Paradise and I decided to go grab food after service."

"Word? Where did you guys go?"

"Friday's."

"Let me guess. Wings, *right*?"

"Of course," I said as I chuckled.

"That's *crazy*! You didn't ask me if I wanted anything, or if I wanted to go."

"Please, Marcus! You play too many games. Tired of playing around with you," I said.

"What do you mean?" He laughed.

"Marcus, what do you want? One minute you're around and the *next* you're not."

"That's not true," he said as he laughed that very comment off.

"Yeah, *OK, Marcus!*"

"No, seriously, Cassie. *I miss you!*" Marcus said. I thought I'd never hear that again.

"Whatever," I said in disbelief.

"I do. I want things to go back the way they used to be between *us!*"

"Me too," I said. I smiled as I clinched the phone just a little tighter.

"I want to see you! Can we see each other tomorrow? Maybe we can work out together in the morning."

"I'll let you know," I told him. As badly as I wanted to see him, I needed him to know that I wasn't going to jump when he said, "Jump." Not *anymore*.

"OK. Well . . . I guess I'll call you in the morning. Hopefully you say *yes*."

"*Hopefully. Good night, Marcus.*"

"Good night. Tell Paradise I said hi."

"I will." Then Marcus hung up.

Maybe this is God. Maybe this is what God wanted. No wonder I felt so heavy about ending things with Mahdi. Maybe this was the right time. Maybe God is finally bringing to pass all that he told me.

I then received a text:

> I hope I get to see you tomorrow. I miss you. I'm going to prove
> myself to you. Let's start over. Let's start fresh. Let's really get

to know each other. Let's give each other a chance to see where things go. Love you. Have a good night, Cassie.

"Love you too, Marcus."

The very next day, I woke up to a few calls and text messages, all from *Marcus*. Marcus sent me a text to see whether or not we could work out. Then he sent me another, asking if we could see each other later on before revival. I decided to not answer back because I promised myself that I wouldn't always make myself available to him. Even though we were starting over, I needed to take my time and not rush into things. I needed to protect my heart this time, and it didn't help that I was having feelings of heating things up between us. I wanted to make love to Marcus *so badly*. It's been far too long. I was ready to end my celibacy. I was ready to throw it all away.

I noticed Mahdi didn't call. Maybe he was still sleeping. I don't know. But what I did know is, if I was starting something fresh with Marcus, then I needed to break things off with Mahdi, and *fast*! After checking my messages, I went on Instagram. I noticed that Nilani wrote me a message in my DM. She sent her number and told me to give her a call. Worried and hoping she was OK, I gave her a call.

"Hello," Nilani answered.

"Hey, Nilani. How are you?" I asked.

"Not good," she said as she started crying.

"Oh my gosh, what's wrong? Talk to me!" I said as I sat straight up in my bed, trying to gather why she was crying so hysterically.

"Marcus played me! He played everybody! He told the whole church that my mom was a crackhead! He told my business to everybody! He lied to me! He told me he would marry me! He met my mom and my best friend and told them he wanted to be with me and I'm the *one*! He talked about everyone. He said that Desmond was gay. He talked sh** about all of y'all. He even said you were *crazy and your family is crazy* and that you're too masculine. He said you think you are his wife and how you even bought your *wedding dress*!" Nilani shouted. Paradise then poked her head in my room, flabbergasted about what she overheard.

"I'm done!" Paradise yelled. "After revival, I'm leaving Powerhouse! I'll be damned to be a part of church with people coming for my sister! Marcus better not say nothing else to me!" She stormed off.

I couldn't believe it. I couldn't believe what was coming out of Nilani's mouth. All that came to mind was all that I shared with him. All that God had told me. All that he entertained. All the times he got down on one knee asking to marry me. All the times he shared to me how the rest of the girls at church were jealous of me and how he kept me separated from them to protect me, when really, he was doing that to portray this picture of me being psychotic.

"He even made me touch myself and used Scripture to prove that foreplay wasn't a sin. He cut me off completely! He wants nothing to do with me. I even called Kim and told her what he did. Nobody believes me!"

But I believed her! I believed every word! Everything she told me, I either told Marcus or he told me. I knew a lot of the church members' business. But playing the role of a First Lady and a "wife," I kept everything to myself. I felt that a husband should confide in his wife and she should cover him. Not only was she saying all the stuff that only he and I should have known, I fell victim to foreplay being justified myself. I felt raped. I felt used. I felt embarrassed.

"I'm going to revival tonight and I am exposing him! I'm telling everyone what he did to me . . . Nobody believes me!" Nilani shouted.

"I believe you, Nilani," I assured her.

I couldn't believe it! Why would Marcus do this to me? Why would he tell her all of this? Why would he break my trust yet again? It was clear he didn't learn from the first go 'round. This was, by far, *worse*! Snapping out of my thoughts and realizing what Nilani said about going to church and exposing him, I started to talk her off the *deep end*.

"*Nilani!* Please don't do that!"

"No! He needs to pay for what he did to me! I'm tearing that church down!"

"Doing that will do what! I know you are upset and Marcus is absolutely wrong. But if you believe in God like you say you do, than you put it in God's hands! He will avenge you! He will repay! You don't want *blood on your hands*. You don't fight evil with evil, Nilani! You overcome it with good!" I shouted, trying my best to convince her.

"Everyone turned against me! Nobody wants anything to do with me!"

"Who cares! Anybody that can walk away from you is not for you! Like the Bible says, Matthew 10:14, 'If *they* don't receive you, shake the dust off your feet!'"

Right when I finished my last statement to Nilani, someone was at the door, knocking.

"Who is it?" I asked in the most *undignified* way. Nobody answered. I then walked to the door and I noticed a finger on the peephole. "I'm not answering until I see who you are!" I shouted. The person took their finger off the peephole. That person was *Marcus*! He was smiling from ear to ear. Little did he know, he walked right into a fire he ignited. "Hold on!" I shouted.

"Is that him?" Paradise asked, poking her head back in my room.

"YEAH, THAT'S HIM!" I answered. I decided to go to Paradise's room because it was farther from the door than my room was. I didn't want to alert Marcus on whom I was speaking to.

"Nilani?"

"Yes!" she said calmly.

"Marcus is at my door right now."

"Cassie! *I swear to God, if he denies anything I told you, I'm going to that church tonight and I'm telling ev-ery-thing!*"

Nearly a half hour went by. As I was still trying my hardest to calm Nilani down, Marcus showing up had her on one hundred *again*. I then received a text from Marcus. It said:

> Hey, Cassie. Sorry for popping up on you like that. I was texting and calling you all morning. I didn't get an answer, so I came by. I wanted to take you to the mall with me. I am going to get an outfit for revival tonight. I really want to see you. I'm going to wait downstairs in my car. Let me know if you want to come. If not, I can see you another time.

"Nilani, I promise I'm going to call you right back. I'm going to speak to him really quick. Stay by your phone."

"OK," she said.

I quickly went to the bathroom and brushed my teeth. I then threw on a T-shirt and some joggers. I had rollers in my hair to keep my hair neat for revival that night. I wasn't looking my best like I normally did when I saw Marcus. But at this point, I didn't care. I was ready to address this *head-on*. When I went outside, I noticed Marcus parked in the driveway. I got inside the car and slammed the passenger-side door. I folded my arms and looked at him and I said, "Do you not care about me?"

"Yes, I care about you!" he said, wondering why I would ask.

"Do you not care about me, Marcus?!"

"Of course I care about you Cassie."

"So why is someone coming to me . . . telling me things that I know . . . that only you should know?"

"Let me guess! Nilani reached out to you, *huh*? She's been calling everyone," he said, rolling his eyes in disgust.

"Yes! And she called me and told me you told her that I am *crazy* and my family is *crazy* and you even told her about my wedding dress."

"She's *lying*! I didn't say any of that!" he yelled. Meanwhile, Nilani sent a whole paragraph to my phone, posing the same threats about exposing him if he continued to lie.

"Well, there is *no way* she made that up, Marcus."

"Cassie, you know how many people know about how you feel about me? You know how many people know about your *wedding dress*?"

"I wonder what could have given them that impression, *Marcus*!" I said with a great deal of sarcasm. "The only person that knew about my dress was Tanya! That's it! You had to have told her. You are the only person that played close with her. Speaking of *close*, she also told me she went down on you!"

"She told you that?" Marcus said in shock.

"Yes she did and how you use Scripture to prove that foreplay wasn't a sin! You would have her, touching on herself right in front of you, and you better not say she's lying because you pulled the same crap with me! *Marcus!* It was like I was having a conversation with myself! I've been dealing with you *off and on* for five years—you don't think I know you by now?" I asked. I then turned away from him, trying my best to hold back tears. I couldn't believe this was all happening. He played me the entire time. Nilani didn't act any different from Jada. They both showed me time and time again that they didn't like me. I wouldn't be surprised if my assumptions of him and Jada were correct. Only God knows. *Shoot!* For all I knew, there could be more women from the church he pulled this with.

"Cassie, please believe me. It's not true. I came back around because I wanted to start fresh with you. As soon as we are in a great space, something always happens. I'm not going to letting the devil win! *Not this time!* Nilani was sent by the devil. She is a Jezebel spirit. She's trying to sabotage me. She's trying to sabotage the church. Let's not give the enemy power to destroy what we are trying to build. It's not by accident that this is all happening now that we are starting over," Marcus explained. I sat there in silence. I didn't believe him, not one bit. This was everything I felt in my gut was happening. I knew all along.

"Can we please enjoy our time together? Come to the mall with me, *please*? Come on. I'll come inside and wait while you get dressed," he said, taking his key out of the ignition. I took him up on the offer. I planned on getting the truth out of him one way or the other.

Marcus followed me inside. He sat in my room as I grabbed a pair of jeans, a sweatshirt, and a jacket to put on. I usually take a shower at night and then again in the morning, but because I was pressed for time, I skipped my morning shower. Last night just had to do.

"Hey, Paradise." Marcus greeted Paradise as she entered my room and noticed Marcus was there. I walked right out of there, knowing that my little sister was not going to hold her tongue. He was about to get all the heat, and I was not about to put my sister on *chill*. Instead, I listened in, as I got dressed in the bathroom.

"No, Pastor. I'm not feeling you right now," Paradise said without hesitation. "After tonight, I'm out! I'm not going to be a part of a church trying to play *my* sister. I watch her go *hard* for the ministry, give her last, going above and beyond, and y'all trying to play her? No! Not happening!"

"Paradise, I'm going to prove it to y'all. Nilani is lying. She is jealous of your sister. She's mad because I didn't want her. She's doing all of this because she tried to come on to me and I denied her. She's been trying to run havoc ever since. You guys are the only ones who believe her. Everyone else knows the truth," Marcus said, trying to convince Paradise.

I walked back out of the bathroom, fully dressed. Paradise walked out of my room, rolling her eyes after hearing Marcus out. She looked at me with such a disapproving look on her face. It was clear that he failed at convincing her. I wasn't surprised. I wasn't convinced either.

"Ready?" I asked Marcus as I headed toward the door. Marcus followed behind.

The mall run with Marcus was very dry. It was as if I wasn't even there. He tried to make light of the situation by making jokes that we'd normally laugh at. He'd ask me for my opinion, here and there, regarding outfits he considered buying. I didn't enjoy being with him at all. He could tell too. Once Marcus found his outfit for the night, the shopping spree was over. He then brought me back home.

"You're still coming to revival tonight, right?" he asked as he pulled back up in front of my house.

"Yes!" I said.

"You promise?"

"I'll be there, *Marcus*!" I said, getting out of the car. I shut the door, then I ran upstairs. I called Nilani right away. By then, she had to have been waiting about two hours.

Nilani and I talked, and talked, and talked. She told me everything. How they would link. Where they would link. How he never let her go to his house. How he convinced her to get her own apartment so they could have more privacy. It all sounded *so* familiar. I'm guessing at the time she had roommates too. We spoke for hours. We spoke so long to where I was late for revival. Paradise had already left. As I was on the phone with Nilani, a text from Marcus came in:

HEY! Where are you? You're still coming, right?

I texted back: "Yeah! On my way."

"Look, Nilani, I have to go. I have to get dressed and head to Revival."

"OK," she said. "Thanks for talking to me. And I'm sorry for *everything*. I'm sorry for how I treated you while I was there at the church. You have such a big heart. You didn't deserve that and he *surely* doesn't deserve you."

"I appreciate your apology. It means a lot. I'll keep in touch."

"I will too," Nilani said. "Later."

"Take care."

I made it just in time for the sermon. Pastor Homes was delivering the Word that night. I noticed Marcus in the front pew, sitting next to Jermaine. I grabbed a seat way in the back. I wanted to leave, the moment benediction was delivered. At that point, I really didn't trust *anybody*. I didn't want anyone phony and in my face. They had been phony enough. As I looked around the room, I noticed quite a few people didn't show up. Desmond wasn't there, this lady named Shameka didn't show—come to think of it, I noticed her and Nilani started getting well acquainted since Nilani stopped showing up. Lastly, my favorite lady, Sister Wells, didn't show either. She and I grew pretty close with the short amount of time she'd been at the ministry. It's sad to say that I had more trust in her than the people I had known there for *years*. Sister Wells was really close to Nilani. Her kids and Nilani went to the same school. I'm almost sure she told Sister Wells everything.

There were a few others missing too. It was pretty *bare* at church. That's not normal, especially with a revival going on. Turning my attention back to the pulpit, I noticed Marcus scanning the room. He then locked eyes on me and smiled. I could tell he was looking for me and relieved that I *actually* came.

Pastor Homes continued to preach: "Eve's biggest downfall in the garden was allowing the serpent to get into her ear! And Adam's biggest downfall was allowing the serpent to do so! Some of y'all have to stop giving the devil your ear! Others got to stop it from happening. Don't let the devil tell you things that God did not say! Stop allowing the devil to get you to do what God did not tell you to do! There is a Jezebel spirit running havoc in our churches, and we have got to kill it!"

Marcus looked back at me! He was shocked that Bishop Homes touched on the same exact thing Marcus stated earlier that day.

"Wow!" Marcus said, with his hand on his head, stunned that Bishop Homes was tapped in to all that had taken place. Little did Marcus know, I was tapped in *too*! All his *lies*. All his *games*. All his *deception*. I knew *everything*! And he would soon find out just how much.

33

OLD THINGS HAVE PASSED AWAY AND ALL THINGS BECOME NEW

The next morning, I received a text from Marcus. It stated:

> Hey, Cassie. Paradise just texted me. She just sent her resignation. She said she is leaving the church and that I am well aware of the reason why. I'm not sure if you feel the same. But if you do, I'd still love for us to stay connected and remain friends as we get to know each other more. I still feel the same no matter your decision. Let me know. Love you.
>
> ~ Best Regards, Pastor Boyd

I decided to call.

"Hello," Marcus said.

"Before we could even explore a friendship and possibly more, we need to address everything!"

"Cassie, I really don't want to revisit anything. I just want to forget all that happened and start over."

"We are not starting anything over until we address what needs to be addressed. I'm not going to be able to move forward without the clarity I need."

"OK. Are you home now?"

"Yes."

"OK. I'm on my way."

I was extremely nervous. But I was ready to address everything. I wanted to know why he had a problem with me preaching. I wanted to know why he was dragging his feet about us. I mean, how long were we going to be *getting to know each other* for? I wanted to know if he would admit to everything that happened with Nilani. Was he the reason that she and the rest of the girls didn't like me at the church? Was he behind all of the drama that went on?

Finally, Marcus was outside. He didn't have to call to inform me. I was already outside waiting for him. I took a deep breath as I walked toward his car. I whispered to myself, "God, please give me the words to say. Amen."

When I got in the car, I asked, "Can we pray?"

"I was just about to suggest that."

"Dear Lord, we thank you this day. We ask for your presence and wisdom right now Lord. Let Marcus and I reason together. Have us to come to an agreement for the best outcome between us. Allow us to be honest to one another in love. We thank you that your will *will* be done. In Jesus's name, Amen."

"Amen," said Marcus.

"OK, first things first. Why this?" I said as I banged both of my fists together. "Why do I feel like we're always bumping heads?"

"I feel like you're always going behind my back and doing things without asking me? That one time, you didn't ask for my permission to preach. You just went ahead and did it."

"Marcus, this is the first time I have ever been *fully* part of a church. At the time, I didn't know protocol. I did what the Bible instructs us to do. We are to go all throughout the world and teach the Gospel. I didn't know I need permission to do what we have *all* been instructed to do. It was your job to come to me as my pastor and correct me. It was not for anyone else to judge me and have something to say about what my pastor should have come to me about."

"You're right. I handled that wrong and I apologize for that."

"OK," I said. "Were you seeing Nilani? And did you tell her that my family and I are crazy? Did you tell her about my *wedding dress*?"

"I felt like your family only joined the church because they knew how you felt about me being your husband. I feel like they only joined in hopes for us to be together," Marcus explained.

"*Marcus, are you kidding me?* Who was the one to ask my mom to join the church and run the children's ministry?"

"I did. And she was not open to it."

"And who kept pressing her about joining?"

"I did."

"What about Paradise? Who put her on the Ushers' Board?"

"Me."

"So what are you talking about, then?" I said, furious that he would even believe that.

"I'm sorry. I just thought they changed their minds because of you?"

"You thought wrong!" I said, rolling my eyes as I looked away. "And Nilani?"

"Yes. I was seeing her. I felt like I was so drawn to her. I don't know why. I felt like she seduced me. The devil knew what I liked. She was so feminine, and I loved that about her."

"Oh yeah? She told me you think I'm too masculine also. Continue!"

Totally ignoring my comment, he continued. He knew he couldn't deny that, because every time I argued with him or spoke passionately on something I would punch my hand and talk very aggressively. I even preached that way. I have a bad habit of doing that. "After a while, she became too clingy. She'd pop up at the church on me. One time, I was doing warm-ups on my voice and she sat on the piano and was looking at me. She just started doing *too* much, so I cut her off."

"Don't you know this girl thought about committing suicide because of you?" I asked, remembering that she disclosed her suicide thoughts, and for someone who battled with that myself, I knew what that felt like all too well.

"She's not innocent either, Cassie," he said, trying to justify his actions.

"I don't care! She is a baby in Christ! You are the *pastor!* You know the Word! 'To whom much is given, much is required!'"

Marcus began to sink in the driver's seat. I could tell conviction had come over him. I never saw a grown man like this, fold. Before my eyes, a man I once saw as my hero instantly became a hopeless victim. "I want to show you something," I said, pulling out my phone. I went on my Instagram page and showed him a picture that reminded me of the church. It was a picture of a church. People were walking in and *falling* out.

I continued. "You see this?" I said as I showed him the picture. Marcus looked over at it and then put his head down. "This is your church! People are going in and then dying out!" Marcus kept his head down. "Marcus, I can't even finish this conversation with you. You need to reach out to Nilani and apologize to her! She is a soul! And if you care for souls like you say you do and love the Lord like I *know* you do, then you need to go make that right! *Right now!* And give her the apology she deserves!" I then got out of the car.

"Thank you for that, Cassie. I'm going to contact her right now," he assured me. I could tell Marcus was very humbled behind our conversation and what he had done. Well, he seemed it anyway.

"Call me when you're done," I shouted as I walked in the house.

A few hours went by before I got word from both Nilani and Marcus. Marcus called me and said that he met with Nilani at the church. He apologized to her over and over again, but she refused to budge. I let Marcus know that if he was sincere, then that was all that mattered. Meanwhile, Nilani was gloating in all of her glory. She told me that Marcus cried profusely as he apologized, but she refused to accept it. I'll never forget how exhausted I felt that day. With all that went on, I didn't know what to do. But at the same time, I knew what had to be done.

The very next morning, I texted Marcus:

> Hey, I decided that I'm going to resign from the Powerhouse Ministry. I just don't see how I can be a part of a church I was called to build up to constantly be broken down. It would be foolish of me to stay when my sister chose to leave on account of me. I wish you all the best. Take care.
>
> ~ Cassie

Shortly after, Marcus wrote back:

> Great morning, Cassie. I accept your resignation. Good luck in your future endeavors. Take care. Don't worry about responding back.
>
> ~ Blessings, Pastor Boyd

I remember how empty I felt after reading what he texted me. It was *over! No marriage! No revelation! No Marcus! Was I wrong, God? Was I wrong? All these years of following you and knowing your voice, did I not get it right?*

A year had passed. It was the beginning of spring. I remember like it was yesterday. It was one late night and I was scrolling through YouTube, on my phone, trying to find a movie to watch. I came across a movie called *It Had to Be You.* Because I am such a *hopeless romantic*, the first genre I tend to gravitate to is romance. I was a sucker for love.

"Bae?"

"Yeah?"

"Check to see if the cookies are done."

"Aight. I gotchu."

I really hope this boy checks on these cookies. Messing with him, they'll probably turn into a crisp playing the game.

"Babe, check them now before they burn! I know you're out there playing 2K!"

"Hold on, booboo. I'm coming."

I loved when he called me that.

"Here, bae."

"Thank you, baby."

"I gotchu."

"Uh-uh! You ate one?"

"I had to check them to see if they were done," he said as he laughed.

"Yeah, OK. That was just an excuse to eat one."

"I'ma eat you in a second."

"You're so annoying!" I laughed.

"You love it though."

"I do."

"I love you, Cass."

"I love you too, *Mahdi!*"

Mahdi gave me a kiss. "Hmm, *my shawty!*"

Mahdi and I hit it off. Who would have known that the man I'd end up with would be the barber next door. We had been together about a year now, and I was loving every moment of it.

"*Bye*! Go play the game!" I said as I chuckled.

"Yeah aight. I'ma be back in a minute for some lovin'."

"Get outta here!" I said, pushing him away. "I'm trying to watch this movie."

I sat in the bed and watched the movie. It was about this man and this woman who went out of town to plan their weddings. Both, the man and woman had fiancés back at home. They bumped into each other in their hotel elevator. They found themselves both at a store to pick out things they needed for their weddings. To their surprise, both of them were pledged to be married. But in this getaway, they fell in love. The man wanted to leave his fiancée for her. Even though the woman wanted to be with this man, she felt like it wasn't right. She told him that she was sorry and was going to marry her fiancé.

About a year later, she was at work as a schoolteacher and was having lunch with her coworker/friend. The coworker happened to be reading a book. The book was written by the same man she met on her *getaway*. He expressed in the book how he loved and wanted to be with her. Both of them assumed they married their fiancés. But they didn't. The woman found out that the man was on duty, trying to save a young girl from jumping off a building to commit suicide. The man came to the girl's rescue, talking her off the ledge. All the people at the scene along with the woman cheered him on for his hero merits. The man made his way through the crowd. As he moved in the crowd, he noticed the woman. He walked toward her. She walked toward him. Then they both began to run. They ran to each other for a warm embrace. As this took place, I heard a song in the background, a *very* familiar song: "*At Last.*"

Right there in that moment, my heart sank. I remember I grabbed my T-shirt, in the area of my heart, as I whispered to myself, *"Marcus!"*

I got out of bed and snuck off to the storage room. I turned on the lights, and I began to rummage through the bins of clothing. After much searching, under a pile of comforters, there was a black plastic bag. I ripped the black bag open and unzipped the garment bag. Peeking out was my beautiful, well-kept, mermaid, off-white wedding dress.

This is the dress. It would be the one I walk down the aisle with. I'd be in marital bliss. I'd live the happily ever after that I have been dreaming of. I'd finally see the fruition of the revelation God presented to me years ago. I'd finally see the man that has been getting down on one knee, popping that question in equivocal attempts, yet dressing it with humor, to finally, finally ask in all sincerity, "Cassie, will you marry me?" *Yesss!* I feel it! It's coming to pass. At last. This is it! Or is it?

9 781664 143586